Witch Is Where Chickens Go To Roost

Published by Implode Publishing Ltd

Chapter 1

"I can't believe you're watching that rubbish," said Wanda, the goldfish.

"We want to go to sleep," Mabel, her companion, chipped in.

"You'll just have to wait another half hour," I said. "I want to see the end of this movie."

"Flesh Eaters of the Red Mist?" Wanda scoffed. "This isn't even a B movie; it's a D movie."

"I don't remember asking for your opinion."

"At least that hubby of yours had the good sense to go to bed."

"I'm not listening to you." I turned up the volume on the TV.

Jack and I had started to watch the movie together, but he kept nodding off, and snoring, so I'd made him go to bed.

When the credits finally rolled, the fish gave a whoop of delight.

"Maybe we can get some shut-eye now," Wanda sniped.

I was just about to power off the TV when the adverts came on.

Oh no! I couldn't believe my eyes.

"Isn't that you in that ad, Jill?" Mabel said.

I desperately tried to manoeuvre myself into a position that would block their view of the screen.

"Sorry?" I said, all innocent like.

"That was you in that advertisement," Wanda said.

"Rubbish." I turned off the TV. "I'm going to bed now."

As I made my way out of the room, I could hear the two

goldfish.

"It was definitely her under all those toilet rolls."

I'd been hoping that the Droza ad wouldn't appear on TV for months, by which time everyone would have forgotten that I'd had anything to do with it. I'd actually told people that I was shooting the ad for DeRosa, the high-end cosmetics company. I hadn't been lying because, at the time, I'd honestly believed it was true. It was only when I turned up for the shoot that I discovered I'd be advertising toilet rolls for Droza. If people saw me being buried under a mountain of toilet rolls, I would never live it down. With a bit of luck, the ads would only be shown in the less expensive slots, late at night, when hardly anyone would see them.

I didn't wake until almost seven-thirty, probably because I'd stayed up so late watching the movie. I expected to find Jack and Florence in the kitchen eating sawdust, but there was no sign of them. I was just about to go back upstairs to check Florence's bedroom when I heard a giggle coming from the lounge.

When I went in there to see what was going on, I couldn't believe my eyes. Florence was standing at the other end of the room, next to the window. Behind her was a small stack of toilet rolls. As soon as she saw me, she pretended to stumble, and knocked them over. At that, the whole room was filled with laughter. Florence was rolling around on the floor, Jack was doing the same on the sofa, and the two fishes were bubbling like crazy.

"Did you two tell them?" I glared at the goldfish.

"Certainly not," Wanda said. "And besides, that husband of yours can't understand a thing we say."

That was true, so how did Jack know about the ad? Before I could ask him, he said, "I got up early to check the results of last night's ten-pin tournament in the US. Why didn't you tell me the ad shoot was for toilet rolls?"

"Because I knew you'd do something like this." I pointed to the toilet rolls that were scattered across the carpet.

"It was funny, Mummy," Florence said. "Was it fun being underneath all those toilet rolls?"

"It was absolutely great."

"I'm going to tell all my friends at school that my mummy was on TV."

"Please don't do that."

"But they'll all want to see it."

"Why don't you go and pour out our muesli, pumpkin," Jack said.

"Okay, Daddy."

"You're not really upset, are you?" he said, after she was out of the room.

"I'm going to be a laughing stock."

"No, you won't. Most people would love to be in a TV ad."

"For toilet rolls?"

"What does that matter? And, besides, you were really good."

"Do you think so?"

"Yeah, I would never have known it was your first time."

"I did feel as though I'd got into the part."

"There you are, then. No one is going to give you a hard time about it. I doubt many people will see it, anyway."

Florence had already finished her breakfast and gone up to her bedroom. I was only halfway through my bowl of Chococandy Pops when Kathy called. At first, I thought we must have a bad line because she didn't speak, but then she said, "Sorry, Jill, I can hardly catch my breath. Are you still there?"

"I'm here."

"You were priceless."

"I take it you've seen the ad?"

"No wonder you didn't want to talk about it."

"Is there a point to this phone call?"

"We've recorded it. I must have watched it a hundred times already. It's even better in slow motion." She laughed.

"Goodbye, Kathy."

Turning to Jack, I sighed. "This is how it's going to be from now on, isn't it? And you made it ten times worse."

"How did I make it worse?"

"You insisted on telling everyone I was doing an ad for a leading cosmetics company."

"That's what you told me. How did the mix-up happen, anyway?"

"It was Talbot's fault. He was the one who led me to believe the ad was for DeRosa."

"Did he actually mention cosmetics?"

"Well, no, but—"

"Did he show you a contract with the name of the customer on it?"

"No."

"So, he just said the name?"

"Yes, but it was the way he said it. I reckon that he deliberately mispronounced it, so I'd think it was DeRosa and not Droza."

"Right."

"You don't believe me, do you?"

"Of course I do."

"I should sue him."

"For what?"

"I don't know. Damage to my reputation?"

"Honestly, Jill, I think the best thing you can do is to forget it. That way it will soon blow over."

"You're right. It'll soon be yesterday's news."

I was just about to get into my car when someone called my name. I looked up to see the vicar hurrying towards me. If that man asked me about the Roomba again, I wouldn't be responsible for my actions.

"Good morning, Jill."

"Morning, Vicar, I'm just on my way to work."

"I won't keep you. I just wanted to compliment you on your performance."

Oh bum!

"Such amazing comic timing. Your expression when the stack of toilet rolls fell down on top of you was thoroughly convincing. If I hadn't known better, I'd have thought you didn't know it was going to happen."

"Err, thanks."

"Will you be doing any more?"

"Ads? No, I wouldn't think so. It was a one-off."

"Pity. I haven't laughed so much for months."

As soon as I saw the grin on Mrs V's face, I knew that she must have seen the ad too, but unlike Kathy and the others, she was too polite to say anything.

The same could not be said about Winky.

"What's that thing?" I screamed at him.

On the wall, behind my desk, was mounted a huge photograph, which showed the moment the stack of toilet rolls had come crashing down on top of me.

"Don't be so coy." He grinned. "That right there is your finest moment captured for posterity."

I was still staring at it when the door behind me opened, and Mrs V walked in. "You didn't say if you wanted a cup of tea." She stopped dead in her tracks and stared at the print. "I'm glad to see you can laugh at yourself, Jill. I was worried that you might be a little embarrassed about the ad."

"I—err—"

"Armi and I have been watching it on loop all weekend. It gets funnier every time I see it. You really are a natural, Jill."

"I will have that cup of tea, please."

"Coming right up."

As soon as she was out of the room, I turned on Winky. "You're so dead."

"I thought you'd be pleased."

"I want that thing gone yesterday."

"It cost me twenty quid to get it framed."

"Why is it still here?"

"Okay, but can I ask you one question?"

"What?"

"Did you know the stack of toilet rolls was going to come tumbling down on you?"

"No, I wouldn't have done it if I had. They tricked me. Everyone tricked me. Mainly Talbot Bottle. He made me believe I'd be doing an ad for cosmetics."

"You should sue him."

"That's what I said, but Jack reckons I should let it lie."

"No way I'd let him get away with it."

"You're right. What he did was unforgivable. I'm going around there right now, to have it out with him." I started for the door. "And that thing had better be gone by the time I get back."

I almost crashed into Mrs V on my way out.

"Do you still want this tea, dear?"

"Yes, put it on my desk, would you? I'm just nipping next door to see Mr Bottle."

I stormed down the corridor, and without stopping to knock, burst through the door of Talbot Talent. There was no one seated at the reception desk, but a voice came from the office behind it.

"Hello?"

"It's me, Talbot. Jill Maxwell."

The office door opened, and Talbot stepped out. Dressed in that awful yellow suit of his, he was all smiles.

Not for long if I had anything to do with it.

"You're bright and early, Jill, I've only just got here myself."

"There's something urgent we need to talk about, Talbot."

"Let me guess." He grinned. "I bet it's about the Droza ad."

His grin made me even angrier. This was clearly just one big joke to him.

"You're dead right it's about the ad. I have never—"

"I was going to pop down to see you later this morning."

"If you think an apology is going to make up for it,

you're very much mistaken."

"Sorry?"

"Isn't that why you were going to come and see me?"

"No, I was going to tell you about the feedback I've been getting."

"I've been getting plenty of that myself."

"I'm not surprised. You were amazing."

He clearly thought that flattery would divert me, but he didn't know Jill Maxwell.

"The thing is, Talbot, I—"

"Droza are over the moon with the reaction to the ad."

"They are?"

"Absolutely. Their early figures show a twenty-five percent uptick in sales since the ad ran."

"But it wasn't aired until yesterday."

"Not true. It's been running for almost a week in the regions where they first tested it. They rolled it out to the rest of the country yesterday."

"That's all fine and dandy, but—"

"How soon will you be able to do the next one?"

"Sorry?"

"That's why I was coming to see you later. Droza want to do another ad in the same series, featuring you and Moo."

"Another one? No chance. I'm not putting myself through that again."

"They know you'll expect more money this time around. From what I hear on the grapevine, they've already agreed a new contract with Moo that is ten times what he got for the first ad. I'm sure I can get them to give you at least as much."

"Ten thousand?"

"At the very least. I'll pitch for fifteen and see what they negotiate me down to. What do you say?"

"Would I have to be buried under a pile of toilet rolls again?"

"They haven't finalised the script yet, so I don't know the details. They're just really keen to recreate the same dynamic between you and Tristan."

"Who? Oh, yeah. Moo."

"What do you say, Jill, can I open a dialog with Droza?"

"Ten grand?"

"Hopefully more."

"Okay, then."

"Great, I'll get straight onto it this morning. Was there something else you came to see me about?"

"Err, no. Not really. I'd better get back."

"Okay, I'll keep you posted."

"Your tea will be going cold, Jill," Mrs V said. "Is everything alright?"

"Err, yeah, I think so."

Winky had had the good sense to remove the print, and he was sitting on my desk.

"Well?" he said.

"Well, *what*?"

"When's the court date?"

"There isn't going to be one."

"Don't tell me you backed down. I thought you were made of tougher stuff."

"I didn't back down. I just changed my mind."

"Why? When you walked out of here, you were ready for lynching Talbot."

"Maybe, I was a little hasty."

"What happened?"

"If you must know, I've been asked to take part in another ad for Droza."

"I assume you told them where they could stuff it?"

"Not in so many words."

"You surely didn't say yes."

"The pay this time is ten grand. That's ten times what they paid last time."

"They must have more money than sense."

"Apparently, sales of Droza toilet rolls have shot up since the ad aired, so they want me to reprise my role."

"How about getting me a part in the ad?"

"You?"

"Just picture it. You're stroking the handsome cat, but then he runs off and knocks over the stack of toilet rolls. Brilliant, eh?"

"Why would there be a stack of toilet rolls in the house?"

"Okay, I admit the plot needs a little work, but including a cat is a definite winner."

"There's no point trying to convince me. I'm just one of the actors in the production."

"*Actor*?" He scoffed. "Getting buried under a mountain of toilet rolls? It's hardly Oscar material, is it?"

"All actors have to start somewhere."

"So, are you going to put a word in for me?"

"No."

Chapter 2

"Do you have to look so smug?" Winky said. He'd been sulking for the last hour, ever since I told him that I wouldn't put him forward for a part in the new ad. "You're getting on my nerves."

"Tough. I have a feeling my part in the new ad is just the start of things."

"I wouldn't hold your breath for Hollywood to call."

"I didn't mean that. I know the ad thing will only be short-lived. I'm talking more generally. I have a feeling that things are starting to turn around for me."

Mrs V came through and closed the door behind her. "I have a Ms Francesca Artichoke out there. She says she needs a private investigator who can take on a major investigation immediately. What shall I tell her?"

"Tell her I'm tied up on an important telephone call at the moment, but as soon as I've finished, I'll be pleased to see her."

"Okay? How will I know when you've finished on the *call*?"

"I'll buzz you on the intercom."

"Okay."

"What did I tell you, Winky? Everything is starting to come together. A major role in a prestigious commercial, and now a major case to investigate."

"*Prestigious*? It's for toilet rolls."

"You weren't saying that when you wanted me to get you a part. I wonder what the major case is that my new client wants me to investigate?"

"You're slipping into Mitty mode again."

"Rubbish, there's nothing wrong with feeling

optimistic." I pressed the button on the intercom.

Ms Artichoke looked every inch the professional businesswoman, and I assumed she must be seeking help for some kind of corporate espionage.

"Francesca Artichoke." Her handshake was firm. "Thank you for seeing me today."

"Jill Maxwell. Please take a seat. Can I offer you a drink?"

"No, thanks, I'd prefer to get straight down to business. This is a matter of the utmost importance."

"Of course. How can I help?"

"My chickens have gone missing."

Winky, who was underneath the sofa, made a spluttering noise.

"What was that?" Francesca looked around.

"It's—err—nothing. They're doing some work in the office next door."

"I see. So, do you think you'll be able to help? As I mentioned to your receptionist, I need someone who can start work on the case immediately."

"I do have some availability at the moment, but I'm not sure that I completely understand the nature of the case."

"Chickens."

"Yes, you said. Are you in the *chicken* business?"

"No, I'm a corporate lawyer."

Now, we were getting somewhere. My hunch about this being a major case was correct.

"And the chickens relate to a case for one of your corporate clients, do they? Acquisitions and mergers, perhaps?"

"No, nothing like that. The chickens are mine. Or at least they were before they went missing."

"They're *your* chickens?"

"Yes, I have a smallholding. After the hustle, bustle and stresses of the corporate law world, I find going back home to my livestock helps me unwind."

"But now your chickens have gone missing."

"Correct."

"And you'd like me to find them?"

"Also correct." She checked her watch. "I'm really sorry, but I'm due in court in a few minutes." She handed me her card. "My home address is on the back. Perhaps you could give me a call and we can arrange for you to visit, to discuss this in more detail."

"Err, sure."

"Excellent, I'll look forward to seeing you then."

As soon as she'd left, Winky came out from under the sofa.

"One word from you, and you'll be on half rations," I said.

"There's nothing I could say that could top that." He smirked, and then started making clucking noises.

"I meant it about the half rations."

Just then, Grandma appeared in my office, which sent the clucking Winky shooting back under the sofa.

"What do you want?" I snapped.

"Charming. Is that any way to greet your favourite grandmother?"

"I'm really busy."

"It looks like it. Still, the chicken case should keep you occupied for a while."

"Why would you listen in on a private meeting with my client?"

"I'm asking myself the same question. It was so boring.

Finding chickens? Really? Is that what you've been reduced to?"

"What do you want?"

"Do you know what day it is?"

"It's Monday."

"It's The Twenty-One."

"No, it's not. It's the seventh."

"I didn't mean the date. Please don't tell me you don't know what The Twenty-One is."

"I have absolutely no idea what you're talking about. Why don't you save us both a lot of pain and just tell me?"

"The Twenty-One comes around once every five-hundred years, so I don't imagine you remember the last one."

"Seeing as I wasn't even born then, no I don't."

"It isn't fun. Take it from someone who was there."

"You still haven't told me what it is."

"The Twenty-One begins the countdown to the day of burning."

"Which is?"

"The day that instils fear in the heart of every witch."

"I'm going to need more."

"You've surely heard of the witch burnings?"

"Of course, but that hasn't happened for hundreds of years."

"Five-hundred years to be precise. Less twenty-one days."

"Are you saying that the witch burnings take place every five-hundred years?"

"Yes, and the next one is twenty-one days from now. Hence why today is The Twenty-One."

"Okay, I think I understand now, but that is just ancient history. No one is going to burn witches today."

"I wouldn't be so sure. My sources tell me that the witch-finders held a secret meeting only last week."

"If it was a secret meeting, how come you know about it?"

"Let's just say I have people on the inside. Anyway, the point is that every witch in the human world is under threat for the next twenty-one days."

"Is that supposed to worry me?"

"It should."

"Have you forgotten that I've seen off witch-finders before?"

"Yes, but you've never had to face this kind of co-ordinated threat."

"If you're so concerned about this, how come you waited until now to mention it? Why not give me more notice?"

"I didn't want to worry you."

"Okay. Well, thanks for the heads-up."

"Is that it? Is that all you have to say?"

"What do you want me to say? I'll keep my eyes peeled for witch-finders for the next three weeks."

"You better had because I have a feeling that you and I will be near the top of their hit list."

"Okay, good talk, but now I really do have to get back to my work."

"Just watch your back, Jill," she said, then disappeared.

"She was even more scary than usual," Winky said, as he came crawling out from under the sofa. "I don't like the sound of the day of burning."

"I wouldn't set much store by that nonsense. Grandma

is still living in the past."

"You're not worried, then?"

"Do I look worried?"

After Grandma's downer, I needed a pick-me-up, so I magicked myself over to Cuppy C.

"If it isn't Purple Myrtle." Pearl grinned.

I might have known the twins would find out that I'd been forced to dress up in a mascot costume at the Purple Festival.

"You told us that you were looking after the coconut shy," Amber said.

"Who grassed me up?"

"Mum."

"How did Aunt Lucy find out?"

"Grandma told her and gave her this photo." Pearl held up her phone.

It was the photo of me, dressed as Purple Myrtle, with Jack, Florence, Kathy, Peter and Lizzie.

"Can I get a caramel latte and a muffin? No, wait a minute, I'll have a cupcake instead."

"Waddle berry?" Amber laughed.

"Hilarious. Just give me a strawberry one."

Once I'd got my drink and cake, I sat at a table as far away from the counter as possible. It didn't do me any good, though, because the twins asked one of their assistants to look after the counter while they came to join me.

"If you two are going to rib me about Purple Myrtle, I'm leaving."

"Not another word about it, I promise," Amber said.

"Pearl?"

"You have my word, too. Besides, we'd much rather talk toilet rolls."

At that, they both dissolved into laughter, and I began to regret my decision to go to Cuppy C.

"Okay, you may as well get it out of your system." I sighed. "Do your worst. You can't say anything I haven't heard already today."

"The look on your face when the stack of toilet rolls crashed down on you." Pearl laughed.

"Comedy magic." Amber slapped the table.

"Have you both done yet?"

"The best part is that you actually thought you'd be advertising cosmetics."

"Any more?"

"Nah, I think that just about covers it," Pearl said.

"You can both mock, but I'll have you know that I've just been signed up for another Droza ad and they're going to pay me ten grand."

"Ten thousand pounds? Just for getting buried under toilet rolls?"

"There's a lot more to it than that. As Moo says, it's all about getting into character."

"*Moo*?"

"The young boy who played my son. His real name is Tristan."

"What about taking your own advice?" Amber said.

"What are you talking about?"

"You said we should concentrate on our core business. It seems like the PI agency is taking second place to your modelling career."

"I prefer to think of it as *acting*."

"Yeah, right. If you say so."

"And it isn't adversely affecting my main business. In fact, I'll have you know that just before I came over here, I landed a major case from a corporate lawyer. You see, girls, unlike you two, I am perfectly capable of wearing more than one hat." I finished the last of my cupcake. "Talking of your core business, you never told me what happened when you went to see the bank manager to fund your expansion plans."

"We're still waiting to hear back from him." Pearl sighed.

"Did it sound promising?"

"He was very non-committal, but fingers crossed."

***

"Are you sure it's nothing to worry about?" Jack said.

We'd just finished dinner and Florence had gone upstairs to play with Jay.

"I'm positive. It was just Grandma trying to scare me."

"The day of burning sounds pretty scary to me."

"Forget it. I'm far more concerned about Braxmore."

"Have you formulated a plan yet?"

"Yes, but I don't want to do anything while Florence is around, just in case."

"Just in case of *what*?"

"Nothing."

"You *are* worried, aren't you?"

"Of course not, but it doesn't hurt to be cautious. Kathy mentioned they were thinking of going to Wonder World for the weekend in three weeks' time, so I asked her if Florence could go with them."

"How come you never mentioned it before?"

"I only spoke to her this afternoon. She says she'd be welcome to go with them."

"I take it you haven't told Florence yet?"

"No, I wanted to tell you first. What do you think?"

"It makes sense I suppose. Do you think she'll want to go, though? She might not like the idea of leaving us at home."

"Yay!" Florence did her happy dance all around the kitchen. "When is it?"

"Not for three weeks," I said.

"Julie Kirkby went to Wonder World and she said it was super wicked."

"You do know that Mummy and Daddy won't be with you, don't you, pumpkin?" Jack said.

If he'd expected her to be upset, he was sadly mistaken because she just shrugged, then said, "Julie said the Wobbler Ride is the best. Can I go on the Wobbler?"

"Auntie Kathy will have to decide which rides you can go on, but if Julie went on it, I'm sure you'll be able to."

"Yay, I'm going to go and tell Jay." She went running upstairs.

"I don't think we have to worry about her missing us," I said.

"It doesn't look like it." Jack frowned.

"You'd better get used to this, otherwise when she leaves home, you'll be a gibbering wreck."

"*Leaves home*?" He looked horrified. "What do you mean *leaves home*?"

"Florence isn't going to live with us all her life. One day, she's going to move out and start a life of her own."

"But that's not going to happen for at least twenty years

yet."

"What if she decides to go to university? That would only be thirteen years from now."

"I don't want to think about it." Jack turned away and if I wasn't mistaken, he had welled up.

Jack was still rather subdued after Florence had gone to bed.

"Are you okay?" I said.

"Yeah."

"Are you sure because you've been very quiet ever since I brought up the subject of Florence leaving home."

"I know it's stupid, but I kind of pictured the three of us being together forever."

"That's not how life works. And, anyway, it'll be a long time before any of that happens. Even when she does leave home, we'll still see her."

"What if she goes to live in another country?"

"I doubt she will, but if she does, it won't be as bad for us as it is for most parents."

"How do you mean?"

"Because she's a witch, and she'd be able to magic herself back home any time she likes."

"I hadn't thought of that."

"That's always supposing she wants to of course."

"Why wouldn't she?"

"Because she'll have her own life by then."

"Can we please change the subject?" He sighed. "I find all this talk about Florence leaving home quite depressing. How much stick did you take today about the toilet roll ad?"

"Quite a bit, actually, but it's water off a duck's back."

"You do seem very relaxed about it all."

"Why wouldn't I be? After all, I've just signed up to do another one."

"Another ad?"

"Yeah."

"Who for this time?"

"Droza again."

"Really? After what happened last time? How did they manage to persuade you to do it?"

"They offered to pay me ten grand."

"Ten thousand? Honestly?"

"Yeah."

"That's amazing."

"For ten grand, I'll be the one who is laughing all the way to the bank."

"Talking of laughing all the way to the bank, did you see that someone in this area won the top prize in the national lottery a couple of weeks back?"

"Anyone we know?"

"That's just it. Whoever it is hasn't come forward to claim their prize yet."

"I don't get it. Why do people bother to buy a lottery ticket if they aren't going to claim their winnings?"

"They might not realise they've won."

"Same difference. Why buy a ticket then not bother checking it? How much did they win?"

"Just under eight million pounds."

"Eight million? Just think what we could do with that kind of money."

"We could buy the village store." Jack enthused.

"Buy the store? With eight million pounds? Are you crazy?"

"What's wrong with that? I like the idea of running that store."

"You can please yourself, but if we win eight million pounds, I won't be working another day in my life."

"You say that, but you'd soon be bored without your work."

"Rubbish. Only people with no imagination get bored. Why don't we do the lottery?"

"I suggested we should do it ages ago, but you shot me down in flames. You said it was a total waste of time, and only something losers did."

"You must be thinking of someone else. I never said that. Anyway, I think we should start doing it."

"Fine by me. You can play online now."

"I don't trust that. I'd rather play the old-fashioned way with the paper tickets. Where can we buy them?"

"The village store sells them."

"Are you sure? I've never seen them."

"They're the first thing you see when you walk through the door."

Chapter 3

The next morning, Jack and I were in the kitchen. He was making a fry-up, and I was assisting by providing words of encouragement when required.

"Good work with the sausages. The bacon is looking good."

He gave me a look. "If you want to help, why don't you stack the dishwasher?"

"Who said anything about wanting to help?"

"Dishes!"

"Okay, sheesh. You're such a slave driver."

"Have you noticed Florence hasn't buzzed once over the last couple of days?" Jack cracked an egg into the frying pan. "Do you think she's come through that phase?"

"I hope not."

"I thought you hated the buzzing?"

"I do, but after all the effort I put into making that costume, she could at least wear it for another month."

"The effort *you* put in? And there was I thinking Kathy had made it."

"If you remember, she made a Bumblebee Girl costume. I was the one who changed it into a Bluebottle Girl costume."

I'd just returned to my seat at the table when Jack said, "What about the pots in the lounge?"

"What did your last slave die of?"

The fish were still transfixed by Florence's yellow blob (AKA a bowl).

"Will your daughter be making any more pieces?" Wanda asked.

"I wouldn't think so."

"I hope you're going to encourage her to continue. It would be a shame to let such a talent go to waste."

"Are you being serious or is this some kind of wind-up?"

"Deadly serious, aren't we, Mabel?"

"Absolutely. I don't think you realise what a talent that daughter of yours has."

"O—kay." I collected the cup and plate that I'd left there the previous night.

"You haven't forgotten about the ornament you promised to buy us, have you?" Wanda said.

I hadn't but I was hoping that they had.

"What ornament?"

"The one you promised in return for us telling you that your husband had been cheating at Scrabble."

"Oh yeah, I remember now."

"So, when do we get it?"

"I'll try and get one sometime this week."

"What's wrong with getting it today?"

"I am very busy at the moment."

"We can always turn on the bubbles."

"Okay, okay, I'll do my best to get it today. What sort of thing do you want? A galleon, maybe?"

"Really?" Wanda rolled her eyes. "No, thank you."

"So tacky," Mabel commented.

"What then?"

"Something pleasing to the eye, like your daughter's piece."

"If you like it so much, why don't I just stick this in your tank instead of buying an ornament?"

"You can't do that. That piece could be worth a small

fortune. You wouldn't want the water to ruin it."

"Okay, I'll pay a visit to Rue Pets and see what I can come up with."

By the time I got back to the kitchen, Jack and Florence were already tucking into their fry-ups.

"I was beginning to think you'd fallen asleep in there," Jack quipped.

"The fish kept me talking."

"What did they want?"

"To remind me that I'd promised to buy them an ornament as payment for telling me about your cheating."

"Snitches."

"What's a snitch, Daddy?"

"It's a tattle tale."

"What's a tattle tale?"

While Jack hesitated, I jumped in, "Mummy and Daddy were playing a game and—"

"What game?"

"It's called Scrabble."

"Can I play Scrabble?"

"When you're older, but if you play with Daddy, make sure he doesn't have his phone with him."

"Why?"

"Mummy is just joking around." Jack shot me a look. "Aren't you, Mummy?"

"Yeah, I'm just joking."

"So, what's a snitch, Daddy?"

***

Before setting off to the office, I was going to call in at the village store to buy a lottery ticket. I was also running low (only two packets left) on custard creams at the office, so I was going to replenish my supplies at the same time. I was halfway there when someone called my name.

"Good morning, Jill."

It was Jack's new hairdresser, dressed in running top and shorts.

"Morning, Z—err—Julian. Going for a run?" My first stupid question of the day.

"I run most mornings. I find a good workout sets me up for the day. What about you, Jill, do you work out?"

"Absolutely. I run most days too."

"You're welcome to join me in the mornings if you like. Amanda isn't a runner; she prefers Pilates."

"Thanks, but I already have a running partner in Washbridge where I work."

"Pity, never mind."

"You should ask Jack, though. He's a mad keen runner, and I'm sure he'd love to join you."

"I'll do that."

Snigger.

"I'd better be making tracks. I need to pick up some—err—protein bars from the store before I go to work."

"Catch you later, then."

Jack was right: The lottery tickets were right next to the door. Winning the jackpot on the lottery would change our lives, so I spent ages choosing what I hoped would be the winning combination. When I had finally completed the three lines on the ticket, I grabbed four packets of custard creams, then made my way to the counter where Marjorie appeared to be doing a crossword.

"Hi, Marjorie."

"Good morning, Jill. What's a five-letter word for

funny?"
"Err—silly?"
"It starts with a D."
"Daft?"
"That's four letters."
"Dafta?"
She gave me a disapproving look; clearly Marjorie took her crosswords seriously.
"No Cynthia today?"
"We've started taking it in turns to cover the early shift. She won't be down for a couple of hours yet."
"I hear you've decided to sell up."
"That's right. It wasn't an easy decision, but I think it's the right one. Neither of us are getting any younger."
"I'll be sorry to see you go. Have you had any interest in the business yet?"
"Not so far. According to the estate agent, this isn't a good time to be selling, so we could be here for some time yet. Just the biscuits, is it?"
"Yes. Oh, and this lottery ticket."
"It's amazing."
"Sorry? What is?"
"The number of people who have done the lottery this week after news came out about the local winner."
"Have they come forward to claim their winnings yet?" I asked.
"Not as far as I know."
"Jack and I were talking about that. Why would someone wait to claim eight million pounds?"
"There could be any number of reasons."
"Nothing would stop me. I'd have been on their doorstep five minutes after the winning numbers were

announced."

"Whoever it is may not even know they've won. They might have lost the ticket. It wouldn't be the first time that's happened."

When I stepped out of the store, I almost bumped into Julian, who stared at the biscuits I was carrying.

"Didn't they have any protein bars?"

"Err, yeah, they're in my pocket. These are for Jack."

"Really?" He shook his head. "There's no wonder he needs to go running."

Mrs V shot me a disapproving look.

"You really should try and cut back on those biscuits, Jill."

"These will last me for at least a couple of weeks."

"That's what you said last week when you brought in four packets of them."

In my defence, I'd had to give some of them to Edna, the surveillance fairy, but I didn't think Mrs V would buy that explanation.

"Any calls?"

"There was a message on the answerphone when I got here."

"Since when did we have an answerphone?"

"I bought it last week. It's so much simpler than that voicemail thingy. A Mr Sandwich left his number and asked if you'd return his call."

"*Sandwich*? That can't be right, can it?"

"Listen for yourself."

She pressed a button on the answerphone.

"*Sandwich speaking. I hate these recording things. Could you call me back as soon as possible.*"

"See," Mrs V said. "He did say Sandwich, didn't he?"

"It sounded like it. He didn't leave a number, though."

"The machine records the caller's number. I jotted it down for you." She handed me a slip of paper.

"Okay, I'll give him a call in a minute."

"Tea?"

"I think I'll have coffee this morning, please."

Winky was staring out of the window and didn't turn around when I walked into the office.

"Good morning, Winky."

"Come and look at this."

"If it's that couple again, I'm not interested. And stop being a Peeping Tom."

"Nah, they've started closing their blinds. Come and look at this."

"What's so fascinating?" It was then that I spotted the helicopter hovering above the heliport that had been built on top of the building opposite ours. "Is it coming in to land?"

"Looks like it." The helicopter descended slowly until it touched down on the helipad. As the rotor blades began to slow down, one of the doors opened.

"I reckon that's Phil Sparks," Winky said.

"Who?"

"Don't tell me you haven't heard of him."

"Should I have?"

"He's the founder and CEO of Fun Rat. He's one of the richest men in the world."

"He doesn't look very old."

"He isn't. He started the business in his bedroom when he was still at school."

The man disappeared into the building and, moments

later, the helicopter lifted off.

Once I'd finished my coffee, I gave Mr Sandwich a call. Someone picked up on the first ring.

"Yes?"

"Mr Sandwich?"

"Who?"

"I'd like to speak to a Mr Sandwich please."

"Who is this?"

"My name is Jill Maxwell; I'm a private investigator. Mr Sandwich left a message on my answerphone."

"That was me, but my name is Sam Rich."

"Ah, right. Sorry for the confusion Mr Rich. The message on the answerphone wasn't very clear."

"Do you find missing persons?"

"Err, yes, I—"

"Good, in that case, we should talk."

"Okay. Do you want to come into the office, or would you prefer me to come to you?"

"It might be better if you came to see me at my office."

"No problem. What's the address?"

"Do you know The Sticks?"

"Funnily enough, I was there recently."

"Excellent. Chicken Enterprises is on Eggshell Road. I'll be out most of today and tomorrow. Can you do Thursday?"

"Err, yeah, sure."

"Is eight-thirty too early?"

"No, that's fine."

"I'll see you then." He hung up.

"Mr *Sandwich*?" Winky laughed. "Brilliant."

"That's what it sounded like."

"Way to make a good first impression."

"Be quiet."

"Another high-profile case?"

"Missing person, he said."

"I suppose that's one step up from missing chickens."

"Maybe, maybe not. His business is called Chicken Enterprises."

"Oh dear."

"And get this, the address is Eggshell Road."

"Someone is winding you up."

"That's what I thought. If you hadn't been here in the room with me, I would have assumed it was you."

I was still wondering why my life was suddenly so full of chickens when Jack called.

"Thanks very much, Jill."

"What for?"

"Why would you tell Julian that I was a keen runner?"

"I didn't say that. Not exactly, anyway."

"So why did he ask me to join him on his morning runs? And why does he think I have a custard cream problem?"

"What's that, Mrs V? Oh, okay. Sorry, Jack, something urgent has just come up."

"I know you're only pretending to talk to Mrs V. We'll discuss this tonight."

"Why are you grinning like a Cheshire Dog?" Winky said.

"It's a cat."

"What is?"

"It's a Cheshire *Cat*. Not a dog."

"Nah, you've got that wrong. So, what was amusing you?"

"Just the thought of Jack running around the lanes of Middle Tweaking."

"I'll never understand two-leggeds' sense of humour."

When my phone rang again, I assumed it would be Jack wanting to continue his berating of me, but it was something much worse.

"Grandma, what a lovely surprise."

"Sarcasm doesn't become you."

"Is it urgent? I was just—"

"I need you over here. Right now."

"At the hotel? I'm not in Middle Tweaking."

"Not at the hotel. I'm in WiFY."

"I'm not sorting out wigs again."

"I don't need any wigs sorting out."

"What then?"

"You'll see when you get here."

"I'm really busy."

"Must I remind you that you owe me a favour?"

"No, Grandma." I sighed. "I remember."

This was all that baby dragon's fault.

"Good, I'll expect you in a few minutes, then."

"I don't know why you don't stand up to that grandmother of yours," Winky said.

"Brave words from someone who hides under the sofa every time she comes to the office."

"What does she want this time?"

"I dread to think."

"Did you speak to Mr Sandwich, dear?" Mrs V asked on my way out.

"His name is actually Sam Rich."

"Oh?"

"Maybe that answerphone wasn't such a good idea."

"I'm sure it'll be fine. It maybe just needs a little tweaking. I'll take a look at the instructions."

"I'm going to see my grandmother. Hopefully, I won't be long."

"Ever the optimist."

Chapter 4

As I walked down the high street, I promised myself that if Grandma asked me to do anything related to bunions, verrucae or warts, I would refuse point blank.

What do you mean, *brave talk*. I'm not scared of Grandma. Okay, maybe a little, but that didn't mean I was going to let her push me around.

"No way! I'm not doing it!" I backed away.

"You have to. You agreed."

"I don't care, I'm not making earwax candles again."

"I'm not asking you to. There's no point, anyway, because the bottom has fallen out of the earwax candle market since they introduced those cheap synthetic imitations. I just need you to get the wax out of my ears because I can barely hear a thing, particularly out of this right one."

"Why can't you go and get it done professionally? I'm sure there are lots of places that do this kind of stuff."

"I'm not having some human poking around in my ears."

"There must be somewhere in Candlefield you could go?"

"There isn't. There's no call for them there. Ear wax is a human world phenomenon."

"I'm not poking around in your ear. I might do you some damage."

"Don't you think I've thought of that? That's why I bought this." She reached under the counter and produced a box.

"Ear wax suction machine?"

"State of the art."

"That sounds even more dangerous to me."

"Nonsense, it's perfectly safe." She opened the box and took out the small gizmo. "I know how squeamish you are, so you'll be pleased to know that the wax is deposited straight into this little compartment, so you don't even need to see it."

Small mercies.

"Ready?"

"Not really."

She took a seat next to the counter.

"Switch it on."

"What if a customer comes in?"

"They won't. I've turned the sign over to say closed. Now, get on with it."

"Okay, what now? There are five different levels."

"Set it to maximum suction."

"Are you sure?"

"Positive. There's quite an accumulation in there, I can tell."

"Okay, what now?"

"Put that bit in my ear."

"If this goes wrong, you can't take it out on me."

"It won't. Get on with it."

I really wanted to close my eyes and pretend I was somewhere else, but I would probably have ended up poking one of her eyes out.

Once the small probe thingy was in her ear, the suction noise grew louder.

"Is that okay?"

"Pardon?"

"I said is that alright?"

"I can't hear you. Keep going, I can feel it breaking

down."

After a few minutes, she had me switch to the other ear.

When it was finally at an end, she opened up the small compartment and peered inside.

"It's a shame the bottom has fallen out of the earwax candle market. There's a good three candles' worth in here. Would you like a drink and a biscuit while you're down here?"

"No, thanks." After that ordeal, I was struggling to hold onto the contents of my stomach. "I'd better be going."

After that horror show, I needed to get some fresh air before returning to the office, so instead of heading straight back, I took a walk to Rue Pets. Rupert greeted me like a long-lost friend, which was hardly surprising given that I was rapidly becoming one of his best customers.

"Lovely to see you again, Jill, what can I get for you today?"

"Those fish of mine insist they need another ornament."

"I'm really impressed with the relationship you have with your pets. It's not everyone that has these kind of imaginary conversations where they tell you what they want."

"You're right. My relationship with the fish is kind of special."

"What kind of ornament did you have in mind? Our galleon range is very popular."

"They definitely don't want anything like that. I'm looking for something more—err—arty."

"Arty?"

"Abstract, I suppose. Do you have anything like that?"

"We do have the Frendear Collection. It was designed

by the award-winning designer Brenda Frendear. You may be aware of her work in street furniture."

"I can't say I am."

"The Aquatics Council commissioned her to design a range of ornaments for them."

"Can I see them?"

"I don't keep them out in the shop for fear of theft. They're very expensive."

"If they aren't out here, how does anyone know about them?"

"So far, I've only sold them to fans of Frendear's work. I'm pretty sure they aren't buying them to put them in fish tanks. Just collectors, really. Would you like to see them?"

"I might as well."

He led the way into a large stockroom.

"They're in the display case over there."

Judging by Rupert's expression, he was as impressed by the Frendear Collection as I was. Although, after seeing them, I was left with a new appreciation of Florence's masterpiece, which was at least as good as those monstrosities.

"I think they're ugly," I said. "Sorry."

"No need to apologise. I agree."

"Do people really pay those prices for them?"

"The hardcore Frendear fans don't blink at them."

"Wow!"

Wanda and Mabel were right; I really should encourage Florence to pursue a career in the arts if you could command that type of money for such rubbish.

"I take it you won't be buying a Frendear, Jill?"

"No, thanks." We were on our way back into the shop

when something caught my eye. "What are these, Rupert?" I pointed to the open box next to the door.

"They're just the rejects: ornaments that were damaged in transit to us, or were broken while out on display."

"Could I take a look?"

"Sure, knock yourself out, but I'll have to go out there, in case there are any other customers."

Ten minutes later, I went back into the shop. "How much for these two, Rupert?"

He shrugged. "One pound for the two?"

"Sure." I handed him a pound coin.

Result! Now, all I had to do was to sell them to Wanda and Mabel.

As I made my way back to the office, I spotted a familiar figure, hobbling along on crutches.

"Hey, Mad."

"Hi, Jill."

"How's the leg?"

"Mending, I hope. I hate these crutches. Don't you have a spell that could repair the break quicker?"

"Sorry, witches aren't allowed to use magic for medical interventions."

"Pity. Fancy a coffee?"

"Sure, why not."

"This is a first for me." Mad petted the sloth clinging to her arm.

"Me too." I had tried to decline the sloth, but Coffee Animal's rules were inflexible: no animal, no drink. "I think they must be a new addition to the menagerie."

"I'm Charlie," my sloth said.

"And I'm Harry," Mad's sloth introduced himself.

"Hi, guys," I said. "Mad and I have a few things to discuss, so if you could talk amongst yourselves, that would be great."

"What's it worth?" Charlie said.

"A bite of my bun?"

"Half of it."

"Okay, half."

"Same for me." Harry nodded.

"I assume you know what they're saying?" Mad said.

"Yeah, that's Charlie and that's Harry. I've asked them to give us a little space, but they want half of our buns to do it."

"Fair enough."

Mad and I both cut our buns in half and placed them on the spare seats. In response, the two sloths began to slide down our arms and onto the seats. It was a slow process, but they made it eventually.

"How's that husband of mine doing?" I asked.

"Jack seems to have really taken to it; he and Brad get on like a house on fire."

"How much longer do you reckon you'll need him?"

"I'm not sure. A couple more weeks at least. Were his blond highlights your idea?"

"Not exactly, but it might have had something to do with my pointing out his grey hairs."

"What has he said to you about the job? Is he enjoying it?"

"He must be. The two sisters who run the store in our village are selling up, and Jack said he wished we could buy it."

"Is that a possibility?"

"We don't have that kind of money. The only way we could do it would be to sell the old watermill and live above the store."

"Would you consider doing that?"

"No way. We could never give up the old water mill. And, besides, it wouldn't be fair on Florence."

"How is she doing? She's started going to CASS, hasn't she?"

"Yeah, but only for a few hours, three days a week. You know what kids are like, she doesn't tell us much about it, but her magic is coming along in leaps and bounds."

"That's good."

"Not always. Some of the stuff she gets up to scares me to death."

"Such as?"

I told Mad about some of the more outrageous spells that Florence had learned recently.

"Sticky feet?" She laughed.

"Yeah, I got home to find her walking on the kitchen ceiling."

"Brilliant."

"The doopcake spell was pretty freaky too."

"Doopcake?"

"It's actually called the *'duplicate'* spell, but Florence insists on pronouncing it doopcake. It lets her make identical copies of herself. The first time she did it, I walked into her bedroom, and there were ten Florences."

"I love it. She's growing up so quickly."

"Too quickly for Jack's liking."

"What do you mean?"

"He's got pre-empty nest syndrome."

"*Pre*?"

"Yeah, we somehow got onto the subject of when Florence eventually moves out."

"That won't be for years yet."

"I know, but Jack is already fretting over it."

"That's so sweet. What about you?"

"When the time comes, I'm sure I'll miss her terribly, but I'm not going to start worrying about it just yet. Anyway, enough about me and my family, what about you? What are you up to?"

"Not much with this leg."

"Have you and Brad started making any plans?"

"What kind of plans?"

"Marriage, kids, that kind of thing."

"Not really. We've got enough on with the shop. Maybe in a couple of years."

"What about the ghost-hunting? Anything new on that front?"

"I don't want to count my chickens, but my boss has decided to take early retirement."

"And you're up for his job?"

"I'm in with a chance, but this hasn't helped." She tapped her leg.

"That won't affect the decision, will it?"

"It shouldn't, but who knows?"

"That was delicious," Harry said.

"Yeah, really nice," Charlie added.

How is it that sloths are slow at everything except for eating?

"If you're angling for some more, you're wasting your time," I said.

"I'll get them another one." Mad stood up. "They're so cute."

Cute? *Sloths*? I was beginning to wonder if her fall on the assault course had affected more than just her leg.

Before heading home, I made a call to Francesca Artichoke. I'd tried to reach her several times earlier in the day, but she'd been in court.

"Artichoke speaking."

"Ms Artichoke, it's Jill Maxwell."

"Who?"

"You came to see me yesterday about your missing chickens."

"Ah, yes. Sorry, I've had rather a hectic day."

"You said I should call to try and arrange when I could come and see you."

"Right, yes, let me check my diary." The line went dead for a moment, then she said, "I was due in court tomorrow afternoon, but it's just been postponed, so I could spare you some time at two o'clock. Does that work for you?"

"Yes, that'll be fine."

"Excellent. I'll send you a text with the address."

"Okay, I'll see you tomorrow."

***

As I drove into the village, the road was partially blocked by a removal van parked outside the house where Donna and family had lived until recently. There was only just enough room to squeeze past the van and the wall on the opposite side of the road. As I edged slowly through the gap, a young woman with long blonde hair came around the side of the van. When she saw my predicament, she stood in front of my car and guided me through. Once I'd made it, she came around to the driver's side and beckoned for me to lower the window.

"I'm really sorry about this," she said. "There's no room to park the van anywhere closer to the house."

"No problem. I take it you've bought this place."

"That's right. We fell in love with it the first time we saw it."

"I'm Jill Maxwell. I live just up the road in the old watermill with my husband and daughter."

"I'm Goldie. I've seen your house. It's so beautiful."

"Thank you."

Just then, one of the removal men came over.

"I'm sorry to disturb you, Ms Locks, but there are a few boxes with no room marked on them. Could you come and take a look and tell us where you want them, please?"

"Sure, I'll be right there. I'd better go and see to this, Jill. Sorry again about the van."

"Good luck with everything."

"Come on, Jack, try and see the funny side," I said.

"There's nothing funny about it."

"It'll do you good. You're always saying that you're out of shape."

"I've never said that. Not once."

"You could have told Julian you didn't want to go running with him."

"I tried, but he's very persuasive. He said I needed to work off the calories from all the custard creams I was eating. Why did you tell him they were mine?"

"I think he must have misunderstood." It was time for a change of subject, so I held out the bag from Rue Pets.

"Look what I've got."
"What are those things?"
"New ornaments for the fish. I got them from Rue Pets."
"What are they supposed to be? They look like they've been thrown against a wall."
"They were in the rejects bin, so I got them both for one pound."
"I'm surprised he didn't pay you to take them off his hands. You're not going to try and fob the goldfish off with those, are you? They'll go crazy."
"Not if I sell them in the right way." I started towards the lounge.
"This I have to see."
"Did you remember our ornament?" Wanda said.
"Of course I did, ladies. In fact, I've bought two for you." I took them out of the bag.
"Wait for it," Jack said in a whisper behind me.
The two fish stared at the damaged ornaments, and I could tell things were in the balance, so I got in first, "These are part of the exclusive Madmoo collection. I assume you've heard of Madmoo?"
"Err, yes of course," Wanda said, hesitantly.
"I was extremely lucky to get these. They were the last two in the shop."
"Such wonderful colours," Mabel said.
"Where would you like me to put them?"
"In the bin." Jack laughed.
Luckily for him, the fish didn't hear him.
"I think we'll have that one over there." Wanda pointed with her fin. "And the other one over there."
Once the ornaments were in the tank, the two fish swam from one to the other, admiring them both in turn. While

they were still transfixed, I ushered Jack out of the room, and followed him into the kitchen.

"Madmoo collection?" Jack laughed. "How do you come up with this stuff?"

"It's a gift. By the way, I bumped into our new neighbour on the way into the village."

"I saw the removal van. Who is it?"

"The young woman I spoke to is called Goldie."

"What's she like?"

"She seems nice enough, but I only spoke to her for a few minutes. You'll never guess what her surname is."

"Rhubarb?"

"Worse than that. It's Locks."

"What's wrong with that?"

"Think about it for a minute."

"I don't get—oh, wait a minute. Goldie Locks?"

"Yeah. What were her parents thinking?"

"Maybe it's not their fault. Perhaps she married a Mr Locks."

"That can't be it. If I was called Goldie, there's no way I'd marry a man with the surname Locks."

"Yes, but not everyone is as shallow as you, Jill."

Chapter 5

"Mummy, the fish have broken their ornaments," Florence said, the next morning.

"They aren't broken, pumpkin," Jack said. "They're Madmoos."

"What's a Madmoo?"

"You'd better ask your mummy."

"What's a Madmoo, Mummy?"

"Daddy just made that word up, darling. They're just broken ornaments."

"Why don't you take them out of the fish tank?"

"I was going to, but the fish seem to like them."

"I told everyone at school that I'm going to Wonder World. Kirsty says she wishes she could go."

"When you're there, you mustn't use any magic."

"I know."

"Promise?"

"I promise. Can I go outside and look for worms?"

"As long as you don't bring them into the house."

"Yay!"

"And don't get dirty because you have to go to school soon."

"Okay." She dashed outside.

"What is it with kids and worms?" I said to Jack.

"I used to love all creepy-crawlies when I was a kid. All children do."

"I didn't."

"Why doesn't that surprise me?"

"Did I tell you I bumped into Mad yesterday?"

"No, you never mentioned it."

"We went for a drink in Coffee Animal. They have

sloths in there now."

"Did she mention me?"

"She said you were a liability and that she wished she'd never asked you to help out."

"Very funny." He hesitated for a moment, waiting for me to laugh, but I kept stony-faced. "She didn't really say that, did she?"

"Of course not. She said you're doing great."

"I'm enjoying it much more than I thought was possible."

"When I was in the village store yesterday, I asked Marjorie Stock if they've had any interest from potential buyers yet."

"Have they?"

"It doesn't sound like it. Do you think they'd take a hundred quid for it?"

"I wish. I can just see myself behind that counter."

Jack had just gone outside to check on the worm-hunter when my phone rang with a number I didn't recognise. I expected it to be a cold-caller trying to interest me in the investment opportunity of a lifetime, but I was wrong—it was Jack's mother.

"Yvonne?"

"Jill, thank goodness I caught you. Roy and I need your help."

"What's wrong?"

"I assume you heard about Lady Tweaking?"

"Caroline? What about her?"

"She's dead."

"Oh no. What—err—when—?"

"About three weeks ago; her heart gave way."

"I can't believe it. When is the funeral?"

"It was last week."

"I feel terrible. I should have been there to pay my respects."

"It was a very small affair, apparently. Her son, Dominic, has inherited Tweaking Manor."

"I met Dominic some time ago when I was working on a case for Lady Tweaking. He seemed like a decent enough guy."

"He plans to turn this place into a hotel."

"How do you know?"

"Because he was here yesterday, talking through his plans with an architect."

"He didn't waste any time. Still, I suppose turning Tweaking Manor into a hotel isn't the worst thing that could happen to it."

"You haven't heard the worst part yet."

"What's that?"

"I overheard him telling the architect that he was getting bad vibes from the place, and that he thought it might be haunted."

"He's not wrong, is he?"

"He's planning to bring in an exorcist. This is a disaster. Roy and I have just settled in here and now we're going to be chased away."

"Like you chased out the colonel and Priscilla, you mean?"

"That's rather unfair, Jill. We didn't chase them away. It's just that the four of us couldn't get along. I know the colonel is a good friend of yours, but he's such an insufferable bore. Anyway, the reason I called you was to ask if there is anything you can do."

This wasn't the first time I'd had to deal with an

exorcism. Several years earlier, the colonel had asked me to help when Murray Murray had been about to bring in an exorcist to rid the colonel's old house of ghosts. On that occasion, I'd taken on the personality of Portia Parkspirit, exorcist extraordinaire. Perhaps, it was time for her to make a reappearance.

"I might be able to help."

"I knew we could rely on you. What will you do?"

I told her about Portia Parkspirit and my previous experience at the colonel's old house.

"That sounds ideal, Jill, but how will we persuade Dominic to hire Portia Parkspirit?"

"Leave that with me."

"Okay, and thanks, Jill."

"Would you like to speak to Jack while you're on?"

"Not just now. Roy is calling me to say breakfast is ready. Give him our love, though, would you?"

"Will do."

I'd just finished on the call when Jack came back inside.

"Did I hear your phone?"

"It was your mum."

"Is she okay?"

"She's still dead, but otherwise she's fine."

"Dad?"

"They're both dead, but okay. Apparently, Lady Tweaking died a few weeks ago."

"Oh no. I'm sorry. I know you were close to her."

"I can't believe I didn't hear about it. I would have liked to have gone to the funeral. Your mother reckons that Caroline's son, Dominic, has inherited Tweaking Manor."

"Lucky guy. That must be worth a few quid."

"Your mother overheard him talking to an architect.

He's planning to turn the manor into a hotel."

"It's a magnificent place. It should do well."

"I agree, but Dominic is worried the place may be haunted, so he's going to bring in an exorcist. That's why your mother called. She wanted to know if there was anything I could do to help."

"Can you?"

"Possibly, but it will take all of my thespian skills."

"They're doomed then."

"Cheek."

"Just joking. Didn't she ask to talk to me?"

"She had to go because Roy had just made breakfast, but she said I should give you their love."

***

As I walked out to the car, I spotted a young man walking into the village.

"Good morning," he called to me. "It's Jill, isn't it?"

"Err, yeah?" I still had no idea who he was.

"I'm Liam Locks. I believe you spoke to my wife, Goldie, when we were moving in."

"Ah yes. Welcome to Middle Tweaking."

"Thanks. This is a beautiful village. Goldie and I fell in love with it the first time we saw it. And your house is amazing."

"Thanks, we think so."

"I've just been for a walk. The air here is so much better than in the city. We used to have a flat in Washbridge."

"I know what you mean. In fact, I'm just on my way there now. My office is in Washbridge."

"What do you do, Jill? If you don't mind me asking."

"I'm a private investigator."

"Really? How exciting. I'm just a boring dentist."

I had never understood why anyone would want to be a dentist. Spending all day, looking in other people's mouths wasn't my idea of fun. It was almost as bad as being a chiropodist.

"Where is your practice?"

"In Washbridge, so I haven't escaped the city altogether. Goldie works there too."

"At your dental practice?"

"No, I meant she works in Washbridge. She's a podiatrist."

"Is that the same as a chiropodist?"

"Yes. Some people still refer to them as chiropodists, but Goldie prefers podiatrist."

"Right."

"Anyway, I mustn't keep you, Jill. It was nice to meet you."

"Likewise."

On the drive into Washbridge, I tried to imagine the conversations that might take place in the Locks' household, as they told each other about their day at work.

"Good morning, Jill," Mrs V said.

I didn't respond immediately because I'd been struck dumb by the sight of the two objects on her desk. Eventually, I managed to say, "I'm probably going to regret asking this, but why do you have a boomerang and a cuddly koala on your desk?"

"Can't you guess?"

"Err, is the Australian embassy holding a garage sale?"

"No, silly. Armi and I are thinking of going to Australia."

"That's the other side of the world."

"Armi's cousin, Petunia, lives there. She's invited us to stay with her for a month. I told Armi I'd have to clear it with you first, obviously. It wouldn't be for a while yet, probably next year."

"Of course. It's just such a long way to travel at your—" I just managed to catch my foot before wedging it into my mouth.

"At our *age*?"

"Sorry, I just meant—err—"

"It's okay. We're neither of us spring chickens, and this will probably be the last chance we get to do something like this. We're both really excited."

"Good for you."

"I'll give you plenty of notice once we have confirmed the dates. Tea?"

"Yes, please."

"Morning, Cobber," Winky said.

"Why are you wearing that ridiculous hat?"

"I thought I'd continue the Antipodean theme." He took off the hat that had corks hanging from the brim. "Do you like it?"

"It looks ridiculous. Where did you get it from anyway?"

"Feline Rent-A-Hat, obviously. They have hats for all occasions."

Mrs V came through the door behind me, and did a doubletake when she spotted the hat that Winky had dropped onto the floor.

"Did you buy that for me, Jill?" She bent down and picked up the hat. "That's so sweet of you. Why didn't you tell me that Armi had already called, to tell you about our plans?"

"I—err—"

"It's a lovely gesture. I just came in to say we're out of teabags. Will coffee do?"

"Coffee is fine."

"Why did you let her steal my hat?" Winky said after she'd left the room.

"It was nothing to do with me. You left it lying on the floor."

"You could have told her you didn't buy the hat for her."

"What was I supposed to say? That you'd hired it from Feline Rent-A-Hat?"

"I'll have to pay for that now."

"Them's the breaks."

"Oh well, at least I won't have to put up with the old bag lady for much longer."

"She doesn't go until next year and then it's only for a month."

"At her age, she'll never survive that trip. They'll be burying her in the land of kangaroos."

"That's a horrible thing to say."

"Can I help you to interview the new receptionists?"

"What? No, you can't because I'm not going to need one."

"But, just for argument's sake, let's say she doesn't make it back, can I help you with the interviews then?"

"In the unlikely event that I need a new receptionist, you're the last person I'd ask to help me choose someone."

"Why not? I have to work with whoever you pick too."
"Forget it. You don't get a say."
"So selfish."

Winky was still pouting when I made a call to the local printer that I'd found in Yellow Pages.
"Print-Lightning, Bobby speaking, how can I help you?"
"Hi, I've just seen your ad in Yellow Pages. It says you can print colour flyers within a couple of hours. Is that correct?"
"Absolutely, provided you can give us details of what you want printing."
"I've just sketched something on paper. If I take a photo and email it to you, would that do?"
"That'll be fine."
"Okay, I'm sending it over now."
"Let me just check our email." The line went silent, and I thought maybe we'd been cut off, but then he said, "Exorcist? Is that the one?"
"Yeah, that's it. Can you work from that?"
"I don't see why not. Are you Portia—err—?"
"Parkspirit, yes, that's me."
"Right. How many would you like?"
"Just one, please."
"One thousand?"
"No."
"One hundred?"
"No, just the one, but it needs to be very eye-catching with plenty of colour."
"O—kay."
"If I pop over in a couple of hours, will it be ready?"
"It'll be here waiting for you."

"Excellent."

"What are you up to now?" Winky said.

"Didn't I tell you? Not only am I Washbridge's premier PI, I'm also an exorcist extraordinaire."

"You're seriously puddled. That's what you are."

Chapter 6

The young man behind the counter at Print-Lightning was wearing a badge with the name Bobby embossed on it. Business was clearly slow because Bobby appeared to be engrossed in a game on his phone. So engrossed, in fact, that he didn't realise I was in the shop until I was standing right next to the counter and said hi.

"Oh, sorry." He quickly put his phone away. "I didn't hear you come in. How can I help you?"

"I'm here to collect a flyer for Portia Parkspirit."

"Is that you?"

"I'm actually Portia's assistant."

"Right."

"Did you manage to get the flyer done?"

"Yeah, it's here." He reached under the counter. "She did say she only wanted the one, didn't she?"

"That's right."

"Is this okay?" He handed me a single flyer, which had been printed on glossy paper.

"Yeah, that's just the ticket. I like your choice of colours."

"Thanks."

"How much is that?"

"Just ten pounds, please." I handed him the cash and was about to leave when he said, "Is your boss really an exorcist?"

"Yes, she is."

"I didn't realise there were such things. Apart from in movies."

"I can assure you that Portia is very much real."

"How does she—err—I mean what exactly—err—?"

"I couldn't begin to explain. I could ask her to pay you a visit, to give you a demonstration, if you're really interested."

"No, thanks. I was just curious, that's all."

"Okay, well, thanks again for this."

From Print-Lightning, I drove straight to Tweaking Manor, and posted the flyer in the post-box next to the main gates. Back in the car, I was just about to head to Francesca Artichoke's house when I got a call from Grandma.

"Have you heard about Belinda?"

"Who?"

"Belinda Berrymore."

"Who's she?"

"She's one of the leading lights on WOW."

I had stopped attending meetings of WOW, Witches Of Washbridge, some years ago because all they seemed to talk about was potions and their bunions.

"What about her?"

"She's disappeared."

"Where has she gone?"

"Do I really have to explain the meaning of the word *disappeared*?"

"Sorry. I'm not sure why you're telling me, though."

"Have you forgotten already?"

"Forgotten Belinda *what's her name*? I don't think I've ever met her, have I?"

"I meant have you forgotten what I told you about The Twenty-One?"

"The burning thingy?"

"*Thingy*? Really?"

"Sorry. Do you think Belinda's disappearance is

connected to that?"

"Of course it is. I would have thought that was obvious."

"Have there been any other disappearances?"

"As far as I'm aware, she's the first, but there will be others. Sixteen witches were burnt at the last burning."

"Sixteen? That's awful."

"That's what I've been trying to tell you. Have you seen anything suspicious?"

"No, but I'll be vigilant."

"What are you going to do about Belinda?"

"*Me*? What am I supposed to do?"

"Finding her would be a good start."

"I'm really busy at the moment."

"Finding lost chickens? I think someone needs to get their priorities right."

"Okay, I'll see what I can do."

"Good, and just be careful. I don't want to have to be the one to explain to Jim that his wife has been burned at the stake."

"His name is—" It was too late; she'd already ended the call.

Francesca Artichoke lived in Little Biggly, which is one of the more affluent suburbs of Washbridge. Her house was in the middle of a tree-lined cul-de-sac, and had the catchy name Too Gusty.

The steel gates were locked, so I pressed the button on the intercom.

"Yes?"

"It's Jill Maxwell."

"I was just about to feed the pigs. Could you make your

way around to the back of the house?"

"Sure."

The gate opened slowly and, as instructed, I made my way to the back of the house. Although Francesca had told me that she kept livestock, I wasn't prepared for the sight that greeted me. From the street, the house looked like any other house in a middle class neighbourhood. From the back, it looked more like Farmer Giles' farm.

And the smell!

"Hi there!" Francesca gestured that I should join her.

If it hadn't been for her voice, I'm not sure I would have recognised her, dressed as she was in dungarees and wellingtons. As I made my way over to her, she began to throw food to the three pigs in the enclosure. By the time I reached her, I was beginning to wish that I'd given more thought to my footwear.

"I adore pigs, Jill," she said. "Don't you?"

"Err, sure."

"Don't sound so enthusiastic," said the fattest of the three pigs.

Francesca then did the introductions. "That's Horace, that's Gerry and that's Norman."

"Those aren't our real names," said the second-fattest of the pigs, "But we find it best to humour her."

"Right."

"Sorry?" Francesca shot me a puzzled look.

"They're great names. You have goats too."

"I do. And a couple of sheep over there."

"Right."

"Come and see where the chickens should be."

I followed her through the mud, trying desperately not to become separated from my shoes. The wooden chicken coop, which was enclosed by a wire metal fence, was at the far end of the garden. Francesca stared at the empty enclosure and began to well up.

"Are you okay?" I felt I should ask.

"I know you shouldn't have favourites, but I really loved the chickens. I had names for every one of them."

"How many did you have?"

"Twenty-four plus Roger."

"*Roger*?"

"The rooster."

"Was he taken too?"

"Yes, all of them."

"Can you tell me exactly what happened?"

"There isn't much to tell. I always set the alarm for five-thirty, to give myself plenty of time to feed all the animals before I go to work. I sensed something wasn't right as soon as I stepped outside, and then I realised there was no clucking coming from inside the coop. When I opened it up, it was empty."

"And you heard nothing unusual during the night?"

"No, but then my bedroom is on the front of the house, and I am generally a deep sleeper."

"Does anyone else live here with you?"

"No, it's just me and the animals. My useless husband and I parted company just over a year ago."

"I see. What about the neighbours?"

"What about them?"

"Have you asked any of them if they saw or heard anything?"

"I don't really have anything to do with the neighbours."

"I see. What about your job? Can you think of anyone,

who you come into contact with in the course of your work, that may hold some kind of grievance against you."

"Plenty." She laughed. "I'm not in the business of trying to make friends."

That much I could believe.

"Quite, but is there anyone in particular who you think might be holding a grudge?"

"It's a very long list, but we're talking about CEOs of major corporations, and other leaders of industry. Hardly the kind of person to get involved with stealing a few chickens."

"Fair enough. Do you have any theories about who may have done this?"

"My gut feeling is that it's someone much closer to home." Her gaze moved between the neighbouring properties.

"Are you saying you think it could be one of your neighbours?"

"No, I'm saying I'd like you to find my chickens and help me bring whoever stole them to justice." She glanced at her watch. "I'm afraid we'll have to wrap this up because I have to go and get cleaned up in time for a meeting later this afternoon. Is there anything else you need from me?"

"No, I think that's it for now."

"Good. I look forward to hearing from you soon."

And with that, she scurried back into the house. There were neighbouring properties to either side and to the rear, but I couldn't actually see them because of the high wooden fence that enclosed the garden. One thing was obvious, though: it wouldn't have been easy for someone to remove a couple of dozen chickens without being seen.

Although Francesca hadn't said so in as many words, I'd come away with the impression that she wasn't exactly on good terms with her neighbours, so I would need to approach them carefully.

***

Jack greeted me at the door, and he didn't look like a happy bunny.

"Is everything okay?" I said. "Is Florence alright?"

"Florence is fine. She's upstairs drawing worms."

"You look upset about something."

"My feet ache and my calf muscles are killing me."

"Is working in the shop getting too much for you?"

"This has nothing to do with working in the shop. Guess who came a calling after I'd dropped Florence at school?"

"Was it the Muffin Man?"

"What? No, it was Julian."

"Had he come to give you a refund for those highlights? I thought they looked a bit dodgy."

"There's nothing wrong with my highlights. He came to ask me to go running with him."

"That was nice of him."

"I should have said no. Every muscle in my legs is aching."

"Poor love." I sniffed the air. "Something smells nice."

"I decided to make one of my world-famous cheesy meatball casseroles. Although, I'm not sure you deserve it after dropping me in it with Julian."

"You'll thank me in the long run." I gave him a peck on the cheek. "I'll go and see what that daughter of ours is up to."

There were no sounds coming from Florence's bedroom, which was either very good. Or very very bad. Hoping for the best, but anticipating the worst, I opened the door and stepped inside. Jay was fast asleep on the bed; Florence was seated at her desk, drawing a worm, just like Jack had said. Unfortunately, there was one minor point he had failed to mention.

"Florence Maxwell, why is there a worm on your desk?"

"That's Ellie."

"I don't care what its name is. Why is it on your desk? I told you that I didn't want any worms in the house."

"But I needed to see it, so I can draw it."

"Okay, but don't let it fall on the carpet, and as soon as you've finished your drawing, I want you to put—err—Ellie out in the garden."

"Okay."

"How was CASS today?"

"Boring."

"What did you do?"

"History stuff. Do you like Ellie, Mummy?"

"She's okay. For a worm. Now, don't forget what I said. Don't let her fall onto the carpet."

"Okay."

The casserole was delicious, and I couldn't resist helping myself to seconds.

"So?" Jack said. "What do you think of it?"

"It's okay." I shrugged.

"Steady on with the praise. What about you, pumpkin, do you like it?"

"It's yummy." Florence had already cleared her plate. "Can I go outside?"

"Yes, but don't bring any more worms inside the house," I said.

"Go on, Jill, admit it, you loved my casserole, didn't you?"

"Yeah, it was nice."

"Wow, steady my beating heart."

"I bumped into Goldie's husband this morning, and you were right, his surname is Locks. Apparently, he's a dentist and she is a podiatrist."

"That's handy. You'll be able to get your corns seen to."

"Cheek. I do not have corns. Grandma might be interested, though. You'll never guess what Mrs V told me this morning."

"Is she going to retire at long last?"

"No. She and Armi are planning to go to Australia next year."

"To live?"

"No, they're going to stay with Armi's cousin."

"Good for them."

"Don't you think they're a bit old for that kind of adventure?"

"Definitely not. You're as old as you feel." He winced as he pulled himself up out of the chair. "Which in my case is about a hundred."

"You're right. When Florence has grown up and left home, you and I should travel the world."

"I told you before that I don't want to think about when Florence leaves home."

Chapter 7

"Are you sure you don't want any breakfast?" Jack said.

"I don't have time." I took a quick slurp of tea. "I have a meeting with my client at eight-thirty."

"Is this the chicken case?"

"It's *one* of the chicken cases." I gave Florence a kiss on the top of her head. "Have a nice day at school, darling."

"Will you teach me to knit, Mummy?"

"*Knit*?"

"Yeah, Nina can knit. She made a scarf. Will you?"

"Err, okay."

"Yay! Can we start now?"

"Not right now. I have to go to work."

"When?"

"We'll need to buy you some knitting needles and wool first."

"Why don't we all go into town on Saturday to buy them," Jack suggested. "We could make a day of it."

"Okay, but I really have to go now."

I had just reached the gate when I spotted Grandma hurrying down the road towards me. If I didn't make eye-contact, maybe I'd be able to get in the car and drive off before—

"Jill! Wait!"

Drat!

"Hi, I didn't see you there. I'd love to stop and talk but I have an urgent meeting at eight-thirty."

"You say that like I care. I want to know what you are going to do about the witch-finders."

"What do you expect me to do?"

"Put a stop to them before they snatch anyone else."

"I'd love to help, honestly, but I'm run off my feet. Why don't you do it?"

"Do you have any idea how many hats I'm juggling? How am I supposed to find the time?"

"And yet, you always manage to find time to berate me. Have any more witches gone missing?"

"Not that I know of."

"And you can't actually be sure that Belinda *what's her face* was taken by a witch-finder, can you?"

"Why else would she have disappeared?"

"People go missing all the time for all kinds of reasons."

"You're not going to help, are you?"

"I can't, Grandma. I'm really sorry."

"In that case, I guess I'll just have to do it myself. What's that saying? If you want something doing–"

"Ask a busy person?"

"No, it's *if you want something doing, don't ask Jill Maxwell because she doesn't care.*" And with those cutting words, she turned and walked away.

Grandma was wrong. I did care, but there was a limit to what I could take on. And besides, I still wasn't convinced that Belinda's disappearance was the result of the so-called twenty-one. As I drove to Chicken Enterprises, I tried not to think about Grandma's attempt to guilt-trip me. Instead, I thought about what Florence had said earlier. I thought her learning to knit was a great idea and something I was keen to encourage. After all, she was likely to get into far less trouble knitting than she would practising random spells from the spell book. When I got to the office, I was going to ask Mrs V if she had any suggestions for how best to get Florence started.

Chicken Enterprises' car park was very small and there were no free spaces, so I was forced to park in the public car park a couple of hundred yards down the road.

Five pounds for one hour? Were they serious? That was daylight robbery. I was debating whether to risk not buying a ticket when I spotted a short man, dressed in a blue uniform, across the road. The vulture was hovering, just waiting for his opportunity to plant a ticket on some unsuspecting motorist's windscreen. The machine didn't accept card payments and I only had four pounds in coins, so I gestured to the vulture to come over.

"I only have four pounds in change."

"Five pounds is the minimum charge," he replied, stony-faced.

"I realise that. I was wondering if you might be able to change a ten-pound note?"

"We aren't allowed to do that."

"Why not?"

"It's the rules."

"Who's going to know?"

"You can pay by app." He pointed to the sign behind the machine.

"I don't have it."

"You could download it."

"I don't have time. I'm already running late for an important meeting. Come on, surely you can break the rules just this once, and split a tenner for me?"

"Sorry, it's not allowed."

He didn't look sorry, not even a little bit.

"Are you seriously telling me that if I go to my meeting, you'll give me a ticket, even though you know I've done my best to pay?"

"If you don't have a valid parking ticket, I'll have no choice."

The vulture might not have any choice, but I did. After a quick check that there was no one around, I cast the 'sleep' spell on him, then laid him on the back seat of my car. As I went along the street, I noticed that everyone who came by me seemed to be walking on tiptoes, which I thought was very strange until I remembered the name of the street.

Underneath the **Chicken Enterprises** sign was the tagline: *Freshly-Laid Technology*. Only then did it occur to me that, when I'd spoken to Sam Rich on the phone, he hadn't actually said what his company did. With hindsight, I probably should have asked, but I had assumed that, with a name like Chicken Enterprises, he bred chickens or something similar.

The young man behind reception looked bored.

"Welcome to Chicken Enterprises. How can I help you?"

"Hi, my name is Jill Maxwell." I wasn't sure if Sam Rich had told the guy that I was a PI, so I decided to play safe and not mention it. "I have an appointment with Sam Rich at eight-thirty. I'm afraid I'm a little late because I had to park down the road."

"Mr Rich called a few minutes ago to say he'd been delayed, and he asked me to convey his apologies. He should only be a few more minutes. My name is Michael. Can I get you something to drink while you wait? Tea? Coffee?"

As I was still only half awake, I asked for a black coffee. While he went to get it, I took the opportunity to take a look at one of the company's brochures that were on the coffee table in reception.

"A fascinating read, don't you think?" Michael handed me the coffee.

"Most of it goes over my head, I'm afraid. What exactly is it that the company does?"

"We design and manufacture all manner of alarm systems."

"Right? I would never have guessed that from the company name."

"It's a fascinating story. Would you like me to tell you it while you wait for Mr Rich to arrive?"

"Sure."

He took a seat next to me on the couch and went into what was a well-rehearsed speech. One that I suspected he'd given many times before.

"Mr Rich's father, Richard, started the company almost fifty years ago."

"Richard Rich?"

"That's right. He was a farmer."

"Now, I'm really confused. How did a farmer end up running an alarm company?"

"Apparently, he was sick of rustlers stealing his livestock, so he created an alarm system to prevent them. It was so successful that when other farmers heard about it, they asked if he could provide them with one. Pretty soon, word got around, and he was getting requests from all over the country and even abroad. Within a year, he'd decided to sell the farm in order to focus on the alarm business, and he never looked back."

"Are all the alarm systems you supply for use on farms?"

"No. The business expanded into other applications and

markets."

"And the name? I assume one of the alarm systems was designed to prevent chickens from being stolen?"

"Actually, no. The original alarm systems were for sheep. When Mr Rich first started the business, he ran it from an old chicken shed. Hence the name."

The door behind me opened, and in walked a tall man sporting a cowboy hat.

"Jill Maxwell? I'm Sam Rich. I'm really sorry to have kept you waiting."

"No problem. Michael has been giving me a potted history of the company."

"Excellent. Let's go through to my office." He turned to Michael. "We're not to be disturbed under any circumstances."

"Yes, sir."

The cowboy theme continued into Sam Rich's office: all of the walls were covered in framed photos and prints of cowboys, and there were several small statues of them on the shelves and bookcase.

"Do have a seat, Jill."

"Thanks."

"In case you're wondering, I'm chairman of the Washbridge Cowboy Appreciation Society."

"I had no idea there was such a high level of interest here in Washbridge."

"Oh yes, the society is going from strength to strength."

We were interrupted by Michael who handed a coffee to Sam, and then scurried out of the office.

"Michael hasn't been with us very long. He's my sister's boy, actually. I wasn't sure he was going to fit in at first, but he seems to be taking to the job slowly."

"He told me how your father started the business."

"Fate is a funny thing. If it hadn't been for those rustlers, stealing my father's sheep, this business probably wouldn't exist."

"You mentioned on the phone that you wanted my help in tracing a missing person."

"That's right. I'm really worried about Cutter."

"*Cutter*? Is that his name?"

"It's just what everyone calls him. His real name is Lorne. Lorne Mower."

If it wasn't for the fact that Sam Rich looked and sounded deadly serious, I might have thought I was being set up for some kind of candid camera TV show.

"O—kay. And is Cutter a relative? Employee?"

"No, he's actually a member of WCAS."

"*WCAS?*"

"Short for Washbridge Cowboy Appreciation Society."

"Of course. Sorry."

"Cutter and I are two of the founding members of the society. No one can spin a lasso quite like him."

"Has his disappearance been reported to the police?"

"I did try to, but they didn't seem particularly interested."

"Is he married?"

"No. He does have a sister, though: Anita."

"Mower?"

"No, she's married. Anita Hedge."

"Right. Does Cutter have any other relatives or friends?"

"No relatives that I'm aware of. And the only friends that he ever mentions are those at WCAS. That's how I knew something was wrong."

"Sorry, I don't follow."

"We hold meetings every other Friday, and Cutter has never missed one since the society started. Even I miss the occasional one, but then I have family commitments."

"I take it there was no word from him to explain his absence?"

"Nothing. I went around to his house the next day, but there was no sign of him."

"Is it possible that he could be inside the house? Ill, injured or—"

"No. We have a key for each other's house, so I was able to let myself in. There was no sign of him."

"Did anything catch your eye?"

"How do you mean?"

"Was there any sign that the property had been broken into? Had anything been disturbed?"

"It hadn't been ransacked if that's what you mean."

"What does Cutter do for a living?"

"He has a stall in the market hall."

"Selling?"

"Sweets."

"Does he work there alone?"

"He has an assistant called Rose Merry. I went to see her after I'd been to his house, to check if she'd heard from Cutter. She hadn't."

"What's happening with the stall?"

"Rose said she'd keep it running until we know what's happened to Cutter."

"Can you think of any reason why this may have happened? Did he have money problems? Had he been depressed? Anything at all?"

"No. Cutter wouldn't just up and leave like this.

Someone must have taken him."

"Possibly, but people who seem perfectly happy on the outside, just up and leave all the time."

"Not Cutter. No way."

"Fair enough. For now, I'll work on the basis that he hasn't voluntarily disappeared. You said Cutter has no family apart from his sister. Has he never been married?"

"He did marry but they were divorced about three years ago."

"Was it acrimonious?"

"He didn't talk about it very much, but from what I could make out, she didn't appreciate him spending so much time on his interest."

"Cowboys?"

"That's right. I've written down his home address for you." He slid a sheet of paper across the desk. "And this is his house key. Is there anything else you need from me?"

"Not at the moment, but I assume I can call you if I think of anything."

"Of course. Finding Cutter is my number one priority."

"Got it."

Chapter 8

The toy koala was still on Mrs V's desk, but there was no sign of the boomerang.

"Where's your boomerang, Mrs V?"

"I was hoping you might know. It had gone when I arrived this morning. I thought maybe you'd taken it home to show Florence."

"No, I didn't take it."

"That's very strange. Do you think it could be one of those people who visit Talbot Talent? There are some very strange individuals who go next door."

"It's possible, I suppose. I'll nip around there later and ask if he's seen it."

As it turned out, I didn't need to pay Talbot a visit because the whereabouts of said boomerang soon became clear.

"Winky! What are you doing?"

"I would have thought that was obvious, even to someone with your limited powers of observation."

He was standing on the window ledge, and before I could stop him, he had launched the boomerang out of the window.

"That's Mrs V's boomerang."

"Relax, I've only borrowed it. I'll give it back in a while."

I hurried over to the window. "You've got no right to—"

"Shush, I need to concentrate."

I watched, transfixed, as the boomerang curved its flight path, and headed back towards the window. Moments later, he grabbed it as it flew by.

"Where did you learn to do that?"

"I have a black belt in boomerang. Want a try?" He held it out.

"I've never thrown one before."

"There's nothing to it. Come here, I'll show you."

"Okay, then." I took it from him.

"You need to grip it like this." He moved my fingers. "That's it. Now, pull your arm back. A bit lower. That's it. Okay, go for it."

I launched the boomerang out of the window and watched as it headed across the road.

"It's not coming back."

"It will," he assured me. "Just give it time."

Sure enough, the boomerang slowly turned back and was heading for the window.

"I did it."

"Don't lose concentration. You still have to catch it."

I kept my eyes on the boomerang as it headed back, and I was just about to grab it when…

"Jill, you didn't say if you wanted a drink or not."

I'd just turned around to see Mrs V standing in the doorway when the boomerang hit me square in the back, sending me crashing to the floor. A little stunned, I looked up to see Mrs V scowling at me.

"If you wanted to play with it, you only had to ask."

What was I supposed to say? I could hardly tell her that Winky was the one who had taken her boomerang.

"I'm really sorry, Mrs V. I couldn't resist it." I picked it up and handed it to her. "I will have a cup of tea, please." I waited until she'd left the room and then turned on Winky. "That's all your fault."

"You should have caught it."

"You shouldn't have taken it in the first place." I rubbed my back. "Now Mrs V thinks I'm a liar and a thief."

"Admit it, though, it was fun."

Before I could respond, my phone rang.

"Is that Jill Maxwell?"

I didn't recognise the voice.

"Yes, speaking."

"I believe you're the owner of a motor vehicle registration MX65 THT, is that correct?"

"Err, yes. Who's this? What's this about?"

"This is the police. My name is Constable Roberts."

My immediate thought was that someone had taken my car from the car park and that it had been found abandoned.

"What's happened? Is my car alright?"

"Your car is fine, but I need you to come down to the car park where you left it, please."

"Why? What's wrong?"

"It would be better if you came down here."

"Okay, I'll come straight over."

"What have you done now?" Winky said.

"I haven't done anything."

"Why are the old bill calling you, then?"

"I don't know. It's probably nothing."

"I thought you wanted a tea?" Mrs V said as I almost knocked it out of her hand on my way out.

"I do. I won't be long."

On my way to the car park, I racked my brain trying to figure out what the police might want with me. It couldn't be non-payment of the parking fee because I had a monthly season ticket for the car park I used at work. And besides, the police wouldn't get involved with non-payment of parking fees. Perhaps someone had broken into my car.

When I arrived at the car park, I saw the police officer standing next to my vehicle, and even from that distance, I could see that none of the windows had been smashed.

"Mrs Maxwell?"

"That's me. What seems to be the problem, officer?"

"We had a report from a concerned member of the public."

"About what?"

"About that." He pointed to the back window of the car.

Only then, did the penny drop. I'd totally forgotten about the car park attendant who I'd put on the back seat. A quick glance through the window confirmed he was still sleeping like a baby.

"Who's that?" I said, trying to look shocked. "How did he get into my car? Was he trying to steal it?"

"We've had a report that a parking warden in The Sticks failed to report in earlier. His employer insists their staff report in on the hour, just to ensure they are safe."

"You surely don't think that I kidnapped him."

"That's exactly what I think. Turn around." Before I had the chance to react, he'd put me in handcuffs and was marching me towards his patrol car. Before he pushed me into the car, I just had time to reverse the 'sleep' spell on the parking warden.

Big Mac took a seat opposite me in the interview room of the police station.

"Well, Maxwell, this makes a pleasant change. Usually when you're around, there's a dead body somewhere in the vicinity. I hear you've decided to try your hand at kidnapping this time."

"That's ridiculous. I didn't kidnap anyone."

"And yet, a public official who went missing earlier today was found on the back seat of your car."

"I don't know anything about that. He must have climbed inside while I wasn't watching."

"Is that really the best you can come up with? Why don't you come clean and tell me what's going on here?"

"There's nothing to tell. I had no idea he was there until your officer called me."

"Do you really expect me to believe that?"

"It's the truth. Think about it for a minute. If I'd really kidnapped him, why would I leave him on the back seat of my car for anyone to see?"

"We'll soon know the truth. Raymond is being checked over in Washbridge hospital as we speak."

"Who's Raymond?"

"The man you abducted and left in the back seat of your car."

"I didn't abduct anyone. It's all a big mistake."

"It will go much better for you if you confess now."

"There's nothing to confess."

"In that case, I guess I'll see you later."

"Does that mean I'm free to leave?"

"Of course not." He scoffed.

I spent the next two hours locked in a small, smelly cell, wondering why this sort of thing always seemed to happen to me. I was eventually returned to the interview room where a young man who I'd never seen before was waiting for me.

"Where's Big Mac?" I demanded.

"Detective Archie McDonald is busy. He asked me to

deal with you. My name is—"

"I don't care. I want a lawyer."

"Why?"

"Because I'm being falsely accused of kidnapping."

"You're not being accused of anything. I'm here to tell you that you're free to leave."

"I don't care what—hang on, did you say I was free to go?"

"That's right. I'm sorry you've been inconvenienced, but I'm sure you realise we have to follow up on this kind of incident."

"What happened? Why the change of mind? Big Mac was all for putting me in jail and throwing away the key."

"I'm sure that's not true. Raymond Hall confirmed that he hadn't been kidnapped."

"He did? I mean, of course he did. What did he say?"

"Just that he remembers coming over very sleepy. He seems to think that you must have helped him into your car. He asked that we pass on his thanks."

"Right. So, that's it, then?"

"Yes, like I said, you're free to go. Your car is in our garage. If you call at the reception desk on your way out, you'll be able to collect your car keys."

***

"Where have you been, Jill?" Mrs V said. "I was beginning to get worried."

"Sorry, something urgent came up."

"Your tea went cold. Would you like another one?"

"No, thanks. I'll be going home soon. There is something you can help me with, though."

"What's that?"

"Florence is keen to learn to knit. I was wondering if you had any advice on the best way for her to go about it?"

"That's excellent news. It's such a lovely hobby for a young person, much better than spending their time looking at computers."

"I agree, so how would you suggest she goes about it?"

Mrs V took a piece of paper out of her drawer and scribbled something on it. "This would be ideal for her."

"Julie Does Knitting? What's that?"

"It's a YouTube video series aimed at kids."

"YouTube? But I thought you just said— oh okay, I suppose I could check it out."

"I didn't think we'd see you again this side of Christmas," Winky said.

"What do you mean?"

"Kidnapping? I thought they'd lock you up and throw away the key."

"I didn't kidnap anyone. It was all just a big misunderstanding."

"Obviously. Haven't we all kidnapped someone by mistake at one time or another?"

"How do you know about it, anyway?"

"I have eyes and ears everywhere. You should know that by now. Anyway, never mind any of that. I have big news."

"What's that?"

"Simon Jewel just visited Fun Rat."

"Really?" I yawned. "That's amazing."

"Please don't tell me you don't know who he is."

"Never heard of him."

"He's the CEO of Drop Jaw."

"Oh, *that* Simon Jewel. No, never heard of him. Or of Drop Jaw."

"Drop Jaw are Fun Rat's biggest competitor. For months now, there have been rumours that Fun Rat were going to buy Drop Jaw."

"Can I ask a question?"

"Sure?"

"Who gives a monkey's about any of this?"

"I do. Don't you realise what this means?"

"I don't care."

"When news of the takeover gets out, Fun Rat's shares will go through the roof."

"Still not caring."

"Don't you realise what a gold-plated opportunity this is?"

"For who?"

"For us."

Winky jumped onto my desk and began tapping away on my computer.

"What have I told you about using my laptop?"

"This is important. If news gets out, it'll be too late."

I walked over to my desk and looked over his shoulder. "Cat Traders? What's that?"

"It's the company I use to buy and sell shares."

"You invest in the stock market?"

"Of course. You didn't think I left all my cash in the bank, earning next to no interest, did you? Only an idiot would do that."

"Err, right."

"You don't have all of your money in the bank, do you?"

"Of course not," I lied. "I have a mixed portfolio of investments."

"I'm glad to hear it. Now, how much should I invest?" He scratched his chin. "Five? Ten? Would fifteen be too much?"

"Hundred?"

"Thousand."

"You're thinking of investing fifteen thousand pounds in Fun Rat? Isn't that a big risk?"

"Not when you have this kind of insider information. When word of the takeover gets out, I'll probably double my money."

When I arrived home, Jack was looking for me through the front window, and if the look on his face was anything to go by, he wasn't very happy about something.

"What's happened?" I said. "Has Florence done something?"

"Florence is fine. She's gone to Julie Kirkby's house for her dinner."

"What's wrong, then? If it's about having to go running with Julian, you should just tell him you don't want to do it anymore."

"I already did. I told him that I'd twisted my ankle."

"So why do you have a face like thunder?"

"As if you don't know."

"I have no idea."

"Nothing you want to tell me, then?"

"I'm too tired for cryptic puzzles, Jack. What's wrong?"

"After work, I happened to bump into Jimmy Cresswell, an old buddy of mine from Washbridge nick. You'll never guess what he told me."

"That he liked your highlights?"

"That my wife had been interrogated on suspicion of kidnapping."

Oh bum!

Chapter 9

The next morning, the three of us were all at the kitchen table, and Florence had something she needed to get off her chest.

"Julie says caterpillars are better than worms. That's silly."

"Some people like worms, and some people like caterpillars," said Jack, ever the diplomat.

"Caterpillars are rubbish!" Florence insisted. "Which do you like best, Mummy?"

"I don't like either of them."

"How long is it until I go to Wonder World?"

"It'll be two weeks tomorrow."

"That's ages."

"It'll soon be here, pumpkin," Jack said. "And tomorrow, we're all going to town to get you some knitting needles and wool."

"Yay, I'm going to knit a jumper for Jay."

"You might have to start with something a little simpler," I said. "Maybe a scarf for Jay."

"What colour?"

"Why don't you go and ask him what colours he'd like?"

"Okay." She shoved what was left of the toast in her mouth and went running upstairs.

"Have you forgiven me for that little misunderstanding yesterday?" I said to Jack.

"By *little misunderstanding,* I assume you're referring to you kidnapping a parking warden in broad daylight?"

"How many more times do I have to explain? There was no kidnapping. The man just happened to fall asleep on the back seat of my car."

"Yeah, that happens to me all the time too. Every time I open the car door, a parking warden pushes his way inside and tries to take a nap."

"There's no point discussing it if you're going to be sarcastic."

"Would you like to continue the worm vs caterpillar debate instead?"

"No, I'd like to talk about our finances?"

"What about them?" He looked puzzled.

"I was just thinking that we aren't making the most of our savings."

"What do you mean?"

"Inflation is getting worse."

"Tell me about it. The price of muesli had gone up again when I bought it from the store yesterday."

"I don't know why you can't eat the same cereal as me. We've got tons of it."

"I'm not eating that teeth-rotting, cholesterol inducing muck."

"Your loss. Anyway, as I was saying, inflation is eating away at the value of our savings."

"There's not much we can do about that. It's in the highest interest account available."

"We could get a higher return elsewhere."

"How?"

"If we were to invest it in the stock market, we could see much higher rates of return."

"We could also lose it all. Share prices fluctuate all the time. It's much too risky."

"Not if you have insider information."

"What kind of insider information?"

"Let's say I knew that a certain major company was about to take over one of its main competitors, and that when news of that takeover gets out, the share price is bound to go through the roof."

"Do you?"

"I do."

"And how did you happen to come across this information?"

"I can't name names for the sake of client confidentiality, but let's just say the source is rock solid."

"Who is the company?"

"Fun Rat?"

"The game company?"

"You've heard of them?"

"Of course I have. They're huge. What did you hear? Who are they going to take over?"

"Drop Jaw."

"Wow!"

"I take it you've heard of them too?"

"Of course, but I had no idea they were up for sale."

"Apparently, no one else does either, but once the news gets out—"

"Fun Rat's share price will go through the roof."

"So, what do you think?"

"About what?"

"Should we invest?"

"I don't know. Are you sure that this source of yours knows what they're talking about?"

"One-hundred per cent."

"I suppose we could risk some of our savings."

"How much?"

"Ten per cent?"

"Ten? It's hardly worth doing."

"Twenty, then?"

"How about half?"

"I don't know, Jill, that's a lot of money."

"Just think how much we'll make when the news breaks."

He hesitated but then said, "Why not? Let's do it."

I was just on my way out of the house when my phone rang.

"Am I speaking to Portia Parkspirit?"

"Yes, this is Portia."

"Excellent. My name is Dominic. Someone put one of your flyers through my letterbox and I was hoping to talk to you about the service you offer."

"What would you like to know, exactly?"

"The leaflet says you do exorcisms."

"That's correct. Do you have a haunting?"

"I believe so, although I haven't actually seen—err—"

"A ghost?"

"Yeah, I just get a really bad feeling whenever I step inside the manor."

"*Manor*?"

"Sorry, I should have said. I recently inherited Tweaking Manor and I'm planning to convert it into a hotel. Do you think you'd be able to help?"

"Absolutely, but I should warn you my services don't come cheap."

"Money won't be an issue, but time is of the essence because I want the ghosts gone before the builders begin their work. What's your availability like?"

"I'm booked three months in advance."

"Oh dear. I was hoping for something much quicker."

"You may be in luck because the booking I had for next week has just been cancelled."

"Oh? May I ask why?"

"The old lady who made the booking died suddenly."

"That's terrible. Does that mean you'd be able to take on my job?"

"I don't see why not. I could come to Tweaking Manor on Monday if that works for you?"

"Absolutely. Nine o'clock?"

"That's fine. I'll see you then."

I loved it when a plan came together.

"Jill!" Grandma was hurrying down the street towards me.

"Good morning, Grandma."

"It most certainly isn't a *good* morning. It's happened again."

"What has?"

"Marsha Downbuggy has been taken now."

"I don't think I know her."

"She works at the launderette in the marketplace in Washbridge."

"I didn't realise there was one there."

"You must have seen it. It's called Washed Up. Anyway, that's not important. She's the second witch to go missing now."

"And I assume you think it's to do with this twenty-one thingy?"

"Obviously."

"It just so happens that I'll probably be talking to Yvonne later today."

"Who?"

"Jack's mother."

"The witch-finder?"

"She's retired. Well, to be more accurate, she's dead."

"Why would you talk to that horrible woman?"

"Yvonne isn't horrible."

"She's a witch-finder."

"*Was* a witch-finder. She and her husband, Roy, live in Tweaking Manor now."

"Rent-free, I assume."

"I suppose so. Anyway, as I was saying, I'll be speaking to her later on another matter, so I could ask her if there's any truth to this twenty-one business."

"Why do you need to ask anyone? Isn't the fact that witches are being snatched off the street enough proof for you?"

"It can't hurt to ask what she knows."

"And what makes you think you can trust anything she says? In case you hadn't noticed, she's on the other side."

"We'll see. Sorry, but I have to get going. I have a busy day ahead."

I'd just got out of my car when I spotted the parking warden, who had spent most of the previous day fast asleep on the backseat of my car. He was making a beeline for me.

"It is you, isn't it?" he said.

"Err—I—err—"

"You were in the car park on Eggshell Road yesterday, weren't you?"

"Yes, I'm really—"

"I'm so glad I've bumped into you again."

"You are?"

"Yes, I was hoping I might get the chance to thank you. When I had my funny turn yesterday, you could have just left me there on the ground. It's not everyone who would have put me into their car until I had come around."

"I suppose not."

"And what did you get for your selfless act?"

"Sorry?"

"I can't believe the police thought you'd tried to kidnap me. How long did they question you for?"

"A couple of hours. Maybe a little longer."

"How awful. Anyway, I'd like to give you something as a small token of my gratitude."

"There's really no need."

"I insist." He reached into his pocket and took out a card which he handed to me.

"What's this?"

"It will give you free parking in any car park in the Washbridge district for the next three months."

"I couldn't possibly accept it."

"I insist. All parking wardens are given a number of these as part of our remuneration package. They're meant for family and friends, but most of us don't have many friends."

"Okay, but only if you're sure."

"Absolutely, and thanks again." And with that, he went on his way.

Free parking for three months—result!

What do you mean you don't know how I had the nerve to accept it? It would have been rude to refuse.

Mrs V wasn't at her desk, but she had left me a note to say that she had an optician's appointment and would be in by mid-morning.

"What are you looking so pleased about?" Winky said.

"I've got free parking in Washbridge for the next three months."

"How come?"

"I bumped into the parking warden from yesterday, and he gave me the free pass."

"For kidnapping him?"

"I did *not* kidnap him. He said he was grateful that I had come to his aid when he'd taken ill."

"He didn't take ill, though, did he? I thought you used magic to send him to sleep?"

"Technically, that's true. That doesn't alter the fact that I could have just left him on the ground in the car park. Instead, I was considerate enough to put him in the backseat of my car where I knew he'd be comfortable."

"Do you know what amazes me most? That you actually believe your own BS. Anyway, never mind that. Did you take my advice on the Fun Rat shares?"

"I talked to Jack about it earlier."

"Don't tell me, he talked you out of it."

"No, he was nervous at first, but when I told him about the upcoming takeover, he could see the sense in it. In fact, he's going to buy the shares today. What about you?"

"My broker confirmed my purchase a few minutes ago."

"You have a broker?"

"Of course. I've used Donny for almost five years now."

"I hope you're right about these Fun Rat shares, Winky. Because we're putting half of our savings into them."

"Fifty quid isn't going to buy you many shares."

"Very funny."

I don't know why, but it always feels a bit weird making a phone call to a ghost, but Yvonne picked up straight away.

"Jill, I was hoping I might hear from you. Do you have any news for me?"

"I do, and there's something else I'd like to discuss with you. Is there any chance I could pop over there sometime today?"

"You can come now if you like. Roy has gone to get some bits and bobs from GT, and there's no one else here at the moment."

"Great. I'll come straight over. Where shall I meet you?"

"I assume you can use magic to get inside?"

"Yeah."

"Okay, I'll be waiting for you in the main entrance hall."

A couple of minutes later, I was standing in the entrance hall of Tweaking Manor, but there was no sign of Yvonne. I was just about to call her name when she appeared at the top of the staircase.

"Gosh, you were quick, Jill. Come on up."

Once upstairs, I followed Yvonne along one of the corridors.

"We use the two rooms at the end," she said. "We have a delightful view over the gardens from there. We'll go in this one."

"I like what you've done in here." I looked around the sitting room.

"I can't take any credit for it. Lady Tweaking furnished all the rooms herself. Take a seat and I'll get us a coffee, unless you'd like something stronger?"

"Coffee is fine for me."

She disappeared out of the room and returned a few

minutes later with two cups of coffee.

"It's only instant, I'm afraid."

"That's fine. Thanks."

"Do you have any news for me, Jill? Roy and I have been on tenterhooks ever since I spoke to you."

"I'm pleased to report that Dominic has hired Portia Parkspirit to carry out the exorcism."

"That's great. How did you manage that?"

"That was the easy part. The difficult part comes when Portia carries out the exorcism."

"I don't understand." Yvonne looked puzzled. "I thought you just pretended to do an exorcism?"

"I do, but if Dominic insists on being present when Portia does her thing, I'm going to need you and Roy to channel your inner thespians."

"What do you mean?"

"Hopefully, Dominic will just leave me to it, but if he does want to watch, I'll need you and Roy to make lots of awful noises."

"What kind of noises?"

"Like the sound of souls being purged."

"What does that sound like?"

"I've no idea, but I'm sure you'll come up with something. The scarier the better. Will you be able to do that?"

"If it's the only way we can stay here, we'll have to. When is the exorcism going to happen?"

"Monday morning at nine o'clock, so I suggest you and Roy practise your tormented soul noises over the weekend."

"Will do. And thanks again, Jill."

"No problem. While I'm here, can I pick your brain?"

"Sure. What do you want to know?"

"It's probably nothing, but my grandmother has got a bee in her bonnet, and I'm hoping you'll be able to help me put her mind at ease."

"About what, exactly?"

"A couple of witches have gone missing recently. There's probably a perfectly innocent explanation, but Grandma is convinced it's related to something called The Twenty-One."

I was hoping Yvonne would ask what that was, but instead, she said, "Oh no."

"Have you heard of it?"

"Of course. It's an important part of our history and is taught to all kids in school. Since I—err—passed away, I've not seen a copy of WF News, and—"

"WF?"

"Sorry, it's short for WitchFinder News which is the leading newspaper read by witch-finders. I'd totally forgotten that the next twenty-one is upon us."

"Does that mean you think the missing witches may have been taken by witch-finders?"

"Almost certainly. All the witch-finders will have been preparing for this for months. They'll be trying to snatch as many witches as possible ready for the—" She hesitated.

"Burning?"

"Yes. I'm sorry, Jill, I know how horrible this must sound to you."

"I was hoping that Grandma was barking up the wrong tree."

"I don't think she is. What about you?"

"What about me?"

"You have one of the highest profiles in the witch community. That will put you in the crosshairs for sure. Your grandmother too, probably. Have you noticed anyone suspicious hanging around?"

"No, but then if I'm honest, I haven't been taking it all that seriously up until now."

"You really must."

"What about the witches who have been taken?"

"What about them?"

"Will they already be dead?"

"Definitely not. They'll be being held somewhere until The Burning takes place."

"Grandma said sixteen witches were killed at the last Burning."

"So history tells us. If I know the leadership, they'll be determined to better that number this time around."

"May I ask you a question, Yvonne?"

"Of course."

"If you were still alive, would you be involved with this twenty-one thing?"

"I'd like to tell you that I wouldn't, but I'd be lying. Every witch-finder will be doing their part to increase the Burning count."

"Great!"

Chapter 10

When Mrs V returned from the opticians, she was wearing a new pair of glasses.

"What do you think of them, Jill?"

I actually thought they were a bit blingy, but I doubted Mrs V wanted to hear that.

"They're very—err—shiny. They're not real jewels, are they?"

"Goodness no. They'd be far too expensive if they were real."

"I thought you were going to swap to contacts?"

"I simply couldn't put up with those dreadful things. I have no idea how anyone can wear them. I was a bit disappointed, but then Armi persuaded me to splash out on new glasses instead. Do you think he'll like these?"

"Err, yeah, I'm sure he will." I glanced at her desk and realised that something was missing. "Where's the answerphone gone?"

"I threw it out."

"How come?"

"Armi showed me an article last night about A.I."

"Artificial intelligence?"

"Apparently, it's in everything these days. If we're not careful it's going to take over the world."

"So, you got rid of the answerphone?"

"I thought it best. Before it had the chance to turn on us."

"O—kay, I'd better get back to work."

"A.I?" Winky was rolling around on the floor, in hysterics. "The old bag lady has totally lost the plot this time."

"She's scared, that's all."

"Of an answerphone? What does she think it's going to do? Speed dial her to death? I can't wait to tell the guys this one."

***

During my meeting with Francesca Artichoke, one thing had become quite apparent: she wasn't on the best of terms with her neighbours. Although she hadn't gone into details, I couldn't help but wonder if her smallholding had been a source of friction. There was only one way to find out and that was to try to talk to them.

I told Mrs V where I was going and that I'd probably go straight home afterwards. When I got to the car park, I spotted something under one of the windscreen wipers of my car. For a horrible moment, I thought I'd been given a ticket, but then I realised that there was a similar flyer on the windscreen of every car in there.

Leeches?

That was the headline on the flyer, and before I could read the rest of it, someone called to me.

"Jill! Coo-ee!"

It was Deli, with a pile of the flyers in her hand.

"Hi, Deli."

"What do you think?" She gestured to the flyer.

"I haven't had chance to look at it yet."

"It's our newest offering. We're the first salon in Washbridge to offer it."

"When you say *leeches,* I assume you don't actually mean *leeches*. Do you?"

"Absolutely."

I took a moment to read the rest of the flyer.

"This says it's supposed to improve your skin tone."

"That's right. The leeches extract all the impurities."

"By sucking out your blood."

"In a manner of speaking, but it's a tiny amount."

"Is this legal?"

"Of course. It's fully licensed by the British Leech Authority on Health."

"BLAH?"

"We were lucky to be approved so quickly. So, what do you think, Jill? It would do wonders for your spots."

What *spots*?

"I'm really busy at the moment. Maybe another time."

"Don't leave it too long. There's bound to be a massive demand because we're offering a forty percent discount for the first month."

"Okay, I'll bear that in mind."

Leeches? Just the thought of it made my skin crawl. I just couldn't convince myself that leech therapy was legitimate.

I tried the house to the right of Francesca Artichoke's property first, but there was no response. I had more luck with the house on the other side where a woman, dressed in dungarees and sporting matching yellow wellingtons, was on all fours, weeding the borders.

"Excuse me," I said over the low wall. "I'm sorry to bother you."

"Not at all." She got to her feet rather gingerly. "I need a break. My back is killing me."

"Your garden is beautiful."

"Thank you. I just wish the weeds would give me a

couple of days respite."

"My name is Jill Maxwell." I handed her my card.

"A private investigator? Gosh. What brings you to Little Biggly?"

"I've actually been hired by your neighbour."

I half-expected her to ask which one, but she said, "Francesca?"

"That's right. Do you have time to talk to me for a few minutes?"

"Any excuse to get away from these dreadful weeds. Why don't you come inside, and we can have a drink. Is tea okay?"

"That would be lovely, thanks."

"My name is Jill, too, but everyone calls me Jilly. Jilly Dilly."

"*Dilly*?"

"I know." She rolled her eyes. "I've only myself to blame for that. Of all the men in the world, I had to fall in love with Kevin Dilly."

Clearly, she wasn't as shallow as me.

Jilly took me through to the lounge which looked out over the garden at the rear of the property. Once we had our drinks, I began by engaging her in a little small talk in the hope that would put her at ease.

"You have a beautiful house, Jilly."

"It used to belong to Kevin's parents. We used to live in a tiny semi in Smallwash, so it was quite a shock to move into this place."

"I used to live in Smallwash."

"Really? Small world."

"We live in Middle Tweaking now."

"That's a beautiful little village. Kevin and I have had

lunch in the pub there a couple of times."

"Your garden looks amazing. If we had a garden like yours, I'd spend all my time out there," I lied.

"You said that Francesca had hired you. Can I ask what it's in connection with?"

"Her chickens."

On hearing that, Jilly's sunny disposition changed. "I might have known it would have something to do with those dreadful animals of hers."

"You're not a fan, I take it?"

"Look, I wouldn't want you to think I have anything against animals." She glanced around. "We have a couple of cats around here somewhere."

"But not farm animals?"

"Again, I have nothing against chickens, pigs or whatever else she has over there, but this isn't the place for them."

"Can you actually see them from your property?"

"No, thank goodness, but we can hear them." She screwed up her nose. "And smell them. Kevin and I used to like to sit in the garden in the summer evenings and enjoy a glass of wine. But the smell was so bad some days that there was no pleasure in it."

"Have you said anything to Francesca about it?"

"Kevin is the diplomat in the family, so he tried to have a polite word with her, but it was a waste of time. She more or less told him to mind his own business. We haven't really spoken to her since then."

"I see."

"We're not the only ones who aren't happy about the animals. Have you spoken to any of the other neighbours yet?"

"Not yet. I did try the house on the other side of Francesca before I came over here, but there didn't appear to be anyone in."

"I'm surprised because Jason rarely leaves the house."

"Maybe I'll try again after we've finished here."

"I should warn you that Jason is a bit—err—eccentric, I suppose. Harmless enough, though."

"Right. Thanks for the heads-up."

"You said something about Francesca's chickens?"

"Yes, they've disappeared, apparently. She's hired me to find them."

"Disappeared? How?"

"That's what I'm trying to find out."

"How strange. Now you come to mention it, though, I haven't heard that awful rooster of hers for a few days. Not that I'm complaining."

"Have you seen any unusual comings and goings on the street recently?"

"Chicken rustlers, you mean?" She laughed. "No, sorry. This cul-de-sac is very quiet. I think I would have noticed."

"Right. Would you mind if I took a look at your back garden?"

"Sure." She opened the French doors and led the way onto the patio. Once outside, she sniffed the air. "The wind is blowing the opposite way today, thank goodness."

I looked in the direction of Francesca's property, but I couldn't see the back garden because of the high fence.

"This fence looks new."

"It is. There was one there before, but it wasn't very high. We had this one put up after the animals arrived. It was Kevin's idea."

"Right, well thanks again for your time. Would you do me a favour and ask your husband if he remembers seeing anything unusual in the cul-de-sac?"

"Yes, but I'm sure he would have mentioned it to me if he had."

"Still, I'd appreciate it. If either of you think of anything that might help me, please give me a call."

"Will do."

Jilly had come across as a perfectly reasonable person, but the same thing has been said about many a serial killer. If I'm being honest, I didn't blame her for being peeved when a lorry load of animals appeared in the garden next-door, particularly with the noise and smell. I decided to try again at the first neighbour's house, but there was still no response from the mysterious Jason, so I headed home.

I'd no sooner walked through the gate than Florence came running down the path to greet me.

"Look, Mummy." She held up what appeared to be a soft toy snake. "Do you like him?"

"Err, I guess so."

"His name is Wormy."

"*Wormy*? I thought he was a snake."

"No, silly, he's a worm."

"Where did you get Wormy from?"

She shrugged. "I found him."

Before I could question her further, she'd turned tail and rushed back into the house.

"Hello, gorgeous." Jack gave me a peck on the lips.

"Where did Florence get that soft toy from?"

"She had him when she came out of school. I assumed that one of the other kids must have let her borrow it."

"Then why wouldn't she just say that? I think I need a word with that little madam."

When I walked into Florence's bedroom, she was hitting Jay with Wormy. Florence clearly found the game hilarious, but Jay looked less impressed.

"Where did you get Wormy from, Florence?" I asked.

"Found him."

"I'm going to ask you again, and this time I want you to tell me the truth. Okay?"

"Okay."

"Where did you get him from?"

"It's Ellie."

"Who's Ell—wait, isn't that the name you gave the worm you were drawing?"

"Yeah. Wormy used to be Ellie."

I tried but failed to process what she had just said. "What do you mean Wormy used to be Ellie?"

"I used a spell to change Ellie into Wormy."

"You changed a real worm into a soft toy?"

"Yeah."

"That's not possible."

"It was easy." She grabbed the spell book from the bookcase, flicked through the pages and then passed it to me.

I stared in disbelief at the spell on the page: **Change a real worm into a soft toy worm.**

Who created these weird-ass spells?

When Jack came downstairs from reading Florence a bedtime story, he joined me on the sofa.

"You were longer than normal tonight," I said. "Is she okay?"

"Yeah, but she didn't want a story from her book. I had to make up a story about Wormy."

"I bet she regretted that. You're hopeless at making up stories."

"Rubbish. In fact, I was just thinking that I could write a children's book based upon stories of a worm."

"Dream on. Talking about creepy-crawlies, I bumped into Deli today. You'll never guess what she's doing now."

"She hasn't put electric eels in the flotation tanks, has she?"

"Worse than that." I went and got the flyer that she'd given me.

"Leeches? This is a joke, right?"

"Apparently not."

"No one is going to pay to have leeches stuck on them."

"Deli seems to think they'll be queuing around the block."

"She's insane."

Chapter 11

"Why, Mummy?" Florence said.

"Because I don't want a worm on the table while I'm eating my breakfast."

Predictably, Jack wasted no time in springing to his daughter's defence. "It is only a soft toy."

"Is it, though? Ellie was real enough when she was wriggling around the floor. Take it up to your bedroom, please."

"Not fair," she huffed, then grabbed the toy and headed upstairs.

"That was a bit harsh," Jack said.

"I might know you'd take her side."

"I'm not taking sides. I'm just saying."

"Doesn't it creep you out to think that toy was once a living worm. Poor little thing."

"You've changed your tune. It's only five minutes ago that you were saying that you hated worms."

"Can we please stop talking about worms? At least until I've finished my breakfast."

"I assume you're going to come into town with us today?"

"I really ought to work. I've barely made a start on the two cases I'm supposed to be working on."

"Florence will be really disappointed if you don't come."

"Okay, I'll come. I assume we'll go after Florence has finished at her dancing class."

"There isn't any dancing this week. The dance teacher is on holiday, so we can go to town as soon as we're ready. Do you need to get anything while we're there?"

"I thought I might get a Gucci handbag and some Jimmy Choo shoes."

"Funny. I need some new jeans."

"What's wrong with the ones you have?"

"Nothing, but I'd like some slim-fit ones."

I laughed.

"What?" He gave me a look.

"Nothing."

"What's funny about that?"

"Aren't you a bit old for slim-fit jeans?"

"No, I'm not. I'm also going to look at t-shirts."

"Why the sudden interest in new clothes?"

"Now I work in a customer-facing role, I need to look presentable."

"Ahh, I get it." I smirked.

"What's that mean?"

"Get a lot of pretty young women in the shop, do you?"

"Don't be ridiculous. It's got nothing to do with that."

"Why are you blushing, then?"

"I'm not, and I'm not having this stupid discussion."

Busted.

Jack's new wardrobe would have to wait because first we had to buy Florence a starter kit for her knitting. The biggest wool shop in Washbridge used to be Ever A Wool Moment, but not long after Grandma sold it, the shop closed. When I'd asked Grandma if she knew why the shop had failed so soon after the change of ownership, she had been quite evasive, and I still suspected she might have had something to do with it. Shortly after Ever A Wool Moment closed its doors, a new wool shop, called Over Your Eyes, opened in the market square. If the window display was anything to go by, they seemed to cater for knitters of all skill and experience levels, so that was encouraging.

Inside the shop, there were three separate areas, each one signposted: New Knits, Experienced Knits and Expert Knits.

"I guess that makes you a New Knit," Jack said to Florence.

"I'm not a nit."

"Let's go and see what they have on offer." I led the way into the New Knit section of the shop, which was deserted except for a young man behind the counter. His face lit up as soon as he spotted us.

"Hi, there." He came hurrying around the counter. "I'm Kit, and you are?" He directed the question to Florence.

"I'm Florence."

"It's lovely to meet you, Florence. Is this your first visit to Over Your Eyes?"

"Yeah. Why does the shop have such a silly name?"

"It is a bit silly, isn't it?" Kit grinned. "It's something people say: Pulling the wool over your eyes. But never mind that. What brings you here today?"

I was very impressed by the way the young man focussed all his attention on Florence; he was clearly very good with kids.

"I'm going to learn to knit," Florence said. "So I need some needles and wool."

"Then you've definitely come to the right place." He looked over to me and Jack. "Maybe your parents would like to take a seat and have a drink while I get you sorted out."

"Err, sure," I said. "That would be nice."

He pointed towards a small area over to the side where there were a couple of colourful sofas and a drinks machine.

"What do you think of this place?" Jack asked once we had our drinks and were seated.

"It's different. I'm not sure Grandma would approve."

"The young guy seems nice enough."

"Florence seems to think so. Just look at her. She's hanging on his every word. I wish she paid that much attention to me when I'm talking to her."

Jack took a sip of his tea. "This isn't half bad considering it's out of a machine. Do we need to get her some kind of instruction book while we're here?"

"There's no need. Mrs V recommended an online course that she reckons will be ideal for Florence. And it's free."

"Great stuff."

Ten minutes later, Florence and Kit came over to join us.

"Look what I've got." Florence held up a pair of yellow knitting needles and six balls of wool: three red and three white.

"The Kid-Knit 272 are the best needles for someone of Florence's age," Kit said. "When she's another year older, she'll need to move up to the Kid-Knit 434."

"Right." Jack nodded enthusiastically.

"Florence told me that she'll be knitting a scarf, so the Scarf-knit Junior wool is ideal."

"Does she really need six balls?" I asked.

"Yes," Florence interjected before Kit had the chance to respond. "I'm going to knit a really, really long scarf."

"Okay, I guess." I shrugged. "How much does that come to?"

"Let me just ring it up for you."

We followed him back to the counter where he tapped away on the till. "That will be forty-one pounds and seventy-three pence."

"How much?" I almost choked. "For a couple of needles and six balls of wool?"

"I'm sure you will appreciate that the Kid-Knit 272s are not just *any* needles. They've been designed specifically with the young knitter in mind."

"Yes, but—"

"That's fine." Jack handed over his credit card.

"Forty-two quid?" I said to Jack once we were outside. "That's outrageous."

"We did get a free drink."

"We should have got a free bottle of champagne. Kid-Knit 72s my backside."

"272s."

"Whatever. There's no excuse for charging that much." I held up the receipt. "And look at the price of the wool. It's not like it's cashmere."

"What does it matter as long as Florence is happy? Do you like your knitting needles and wool, pumpkin?"

"Yeah. I'm going to start knitting as soon as I get home."

"Right, so who's ready for a burger?" Jack asked.

"Can we afford to eat now we've bought that lot?"

"Of course we can, and I'm starving."

"I suppose I could manage a Supermax burger." I sighed.

"Actually, I thought we'd give Big Burger a miss," Jack said.

"Why? What's wrong with Big Burger?"

"There's a new place opened just down the road from Kathy's bridal shop. I'm surprised you haven't seen it. It's called Tough, and I hear their burgers are out of this world. Mad and Brad are obsessed with them. What do you say? Shall we give it a try?"

"What kind of name is *Tough*? I hope that isn't a description of their burgers."

"What about you, pumpkin?" Jack was obviously hoping for more enthusiasm from his daughter.

"Do they do the Kid's Box?"

"I'm sure they'll do something similar. Come on, let's give it a try."

Jack led the way down the high street, around the corner and past Kathy's shop. As we walked by, I peeked inside but there was no sign of her. Tough was twice the size of Big Burger and extremely busy, but we managed to grab a window table just as another family were leaving.

"Where are the order consoles?" I asked.

"The notice over there says it's table ordering. They come to us."

Florence had taken everything out of the bag and was wrapping wool around one of the needles.

"Is this how you do it, Mummy?"

"No, darling, you have to do something called casting on."

"Can you show me?"

"Not in here. I'll do it as soon as we get back home."

Just then, a young woman dressed in a candy-striped uniform appeared beside our table. Without so much as a word, she threw three menus down on the table and then walked away.

"What was that all about?" I glared at her as she

disappeared into the distance.

"She's probably run off her feet," Jack said.

"That's no excuse." I studied the menu. "They have a lot of different burgers."

"I think I'll have a Whizz Burger," Jack said.

"Who came up with these names?"

"Can I have the Kid's Bang Box?" Florence said. "You get a surprise toy with it."

"Sure, I'll have the Buzz Burger." I looked around. "How are you supposed to get service in here?"

"Somebody will be over soon, I'm sure," Jack said.

"We should have gone to Big Burger. At least you can get served in there."

"Look." Jack pointed. "That young man is coming over."

A spotty young man, wearing the same candy-striped uniform came up to our table. "Ready?"

"We are." Jack picked up the menu. "Can we get one Whizz burger, one Buzz burger and a Kid's Bang Box, please?"

"That it?"

"We'll need some drinks too," I chipped in.

"What drinks?" He sighed.

"I'd like orange," Florence said.

"Coke for me," Jack added.

"Same." I nodded.

"Right."

Before he could walk away, I asked, "Does the Buzz burger come with fries?"

"Says it does, doesn't it?" he said and then turned away.

"Did you hear that?" I looked at Jack. "What an attitude. I've a good mind to report him to the manager."

"Relax, Jill, he didn't mean anything by it."

Colour me unimpressed. The food would have to be out of this world to compensate for the abysmal service.

If we ever got to eat it, that was.

"It's been twenty minutes," I said. "This is ridiculous!"

"It is really busy in here." Jack shrugged.

"That's no excuse. This is supposed to be fast food."

"I think ours is coming now." He gestured to the young woman who had brought our menus earlier. She was heading our way with a tray full of food and drinks.

Before I had the chance to comment on how long it had taken, she practically threw the food onto the table. Not satisfied with that, she slammed each cup down in turn. Enough was enough! I wasn't going to put up with this for another minute.

"Excuse me, young lady."

"What?" She said then blew a gum bubble.

"This simply isn't good enough."

"What's up?"

"*What's up*? Where do I begin? We've been waiting for ages and then you come over here and practically throw the food at us."

"So?"

"So, I'd like to speak to the supervisor."

"I am the supervisor."

"In that case, I'd like to talk to the manager."

"You can't."

"Why not?"

"Because he's busy."

"Then you'd better tell him to get unbusy and come over here."

"No."

"What do you mean *no*?"

"He's on a cigarette break. I'm not allowed to disturb him."

"That's simply not good enough."

"Tough."

"Jill." Jack grabbed my arm. "Leave it."

"I won't leave it."

"Jill, please, there's something you should know."

"Why are you laughing?"

"Read this." He held out one of the menus.

"I don't want to order anything else. I want to talk to the manager."

"Read the back page." He pushed the menu into my hand.

"I definitely don't want a dessert."

"Not that. The bit at the bottom."

Tough is a theme restaurant where all the staff are encouraged to be as rude and obnoxious as possible to all customers. Please note that this is done in fun, and customers are requested not to take anything the staff do or say personally.

I glanced at the young woman who was still standing next to the table. "This is all an act?"

"Yeah, sorry, I thought you knew and that you were playing along with it. If you really do want the manager, I can get him for you."

"No, it's okay."

"I hope you enjoy your meal."

"Right, thanks."

Florence burst into laughter and she and Jack high-fived one another.

"You both knew about this before we came in here, didn't you?"

"Yeah, I saw an article about this place in the paper and I thought it would be a good laugh."

"And you conveniently forgot to mention it to me."

"Come on, Jill, you must see the funny side."

"Oh yeah, hilarious. This food had better be good."

That evening, Jack and I sat in front of the TV, waiting for the lottery numbers to be drawn.

"This is it," I said. "I can feel it in my water. We're going to win the jackpot."

"Do you know what the odds of doing that are?"

"I don't care. Someone in this area won it recently, didn't they? If they can win it, why can't we?"

"Did you hear that they've finally come forward to claim their prize?"

"No, I didn't. Who was it?"

"I don't know. They chose to remain anonymous."

"Shush! They're drawing the numbers now."

Five minutes later, we were both still sitting on the sofa.

"How did we not manage to get even one number?" I screwed the ticket up and threw it across the room.

"I told you the odds were against us. We can try again next week."

"Forget it. It's a waste of money."

Chapter 12

It was Monday morning and the three of us were at the breakfast table. Florence had spent a good part of the previous day watching the videos that Mrs V had recommended. I'd watched the first two with her, and I have to say that I thought they were very good. The woman in the videos, Ginger Vitis, was excellent in my opinion. The way she explained everything step-by-step was ideal for young kids, like Florence. Unfortunately, despite Florence's many talents, knitting apparently wasn't one of them.

"Why doesn't this look like a scarf?" She threw it onto the table.

"I think you've dropped some stitches," I said. And by *some*, I meant almost half of them.

"I didn't drop anything. Look!" She pointed to the kitchen floor.

"It's not that kind of dropping."

"Why can't I do it?"

"You will be able to, pumpkin," Jack said. "It just takes lots and lots of practice."

"I've done lots of practice already."

"You've only been doing it for one day," I said. "It takes much longer than that."

"How long?"

"I don't know. It's different for everyone."

"If I take it to school, Nina will laugh at me."

"You'll just have to keep practising until you get better at it. Then, you'll have something you can show Nina."

"Can I go upstairs and practise again now?"

"Have you finished your muesli?"

"I don't want any more."

I couldn't say I blamed her for that. "Okay, off you go."

"Poor little sausage," Jack said. "She really wants to be able to do it."

"She'll be able to soon enough. She just needs a little patience."

"Says the most impatient woman on the planet."

"Rubbish. I'm renowned for my patience. Anyway, how much longer are you going to stay in denial?"

"I don't know what you're talking about."

"When are you going to admit that you bought the wrong size jeans?"

"They aren't the wrong size. They fit me perfectly."

"So why have you been standing up while you eat your muesli?"

"I don't want to crease them."

"Admit it. You can't breathe when you sit down, can you?"

"I can sit down."

"Go on then."

"I will."

"Still waiting."

He slowly manoeuvred himself down onto the chair, but not before breathing in.

"See," he managed to say, with a strained expression.

Florence came running downstairs. "What's wrong with Daddy?"

"His new jeans are too tight."

"Take no notice of Mummy, pumpkin, my jeans are just fine."

"I've mended my scarf." She held up the knitting needles from which there now hung a perfect scarf.

"And how did you do that?" I asked.

"I just—err—mended it." She shrugged.

"Did you use magic?"

"No."

"Do you remember what I told you happens to children who tell lies? I'll ask you again. Did you use magic?"

"Only a little bit. I'm going to take it to show Nina."

"Wouldn't it be better to wait until you have managed to knit a scarf without using magic?"

She considered that for a few seconds before saying, "No, I want to show her this one. It's much better than the one she made."

"It's time you went upstairs and got ready for school, pumpkin," Jack said.

"Okay." She ran back upstairs.

"I'm not very happy about her taking credit for something she didn't do," I said.

"Like you did with the Bluebottle Girl costume, you mean?"

"That was totally different. Anyway, I'd better get going. I have an exorcism to perform."

"If you see my mum and dad, give them my love."

"Will do."

***

It was a tragedy that Caroline had died not long after spending a small fortune on restoring Tweaking Manor. And now, it seemed that it was to be converted into a hotel by her son, Dominic. For some reason, he'd got it into his head that Tweaking Manor was haunted, which is why my alter ego, Portia Parkspirit, had been hired to perform an exorcism. I'd met Dominic before when Caroline had hired me to find out who had stolen the Tweaking Goblet, so I would have to change my appearance. The beauty of the 'doppelganger' spell is that I could change my appearance to match anyone, even a random stranger. In fact, that's exactly what I did. As I was approaching Tweaking Manor, I saw a woman, about my age, walking along the road, so I made myself look like her.

Dominic hadn't kept on Sears, Caroline's trusty manservant, so it was Dominic himself who answered the door. I expected him to offer his hand in greeting or at least to say hello. Instead, he just stood there, open-mouthed, so I thought I'd better do the honours.

"Hi, I'm Portia Parkspirit. Are you Dominic?"

"I—err—yes, sorry."

"It's very nice to meet you." I decided to offer my hand, as he was showing no sign of doing so.

"Err, yeah." He took my hand but was still staring at me like he'd seen a ghost.

"Are you feeling alright? If this is a bad time, I could always come back later."

"No, it's fine. It's just that—"

"Yes?"

"You're the spitting image of my girlfriend, Catherine."

"Really?"

"Absolutely. She was here just a few minutes ago; she left just before you arrived."

Oh bum!

"How strange, but then they do say that everyone has a double somewhere, don't they?"

He took out his phone. "You have to see this." He

tapped away for a minute, then held it out for me to see a photo of his girlfriend. Needless to say, it was the woman I'd seen earlier.

"I suppose there is a slight resemblance," I said.

"You could be twins. I can't wait to tell her. I don't suppose I could take a photo of you, could I?"

"I'm sorry." I put my hand in front of my face. "I'm very superstitious when it comes to photographs. I have to be careful in case the spirits try to get their revenge."

"Right?" He clearly didn't have the first clue what I was talking about, which wasn't all that surprising because neither did I.

"Shall we make a start?" I suggested.

Lesson learned. From now on, there would be no more basing the 'doppelganger' spell on random strangers. I would just have to stick to making myself look like Kathy.

"Please do come in."

"This is a magnificent building."

"Thank you. It's been in my family for generations. My mother, the late Lady Tweaking, recently spent a small fortune having it renovated."

"I believe your mother passed away recently?"

"Yes, that's right."

"I'm sorry for your loss. Tell me, do you suspect that she might be the one who is haunting the building?"

"I hadn't actually considered that possibility, but I wouldn't have thought so. I get the sense that these spirits are—err—how can I put it? Rather common."

Common? I hoped Yvonne wasn't listening in on this conversation.

"Does that mean you have been able to make contact with the spirits?"

"No, nothing like that. It's just the sense I get, Ms Parkspirit."

"Call me Portia, please."

"As I said, Portia, I plan to turn Tweaking Manor into a hotel, so it's essential that I make sure the place is free from ghosts."

"Are you sure you want to do that? After all, there are some hotels that are able to charge a premium precisely because they *are* haunted."

"I'm positive. I intend Tweaking Manor Hotel to cater to the more discerning customer. We'll be building a swimming pool and spa. I don't want to rely on anything gimmicky like ghosts."

"Very well. You know best. Do you have a sense of which rooms in the manor house they might be frequenting?"

"There are a couple of bedrooms in the east wing which seem unusually cold, but I suppose that could just be my imagination."

"Why don't we start there, and I'll see if I pick up on anything?"

He led the way up the grand staircase, which was even more impressive after the renovation. As we approached the end of the corridor in the east wing, I sensed that Yvonne and Roy were close by. Sure enough, they were standing either side of the four-poster bed.

"Did you feel the temperature drop?" Dominic shivered.

"I did. I think you may be right about this room." I tried not to appear distracted, but it wasn't easy because both Roy and Yvonne were waving to me.

"Can you get rid of them?" he asked.

"Yes, if you're sure that's what you want."

"I'm positive. Where shall I stand?"

"It might be better if you left the room."

"No, I want to stay."

"Okay, if you're sure."

He didn't look very sure, but, unfortunately, he chose to stay.

Now, as you will no doubt already be aware, I am something of an accomplished thespian, but I would need to be on top form if I was to put on a convincing performance for Dominic. Before my visit to Tweaking Manor, I had prepped Yvonne for the part she and Roy would need to play in this charade. Although Dominic couldn't see or hear the ghosts, he should be able to feel the vibes that Yvonne and Roy gave off, and hopefully that would be enough to convince him of the veracity of the exorcism.

"How does this work, exactly?" he asked, nervously.

"In a moment, I will invoke the spirits of the Magnas. They will drive the ghosts back to the other side."

"*Magnas*? What's that?"

"Please, I need complete silence if this is to work."

"Sorry."

I closed my eyes, contorted my face and began to make weird moaning sounds. Right on cue, Yvonne and Roy began to writhe in faux agony, screaming at the top of their voices. If I'm honest, it was all a little over the top, but it was obviously having the desired effect.

"What's that?" Dominic took a step backwards. "I felt something. A shift in the air."

"That means it's working. What you described is the energy expelled by the ghosts as they transition back to the other side."

Good, eh? That Oscar was long overdue.

"Have they gone?" Dominic asked.

"Wait a moment." I closed my eyes for a few seconds, then reopened them and smiled. "They have left."

"That was amazing," Dominic said. "I wouldn't have believed it if I hadn't been here to witness it. That blast of energy was like nothing I've ever felt."

"The spirits who had taken up residence here were some of the most powerful I've ever encountered."

"Will they come back?"

"Definitely not."

"That's great. Thank you so much."

"My pleasure."

"Let's go to my office and I'll settle your account."

As I made my way out of the room, Yvonne gave me a thumbs up.

***

I left Tweaking Manor feeling very pleased with myself. Apart from the initial hiccup with the 'doppelganger' spell, everything had gone perfectly. Dominic was satisfied that the ghosts had been exorcised, which meant that Yvonne and Roy didn't have to worry that a real exorcist might be brought in. And, as an added bonus, Portia had been paid a tidy little fee for services provided.

To celebrate my little windfall, I decided to try a new coffee shop, which had opened the previous week, close to my regular car park in Washbridge.

"Hi, welcome to The Corner Coffee Shop." The woman behind the counter beamed.

"Hi." I was a little distracted by the magnificent array of cakes on display in the glass cabinet beneath the counter.

"See anything you fancy?"

"They all look delicious."

"They're all homemade."

"You made these?"

"Not me. My mother. I can definitely recommend the Victoria sponge."

"I really shouldn't."

"I won't tell anyone."

"Go on, then."

"And to drink?"

"I think I'll have a cappuccino for a change."

"Coming right up."

"How's business been?"

"A little quiet so far, but I'm hopeful that will change when word gets around. I'm Marcy, by the way, I own this place."

"I'm Jill. Can I ask you a question?"

"Sure?"

"The shop name? It's called The Corner Coffee Shop, but you're in the middle of a row of shops?"

"Right. A few people have asked about that. We used to be based on the other side of Washbridge, on the corner of the street. We had to relocate because that whole area is being redeveloped, so we decided to take the name with us. I'm beginning to wonder if that was the right call."

"I see. Well, good luck with the new venture."

"Thanks."

I took my drink and cake, and sat at a table just to the left of the counter. The cake was amazing and melted in my mouth.

A few minutes later, a middle-aged man came into the shop. Well-dressed, he could have passed for a solicitor, accountant or other professional, had it not been for one thing. He was holding a fishing rod. I could tell by the expression on Marcy's face that she was as confused as I was, but to her credit she never reacted.

"Hi, welcome to The Corner Coffee Shop."

"Good morning. Is there somewhere I can put my fishing rod?"

"You can lean it over there in the corner?"

"Hmm, will it be safe there?"

"I'm sure it will be. I'll keep an eye on it."

He considered it for a few seconds before saying. "Okay."

As he was storing his rod in the corner, Marcy made the mistake of looking my way. She must have seen the expression on my face because she almost cracked up, but somehow she managed to compose herself in time for when he returned to the counter.

"What can I get you, sir?"

"A latte, please."

"Coming up."

"Not too much milk."

"Err, you did say a latte?"

"That's right, but not too much milk."

Unsurprisingly, Marcy looked a little confused by that request. "Did you mean you don't want full cream milk? We have skimmed, semi-skimmed, soya, oat or coconut if you'd prefer any of those."

"Whole milk is fine. Just not too much of it."

"Right."

Moments later, Marcy handed him what appeared to be

a regular latte. The man studied the coffee for a moment, then said, "Perfect. Just as I like it."

He took his drink to the table closest to his fishing rod, no doubt to deter anyone from rushing into the shop and stealing it. Marcy looked my way and rolled her eyes.

I'd just finished my drink and was about to leave when I got a phone call from Aunt Lucy who was in tears.

Chapter 13

I found Aunt Lucy seated on the sofa, blubbing into her handkerchief. She was flanked by Barry and Buddy, both clearly concerned about her.

"What's the matter with Lucy?" Barry said.

"Why don't you two go upstairs while I try to find out?"

"Will she be okay?" Buddy asked.

"I'll be fine." Aunt Lucy wiped her eyes. "You two don't need to worry."

The two dogs still looked concerned, but they did as I asked and headed upstairs, allowing me to take a seat next to Aunt Lucy.

"What's wrong?" I put my arm around her.

"It's Alice." She sobbed.

"Alice?"

"Alison."

"Alice's Son?"

"No, Alice Alison."

"Right. Who—?"

Aunt Lucy dissolved into tears again.

"Why don't I go and make us both a cup of tea?" I stood up. "Then you can tell me all about it."

She nodded.

By the time I returned with the drinks, she'd managed to stem the tears.

"Here, drink this and then we can talk."

"Thank you, Jill." She took a sip of tea. "I'm okay now."

"Take your time. There's no hurry."

"Alice and I have been friends forever. We were at school together. I couldn't believe it when I heard the news. They've taken her, Jill."

"Who has? Taken her where?"

"Those awful witch-finders. They're going to burn her."

"Are you talking about the day of burning?"

"Yes."

"Where was she when she was taken?"

"On her way to her office in Washbridge, at least as far as anyone can make out. The last time she was seen was when she stepped off the bus. Her office is only a five-minute walk from the bus stop, but she never made it there. Poor Andrew is beside himself."

"Andrew?"

"That's her husband."

"How long have they lived in the human world?"

"Almost twenty years now, but she pops back here regularly to visit her relatives, and she always drops in on me. I can't bear the thought that I might never see her again."

"It's too soon to be thinking like that. The day of burning isn't for ages yet."

"It's only two weeks away, and no one knows where the witches have been taken."

"I'll find her."

"You will?" Aunt Lucy's face lit up. "Do you really think you'll be able to save them?"

"Of course I will. I've dealt with witch-finders before, and I can deal with them again."

"Oh, Jill." She threw her arms around me. "Thank you so much. What are you going to do?"

"I haven't figured that out yet, but don't worry, I will. Now, finish your tea and let's have no more tears."

Only when I was satisfied that Aunt Lucy was okay, did

I leave her in the capable paws of Barry and Buddy, who had come down to check on her.

"You'll let me know how you get on, won't you, Jill?" Aunt Lucy said.

"I'll keep you posted, but don't worry, everything is going to be okay."

After I'd left Aunt Lucy's house, I made a phone call.

"Grandma, it's me."

"Who's *me*?"

"You know who it is. Are you busy?"

"I'm always busy. My life is one of perpetual motion."

"Can you spare me a few minutes?"

"If I must."

"Are you at the hotel?"

"No, I'm at the chiropractors."

"What are you doing there?"

"Getting my hair done. What do you think?"

"Are you okay?"

"You know me. I don't like to complain, but I'm a martyr to my back. If I didn't have these regular sessions with Ray Ray, I'd barely be able to walk."

"Ray Ray?"

"He's the best. If you're ever in need of some spinal manipulation, he's your man."

"When will you be done with Ray—err—the chiropractor?"

"In about ten minutes."

"Could we meet somewhere for coffee?"

"To discuss what?"

"I'd rather we spoke face-to-face."

"Very well. I'm close by that animal coffee place."

"Coffee Animal?"

"Yes. Meet me there in twenty minutes."

"Will do, and thanks."

"Shut up!" Grandma yelled at the parrot in the cage by her side.

"I only asked for a bit of your cake." The poor parrot backpedalled to the opposite side of the cage.

"That was a bit harsh," I said.

"I don't know why they insist on foisting these animals on us every time we come in here for a drink. Now, hurry up and say what you have to say because I have a meeting with my accountant in thirty minutes."

"I wanted to talk to you about what we can do to get the witches back from the witch-finders."

"Sorry?" She made a show of cupping her ear. "What did you just say?"

"I want to talk about the witches who have been taken for the burning. I thought we could discuss how we can rescue them."

"That's what I thought you said. Would that be the same witches that you didn't give two hoots for only the other day?"

"That's not true. I just said I was too busy to help."

"So what changed your mind?"

"One of Aunt Lucy's friends has been taken."

"That Alice Alison woman, I assume you mean?"

"You heard about it, then?"

"Of course I heard about it. What do you think I've been doing these last few days?"

"Do you have any leads so far?"

"Not a thing. Those awful witch-finders seem to be very well organised this time. They don't appear to have left any clues behind."

"So what are we going to do?"

"*We*? It's *we* now, is it?"

"I promised Aunt Lucy that I'd find her friend and bring her back alive."

"So, that's how it is. When I ask for your help, you tell me to do one, but when Lucy cries on your shoulder, suddenly you're all-in."

"I'm sorry I wasn't more responsive before, but I'm here now. Tell me what I can do to help."

"I think it's time we convened a meeting of the WOW committee."

"But I'm no longer involved with WOW."

"That doesn't matter. This affects all witches. I'll make some calls and let you know what time the meeting is." She stood up. "You can take this stupid parrot back for me."

"Will do. Oh, and Grandma—"

"What?"

"I'm sorry I didn't take this more seriously earlier."

"So am I." And with that, she made her exit.

***

Mrs V was reading a book titled What To Do In Australia.

"Any calls, Mrs V?"

"Only some stupid joker who said his name was Walter Rang."

"What did he want?"

"He wanted to know if you could find his brother, Boomer."

"What did you say?"

"I'm afraid I was rather rude to him, dear. I told him to get lost."

"Good for you. Nothing else?"

"No, it's been very quiet so far today."

Winky was tapping away on my computer.

"What have I told you about using that?"

"I'm done now. I was just checking if there's been any news on the Fun Rat takeover bid."

"And has there?"

"Nothing yet."

"You'd better be right about this."

"Of course I'm right. The news will break any day now."

"I assume you're Mr Boomer."

"At your service." He took a bow.

"How many times have I warned you not to wind Mrs V up?"

"But it's so easy. Come on, you have to admit it was funny."

"Hilarious. Get off my desk because I need to do some work."

"It's a bit late in the day to be starting now, isn't it?"

"I'm not just starting. I'll have you know that I carried out an exorcism this morning."

"Creepy stuff that. You shouldn't get involved with it."

"It wasn't a real exorcism. I was just playing a part."

"A fraud, you mean?"

"The client was very happy, and I received a nice fee for services provided."

Mrs V came through to my office.

"Mr Bottle is out there. He wonders if you can spare

him a minute. He said it's about the Droza ad."

"Absolutely, send him through, please."

Talbot had discarded his usual yellow suit in favour of a bright orange one. If I'd had my sunglasses with me, I'd have been tempted to put them on.

"Thanks for seeing me, Jill, I know how busy you are."

"No problem. Mrs V said you had news about the next ad shoot?"

"That's right. Droza have just sent the details through. As you might imagine, they're keen to capitalise on the success of the first ad, so they want to shoot the next one ASAP."

"How soon?"

"Next week. They've provisionally booked the studio for a week today. Will you be able to fit that in with all your other commitments?"

"I'll make it work somehow. Did they send you a script yet?"

"No. I did ask them, but they insisted that they don't want you or Moo to have sight of the script until the day. They reckon your reactions will be more authentic that way."

I would have preferred to know what I had let myself in for, but I figured that it couldn't be any worse than being buried underneath a mountain of toilet rolls.

"Fair enough. Where is the shoot? And what time do they want me there?"

"All the information is in there." He handed me a large white envelope. "If you need clarification on anything, let me know, and I'll contact them."

"Okay, will do."

"Great. I'll not take up any more of your time. Break a

leg next Monday."

"That sounds a bit ominous," Winky said after Talbot had left. "They must have something pretty awful planned if they daren't tell you in advance."

"It's not like that. They want to make sure our reactions are as authentic as possible. Whatever they have planned, can't be any worse than the first ad."

"Are you sure about that?"

"It'll be fine."

"I still think you should have suggested using me in the shoot."

"We've been over that already. Neither Talbot nor I have any say in the ad."

"Droza's loss. Do you reckon he wears those suits for a dare?"

***

Florence came running down the path to meet me at the gate.

"Everyone said my scarf was better than Nina's, Mummy."

"I thought I told you that you couldn't take the scarf you'd magicked to school."

"I forgot." She shrugged. "Katy said mine was the best scarf she'd ever seen."

"Hmm."

"I'm going to make another one now." She went charging back into the house and up to her bedroom.

"Hi." Jack gave me a peck on the lips.

"I thought we'd agreed that you wouldn't let her take that scarf to school?"

"We did. She must have sneaked it into her bag when I wasn't watching. How did the exorcism go?"

"Pretty good, I'd say. Mind you, your mother and father went a bit over the top with the amateur dramatics. How was your day?"

"Fantastic. Brad reckons there's a chance he might keep me on even after Mad is back fulltime."

"Really? How do you feel about that?"

"I'd be over the moon. I'm enjoying it far more than I ever expected to."

Our conversation was interrupted by a phone call from Grandma.

"Tomorrow morning at eight o'clock."

"What is?"

"The meeting between you, me and the WOW committee."

"Oh, okay."

"Don't be late."

"Hang on. Where's the meeting?"

"At the hotel of course."

"What—err—"

Too late. She had already ended the call.

"Problem?" Jack said.

"I'll have to leave early tomorrow morning. Grandma has set up a meeting about the witch burnings."

"I thought you said there was nothing to worry about?"

"Turns out that there is. A few witches have been abducted including a friend of Aunt Lucy's."

"What are you planning to do about it?"

"I'm not sure. That's what the meeting is about."

Chapter 14

"Not fair." Florence pouted.

"You're not taking that scarf to school," I said. "Daddy will check your bag before you leave, won't you, Daddy?"

"Err, yeah. Mummy's right, pumpkin."

"Why can't I take it to show Nina?"

"Because it's almost six feet long and everyone will know that you couldn't possibly have knitted that overnight."

"I can tell them I'm a really quick knitter."

"I said no, and that's final. Now, I have to get going or Grandma will have my guts for garters."

"What are garters?"

"Daddy will explain that." I gave her a peck on the top of the head, blew Jack a kiss, and then headed out.

I arrived at the hotel one minute after eight o'clock.

"They're in the Scarlet Room," the receptionist said. "Down that corridor, second door on the left."

"You're late!" Grandma said.

"Sorry."

There were two other witches at the table, neither of whom I recognised.

"Ladies, I apologise for my granddaughter's tardiness." Grandma shot me her infamous death stare. "Perhaps you would be kind enough to introduce yourselves."

The taller of the two witches stood up. She was wearing one of the prettiest summer dresses I'd ever seen.

"Hi, Jill, I'm Zoe Rabbendeckermouse."

"Rabbendecker—?"

"Mouse. Please just call me Zoe. Before we get into the guts of the meeting, can I just say that I do hope you and your grandmother will one day return to the WOW fold. I know that—"

"Can we please stay on point, Zoe," Grandma snapped.

"Sorry." Duly reprimanded, Zoe retook her seat.

The second witch, who had unruly hair and was wearing purple dungarees, took to her feet. Having witnessed her colleague's dressing down, she kept her introduction short and sweet.

"I'm Doris, the vice chair."

"Okay, let's get to the matter in hand," Grandma said. "Four witches have already been abducted from Washbridge, and that number is only likely to increase between now and the day of burning. Our mission, therefore, is very straightforward: We have to ensure there are no further abductions, find the witches who are being held against their will, and destroy the witch-finders who are responsible for this atrocity. Agreed?"

Everyone nodded.

"Grandma continued, "Good. In that case, we'll go around the table, so each of you can outline your suggested plan of action."

Plan of action? What plan of action?

"Jill, we'll start with you."

"I—err—I don't have a plan. Sorry."

"What are you doing here, then?" Grandma demanded.

"You only invited me to this meeting last night, and you didn't mention anything about coming up with a plan."

"Typical." She sighed. "Zoe?"

The poor woman looked like a deer caught in the headlights.

"I—err—thought we could look out for anyone with a tattoo of a goblet on the back of their neck."

"And?" Grandma prompted.

"I hadn't really thought beyond that."

"And how are we supposed to check the necks of everyone in Washbridge?" Grandma asked.

"It was only a suggestion."

"And if we find someone with the tattoo on their neck, what then?"

"Sorry." Zoe looked close to tears. "I hadn't really thought it through."

Grandma turned her gaze on Doris. "What about you? What did you come up with?"

"Could we offer them money? To release the witches they've taken."

"Pay the witch-finders?"

"Err, yeah."

"A sort of reward?"

"Err, no. I just thought—"

"Did you, though? Are you honestly telling me that you thought this through and that was the best you could come up with?"

"Sorry."

"I knew this is what would happen, which is why I came up with a plan." She opened her bag and took out a number of small black plastic cubes, which had a red button on one side. "Voila!"

"What are they?" I asked.

"The four of us are amongst the highest profile witches based in Washbridge, which is why the witch-finders are bound to target one or more of us." She turned to me. "Agreed?"

"I guess so."

"When they make a move on you, what will you do?"

"It won't be my first rodeo, going up against a witch-finder. I'll make them regret the day they were born."

"Wrong."

"What do you mean *wrong*?"

"I mean that if they make a move on any of us, you should let them take you."

"Why? Are you crazy?"

"Far from it. Once they have taken you to wherever they're holding the other witches, you press the red button on this gizmo. That will immediately alert the other three of us, and show the GPS coordinates of where you're being held." She picked up one of the gizmos and handed it to Zoe. "Press the red button."

Zoe did as she was told, and the other three gizmos began to buzz.

"Take one," Grandma said to me. "And look underneath."

I did as she said and saw a display showing GPS coordinates, which I assumed corresponded to the hotel's location.

"Well?" Grandma said.

"That's brilliant," Zoe gushed.

"Amazing," Doris agreed.

I said nothing.

"Jill?"

"What happens when the buzzer goes off? What do we do then?"

"I would have thought that was obvious. The other three of us will head straight to the location given by the GPS coordinates, rescue the witches who are being held there, and deal with the witch-finders."

"Define *deal*."

"I'll leave that to your imagination. Now, Zoe and Doris, I also need you to speak to as many witches in Washbridge as possible. Right now, they're bound to be feeling nervous. It's your job to put their minds at ease by telling them that we're doing everything possible to resolve this situation. You don't need to go into details about our plans, but you should tell them to remain vigilant at all times." Grandma stood up. "Okay, that will do. I have a hotel to run."

I hung back and waited until Zoe and Doris had left before confronting Grandma, "Your plan is full of holes."

"Like what?"

"What if they don't come for any of us four?"

"They will."

"How can you be so certain?"

"Because I have eyes and ears everywhere. My sources tell me that there is a lot of discontent amongst the rank-and-file witch-finders in respect of their current leadership. To avoid a challenge to their position, the leaders need a big score on burning day. And we four are about as big a scalp as they could hope to secure."

"And these things." I held up the gizmo. "Are you sure they'll work?"

"You've just seen they do."

"Hmm." I wasn't convinced, but I slipped it into my handbag.

"Just be careful, Jill."

"I will."

I had just turned to walk away when I felt a sharp pain on the back of my neck. I spun around and realised that Grandma had just slapped me.

"What did you do that for?"

"There was a wasp in your hair. I didn't want it to sting you."

"A sting would have been less painful." I rubbed my neck.

"Don't be such a cry-baby."

I left the hotel in something of a daze, and not just because of the crack on the neck that Grandma had given me. I'd expected the four of us to spend the morning trying to hatch a masterplan to rescue the abducted witches. Instead, I'd been given a little black box with a red button, and told that if they came for me, I should allow myself to be kidnapped.

No chance. If Grandma thought I was just going to roll over for a witch-finder, she was sadly mistaken. I had other plans.

***

Although I'd been busy with the missing chicken case and distracted by the burning day saga, that was still no excuse for neglecting Sam Rich's case. Since visiting his offices on Eggshell Road, I'd done virtually nothing to find his missing friend, Lorne Mower, AKA Cutter. I was determined to put that right, so I'd set up meetings today with Cutter's sister, Anita Hedge, and his assistant on his sweet stall, Rose Merry.

The first of those meetings wasn't until ten-thirty, so I had time to nip into the office first. After parking my car, I glanced across at The Corner Coffee Shop, and considered popping in there, but I didn't want to get into the habit of doing that every day.

Mrs V was at her desk, but she seemed distracted.

"Good morning, Mrs V."

"Sorry, Jill, I was miles away."

"Are you okay?"

"Err, yes."

"Are you sure?"

"Did you know that there are deadly spiders in Australia?"

"I might have seen something about it on TV."

"Lots of them, apparently: Funnel-webs, Redbacks, Trap door."

"It hasn't put you off going there, has it?"

"Err, no. Of course not. Armi says we'll be fine, but we'll have to be vigilant. Tea?"

"I think I'd like a coffee this morning, please."

"What did I tell you?" Winky said.

"About what?"

"The old bag lady. She has no chance of making it back here. If the flight doesn't kill her, the spiders will."

"Nonsense. Mrs V is one tough cookie."

"We'll see. I have a request."

"The answer is no."

"I haven't even told you what it is yet."

"You don't need to. The answer is no, anyway."

"It isn't for me."

"If it's for Socks, the answer is definitely no. I've done enough for that brother of yours already."

"It isn't for him. It's for charity."

"Oh yeah." I scoffed. "The Winky Charity Foundation?"

"It's for the Abandoned Kittens Shelter." He handed me a small brochure.

It looked genuine enough, but I still wasn't convinced. This was Winky after all.

"What do they do?"

"It's kind of in the name. They take in abandoned kittens and look after them until they can find them a new home."

"Is it run by humans?"

"What? No, it's run by felines. So, will you sponsor me?"

"To do what?"

In response he handed me a form.

"Sponsored parachute jump? Are you serious?"

"Deadly."

"You're going to jump out of a plane?"

"They'll probably have to push me, but yeah."

"Are you insane?"

"Probably."

"Who else is taking part?"

"There's three of us altogether."

"All cats?"

"Yeah."

"Who's piloting the plane? Not a cat, surely?"

"Why shouldn't a cat pilot a plane?"

"I—err—"

"As it happens, it's a wizard called Alfie. He has a pilot's licence."

"And how did Alfie get roped into this?"

"Tommy lives with him."

"Tommy is a cat, I assume?"

"Yeah, he's one of the others taking part in the jump. So, will you sponsor me or not?"

"I suppose so. How does it work?"

"It's really simple. You commit to paying a certain amount if I make the jump. If I back out, then you pay nothing. It's an all or nothing kind of thing."

I took a closer look at the other entries on the form.

"Are these real or did you just write them in yourself?"

"When did you get so cynical?"

"It comes from sharing an office with you."

"Those are all friends of mine. Come on, you know you want to."

Every other entry on the form was for twenty pounds, so somewhat reluctantly, I followed suit, then handed the form back to him.

"Thank you, Jill. The kittens will be grateful to you."

"I do have one question."

"Shoot."

"You said if you back out that no money is due."

"Correct."

"What if you jump but the parachute fails to open, and you plunge to your death?"

What? It was just a joke. Sheesh!

Chapter 15

Anita Hedge's bungalow was nothing out of the ordinary, just a simple semi in a row of near identical properties. What made it stand out from the others on the street was the front garden, and more specifically the topiaries. I'd seen topiary before but nothing on this scale or to such a high standard: a dog, a squirrel, a horse, and my personal favourite, a giraffe. I was still busy staring at them when someone called my name.

"Jill?" The woman stepped out of the house and walked down the path to greet me.

"Hi, I was just admiring your topiary. It's amazing."

"Thank you."

"Did you do all of these yourself?"

"Me? No, I can barely cut a straight hedge. These are all the work of my hubby, Rolly."

"He's very talented. I assume he does this for a living?"

"No, it's just a hobby. He's an electrician by trade."

"Well, they're amazing."

"Thanks. Would you like to come inside? I'll make us a cup of tea. Unless you'd prefer coffee?"

"Tea is fine, thanks."

A few minutes later, we were seated in the lounge, and Anita handed me the biscuit barrel.

"I'm afraid custard creams are the only biscuits I have in at the moment."

"That's okay." I grabbed three. "I am partial to the occasional custard cream."

"This is all terribly upsetting. Do you think you'll be able to find him?"

"I hope so. Are you and your brother close?"

"Very. We always were, but more so after Mum died."

"How old were you at the time?"

"I was eight. Cutter would have been ten."

"You were brought up by your father?"

"He did his best. He wasn't a natural parent. Cutter and I more or less raised ourselves."

"When was the last time you saw your brother?"

"He always comes here for his dinner on a Friday night after work, so it would have been about two weeks ago."

"How did you learn he'd gone missing?"

"Sam Rich called to ask me if I'd seen him because he hadn't turned up to that silly cowboy society thing."

"You don't share your brother's enthusiasm for cowboys, I take it?"

"They're like big kids if you ask me. Cutter absolutely loves it, though."

"How was your brother the last time you saw him?"

"Same as always."

"There didn't seem to be anything bothering him?"

"Not that I noticed. He was moaning about the sweet stall, but that wasn't unusual."

"Anything in particular?"

"He was barely breaking even. I'd told him a dozen times he needed to let Rose go, but he couldn't bring himself to do it."

"Do you think it's possible that your brother has deliberately disappeared?"

She didn't hesitate. "Definitely not. Cutter would never do anything like that because he knows how much it would upset me."

"Fair enough. I understand your brother lives alone."

"That's right."

"He never married?"

"No."

"Was he seeing anyone?"

"No. Well, maybe. I'm not sure."

"Go on."

"He told me that he'd been out with a woman from the market a couple of times."

"A customer?"

"No, one of the other stallholders. Sarah, I think her name is, but nothing came of it as far as I could tell."

"Sam Rich gave me a key to your brother's house, but I didn't want to go around there until I'd asked your permission first. Would you have any objections?"

"None at all."

"In that case, I think I'll head over there now. You're welcome to accompany me if you wish."

"Thanks, but I have my weekly Zumba class in an hour's time."

"Right, well thanks for your help."

"Can I ask you something, Jill?"

"Sure, fire away."

"I assume you've dealt with a lot of missing person cases?"

"A few."

"Does the missing person usually turn up? Alive, I mean?"

"Most of the time," I said, not because it was necessarily true, but because it was what she wanted to hear.

The nameplate on Cutter's house was shaped like a cowboy hat and bore the name: The Ranch.

"He isn't in."

I turned around to find an elderly woman walking across the road towards me. She had a small dog under one arm and a cigarette hanging out the corner of her mouth.

"Do you know Lorne?" I asked.

"Who? Oh, you mean Cutter. Yeah, we've lived across the road from one another for nearly ten years. Who are you?"

"My name is Jill Maxwell." I handed her one of my cards.

"Private investigator? What's he done?"

"Nothing as far as I'm aware. He's gone missing."

"I thought it was strange I hadn't seen him for a while."

"Do you see him often?"

"My hubby doesn't like me smoking in the house, so I come out here every few hours for a ciggy. Cutter always stops for a chat when he sees me. You don't think anything has happened to him, do you?"

"I've no reason to believe so, but it has been a while since anyone has seen him. Tell me, err—sorry, I don't know your name."

"Amy."

"Tell me, Amy, have you seen anyone else come to his house over the last week or so?"

"I don't think so." She took a long drag on the cigarette. "Oh, hang on. I did see that lady friend of his."

"Sarah?"

"I don't know her name. I just saw her with Cutter a few times."

"Can you describe her?"

"About the same hight and age as you. Blonde hair, but not natural, I don't think."

"Can you remember when you saw her?"

"About a week ago, but I couldn't be sure of the exact day."

"Okay, thanks. Could I ask you a favour?"

"As long as it doesn't cost me anything." She stubbed out the cigarette under her foot, immediately took out another one, and wedged it in the corner of her mouth.

"Would you give me a call if you see anyone come to this house?"

"Sure, no problem."

Using the key that Sam Rich had given me, I let myself into Cutter's house. The first thing that struck me was how clean and tidy it was for a man living alone. The second thing was the sheer volume of cowboy memorabilia. Posters from famous cowboy movies, most of them from the sixties, adorned the walls of the hallway. There were two glass display cases in the lounge, both full of cowboy figurines. The wallpaper in that room was also cowboy-themed and wouldn't have looked out of place in a young boy's bedroom. There was a DVD player underneath the TV, and next to it was a storage unit containing hundreds of DVDs, stored in alphabetical order. All of them cowboy movies.

Thankfully, the cowboy theme appeared to be restricted to downstairs. Upstairs, were two bedrooms and a bathroom. I carried out a cursory search of the cupboards and wardrobe in the main bedroom, but I found nothing of interest. The spare bedroom, like ours, was used as a dumping ground, so I didn't even try to sort through that lot. There was nothing to see in the bathroom, other than a dripping showerhead.

Twenty minutes later, having found nothing of interest

upstairs, I made my way back downstairs and into the kitchen. The cupboard units were dated but in reasonable condition. The washing machine looked new, but the fridge freezer looked like it had seen better days. In addition to his fascination with all things cowboy, Cutter obviously had a thing about fridge magnets because the fridge freezer was covered in them. A few of them displayed place names, but most were just random: animals, jokes, fast food. Under one of the magnets was a business card for a plumber called Dan Tapp, and under another was a handwritten note that contained a string of numbers. I thought at first it might be a phone number, but when I tried to call it, I got a message that no such number existed.

Minutes later, I headed out of the house, no wiser about Cutter's whereabouts or the reason for his disappearance.

***

On my last visit to Francesca Artichoke's neighbourhood, I'd been unable to get a response from one of her next-door neighbours. The man, called Jason, had been described by another of the neighbours, as being eccentric. I was fairly sure he'd been at home when I'd called before, but he hadn't answered the door. This time, I was determined that he and I were going to have a conversation, whether he wanted to or not.

I rang his doorbell. No response.

I knocked on the door several times with the same result, but then out of the corner of my eye, I saw movement at one of the upstairs windows.

I opened the letterbox and shouted through it, "Jason, I

know you're in there. It's important I speak to you. Would you open the door, please?"

There was still no response, so I tried again, "I can stay here all day, and that's what I'll do if necessary. Why don't you open the door, so we can have a quick chat and then I'll be on my way."

I wasn't hopeful, but then I heard footsteps coming from inside and moments later, the door opened. A fraction.

"What do you want?" said a high-pitched voice.

"Do you think you could open the door a little wider so that I can see you?"

"Who are you?"

Cautiously, in case he slammed the door closed on my arm, I held out my card. Moments after taking it, he opened the door to reveal himself in all his eccentric glory. I found it difficult to assess his age; he could have been anywhere between thirty and fifty. He was wearing purple sequined trousers with a matching waistcoat, under which he was bare-chested. And, as if that wasn't enough, he was wearing odd slippers: one purple, the other green.

By way of explanation, he said, "I've misplaced my other purple slipper."

"Right."

"You were here the other day."

"I was, but you didn't answer the door."

"I don't have visitors." No surprises there. "What do you want?"

"I've been hired by Francesca Artichoke."

"Who?"

"Your next-door neighbour."

"Oh. What do you want with me?"

"Just a chat, really. I don't suppose I could come inside, could I?"

"No one comes in the house."

"Right. I just thought it might be more comfortable."

"No one comes in the house."

"Okay. You're probably aware that your neighbour keeps animals in her back garden."

"Pigs."

"That's right."

"Goats."

"Correct."

"Hedgehog."

"What? No, I don't think so."

"I've seen it."

"Right, maybe there was a hedgehog, but I'm actually here about the chickens."

"They wake me up."

"That's Roger."

"Who's Roger."

"The rooster's name is Roger. He's the one that you can hear in the morning. The reason your neighbour hired me is because her chickens have disappeared."

"Where have they gone?"

"She doesn't know, that's why she has hired me. The reason I wanted to talk to you was to ask if you might have seen anything."

"Like what?"

"Someone taking the chickens?"

"No."

"Have you seen anyone acting suspiciously around here in the last week or two?"

"You."

"Apart from me."

He considered that for the longest moment and then said, "There was a man in a black van who parked across the road a week or so ago."

"What did he do to make you say he was acting suspiciously?"

"When he arrived, his face and hands were clean, but when he left, they were dirty."

At last. Maybe now we were getting somewhere.

"Did you see him carrying any chickens? Or cages, maybe?"

"Now you mention it, he was carrying something."

"Chickens?"

"Brushes."

"I don't suppose you took a note of the registration number of the van?"

"No."

"Okay, never mind. It was just a longshot."

"There was a name on the van, though."

"What name?"

"Edward Soot, chimney sweep. I don't think that's his real name, though."

Please, beam me up now.

"Okay, well, thanks for your time."

"Will you be coming back again?"

"I don't think so."

I've said it before, and I'll say it again: there are days when it feels like I'm a nutter magnet. I had now talked to the neighbours on either side, which left just the property that backed onto Francesca's house. It was getting late, and I was exhausted after my session with Jason, so I decided to leave that for another day.

***

Jack stared at me in disbelief. "A sponsored parachute jump?"

"Yeah."

"For cats?"

"Correct."

"Just when I thought nothing else you told me could surprise me. How much have you sponsored him for?"

"Twenty pounds."

"*Twenty*?"

"That's what everyone else had sponsored him for, and besides, it's for abandoned kittens."

Chapter 16

The next morning, Jack and I were at the kitchen table. Florence had yet to make an appearance, although I could hear her moving around upstairs.

Jack glanced over at the stairs. "What do you reckon that little madam is up to?"

"Nothing good." I stood up. "I'll go and check."

I'd expected to find Florence in her bedroom, but it was empty. I was about to start panicking when I heard sounds coming from the bathroom. It was the sound of vomiting.

"Florence, are you okay?" I pushed the bathroom door open and stepped inside.

"I'm okay, Mummy. It's Jay."

Florence had her arm around the jelly monster who had his head over the toilet bowl.

"What's wrong with him?"

"Don't know. He said he didn't feel well and then he came in here."

Jay lifted his head. "Sorry."

"Don't be silly." I put my hand on his.

"I think I'm okay now." He stood up slowly.

"Are you sure?" He still looked a little green around the gills.

"I think so, but I'd like to lie down."

"Come on." I took his hand and led him towards our bedroom.

"Why isn't he going in my room?" Florence asked.

"If he has a bug, I don't want you to get it."

"What about you and Daddy?"

"We'll be okay. You go down and have your breakfast

or you'll be late for school. I'll see to Jay."

"Okay. Hope you're better soon, Jay."

I helped Jay onto our bed, and I was pleased to see his colour was already starting to return to his cheeks.

"Do you want anything, Jay?"

"No, thanks, I think I'd like to sleep."

"Good idea. A good sleep will do you the world of good."

After tucking him in, I went downstairs.

"Is he okay?" Florence said.

"Yeah, he's going to have a sleep."

"What's wrong with him?" Jack asked.

"No idea."

Florence shovelled down her breakfast in double quick time, and then jumped down from the table.

"I'm going to check on Jay," she said.

"If he's asleep, don't wake him up. He needs to sleep."

"Okay." She tiptoed up the stairs.

"Was it a good idea to put him in our bed?" Jack said.

"I couldn't leave him in Florence's room."

"I know that. I just meant we might catch whatever he has."

"Hopefully not. What else could I do? It's not like there's a bed or even any room for him to lie down in the spare room."

"We really should sort out that room."

"Are you volunteering?"

"Why don't we tackle it together this weekend? If we can get it sorted, we could use it as a guest room."

"We never have guests."

"We might do if we had somewhere for them to sleep. Come on, Jill, it's needed doing forever."

"Okay. It's not like I was looking forward to a restful weekend or anything."

Before setting off for Washbridge, I gave Grandma a call.

"Have they made contact?" she said, before I'd had chance to get a word out.

"Who?"

"The witch-finders. Who do you think?"

"No, I haven't seen any of them."

"Why are you bothering me, then? Don't you know early mornings are the busiest time for a hotel?"

"Sorry, it's just a quick question. What do you know about jelly monsters?"

"About *what*?"

"Jelly monsters. You remember Florence's friend called Jay?"

"Are you talking about that green blobby thing?"

"Yeah, that's Jay."

"How am I supposed to know anything about him?"

"I didn't mean Jay specifically. I meant jelly monsters in general."

"That thing was created by Florence; he's a one-off. There aren't any other jelly monsters unless some other child has conjured up the very same monster, which I very much doubt."

"I guess you're right. I should have realised."

"If you don't have any more stupid questions, I have work to do."

"Sorry, I—err—"

She had already ended the call.

"I don't know what that cat is up to," Mrs V said. "But I've been hearing thudding sounds coming from your office ever since I arrived."

"I'll sort it out. Have you had any more thoughts about the Australian spiders?"

"Armi says I'm worrying unnecessarily, and that we're unlikely to encounter them where we'll be staying."

"Has that put your mind at ease?"

"Not really."

As soon as I stepped into my office, I realised what was making the thudding sound: Winky, who had been standing on my desk, jumped off it, landed with a thud, and then dropped onto his side and rolled across the floor.

"What do you think you're doing?"

"Isn't it obvious?"

"It looks like you're standing on my desk, which by the way, you shouldn't be doing, and jumping down onto the floor. What I can't figure out is why."

"I'm practising for the parachute jump, obviously." He climbed back onto my desk. "Imagine this is the exit door of the aircraft. Three, two, brace, go, go, go." He launched himself off the desk, and landed on his feet before dropping onto his side again.

"I really don't see how that's going to help. It's nothing like the real thing."

He stood up and brushed himself down. "Our instructor said we should do this."

"And what's that on your back?"

"It's my parachute pack of course."

"That backpack looks nothing like a parachute. And that bit of string isn't fooling anyone." I reached out for it.

"Don't pull—"

What I thought was a backpack burst open and the next thing I knew I was engulfed in white fabric.

"Help!"

Winky managed to pull the fabric off me, and then helped me to my feet.

"Thanks very much, Jill, I'll have to repack that thing now."

"It's a real parachute."

"What did you think it was?"

"I just thought it was a backpack with your lunch in it."

Naturally, Mrs V chose that precise moment to walk into the room.

"Jill? What—err—"

"You're probably wondering what's going on?"

"I was rather."

"I can explain."

"Really?" Winky grinned. "This I have to hear."

"You remember my new client, Mr Rich."

"The cowboy?"

"That's him. It turns out that he also likes to parachute jump."

"Dressed as a cowboy?"

"No, I don't think so. Anyway, he gave me one of his parachutes."

"Why?"

Good question.

"Because I'd told him that I might like to try it sometime."

"I don't think that's a good idea, dear. I don't hold with jumping out of planes. Why did you release the parachute here in your office?"

"Sam says it's important that everyone is able to pack

their own parachute. I was just about to do that when you walked in."

"What does Jack think about you jumping out of a plane?"

"He's very supportive. Did you come in for anything in particular?"

"Only to ask if you wanted a drink."

"Not right now. Maybe when I've repacked the parachute."

"Very well, dear."

"You should run a masterclass," Winky said.

"In what?"

"Lying. It comes so easily to you, doesn't it?"

"It's a good job it does. I could hardly tell her that you're the one doing the parachute jump, could I? Now, will you repack this thing?"

"Me? I don't know how to do it. You'll have to help me."

"Great."

Between the two of us, it took almost an hour to get the parachute back in its pack, and even then, I wasn't convinced we'd done it correctly. Let's put it this way, you wouldn't have got me to jump out of an aircraft with that thing on my back, but then you wouldn't have got me to jump out of an aeroplane at all. Ever.

Still exhausted from the parachute packing, I paid a visit to Washbridge market hall. It was years since I'd last stepped foot in there, and it didn't get any better. The building was over one-hundred and fifty years old, and in desperate need of a major renovation. According to the sign outside, there were over one-hundred stalls inside, but not every one of them was occupied. The variety of goods on offer was amazing, everything from cat food to doilies. I counted at least four other sweet stalls before I found Cutter's, which had the catchy name Sweets. The woman behind the counter was sitting on a stool, and she appeared to be engrossed in something on her phone.

"Excuse me."

She didn't react because she had an earpiece in each ear.

I tried again, and this time waved my hand close to her face. "Excuse me."

She removed the earpieces. "Sorry, love, I didn't see you there. I was engrossed in Game of Thrones. Do you watch it?"

"It's not really my thing."

"I enjoy a bit of fantasy. Anything to get away from this humdrum world. What can I get for you? Chocolate limes are on offer this week."

"Actually, I was hoping to have a word with you. You are Rose, I assume?"

"Err, yeah." Her smile had faded, and she was obviously on her guard. "What about?"

"Cutter."

"Have they found him? Is he alright? Are you the police?"

"I'm not the police, and he's still missing. My name is Jill Maxwell and I've been hired to try and find him."

She let out a sigh of relief. "For a horrible moment there, I thought you were going to tell me that—never mind. I'll get someone to watch the stall and we can talk over a cup of tea if you like."

"Sounds good."

"Hey, Ricky," she shouted to the neighbouring

stallholder. "Can you watch the stall for a few minutes while I go and talk to this lady. She's trying to find Cutter."

"Sure, Rose, no problem."

She led the way to a small café at the opposite side of the market hall, which was doing a roaring trade.

"Hey, Mac." Rose caught the eye of the man behind the counter. "Could you rustle us up two teas and bring them over?"

"We don't do table service." The tall guy grinned. "But seeing as it's for you. Where are you going to sit?"

"Over there next to the highchairs."

"Be with you in a couple of ticks."

"You said you were trying to find Cutter," Rose said. "Are you some kind of private investigator or something?"

"Yeah." I handed her my card.

"Who hired you? His sister?"

"No, a guy called Sam Rich. He's the chairman of the Washbridge Cowboy Appreciation Society."

"I wouldn't trust those guys as far as I could throw them."

"Why do you say that?"

"A couple of them come to the stall occasionally, dressed in the full cowboy gear. They're very loud and can be pretty obnoxious at times."

"In what way?"

"They're always condescending towards me, which doesn't bother me, but I also got the feeling that they were making fun of Cutter sometimes, but he never seemed to notice."

"You don't happen to remember their names, do you?"

"They went by the names of Tex and Hank, but I doubt those are their real names."

"Did Cutter ever wear his cowboy outfit?"

"Not here in the market hall. Not the full gear, anyway, but he did occasionally wear one of his hats. He's shown me photos of their meets, though. Do you reckon Cutter is okay?"

"I don't know. How was he before he disappeared?"

"Pretty miserable."

"Really?"

"Yeah, but don't go reading too much into that. Cutter has been a misery guts as long as I've known him. It's just how he is. I know he's been worried about the stall. Takings have been down for a while now."

"Any particular reason?"

"It's not just our stall. Most of the stallholders are experiencing the same thing. It's this place." She looked around. "Look at the state of it. It needs a lot of work and has done for years, but the owners don't want to know. People don't come in here in the numbers they used to."

"And you reckon that was starting to get Cutter down?"

"I know it was. He didn't talk to me about the accounts, but I know how much we're selling, and I reckon he's only just about breaking even some weeks. To tell you the truth, I've been feeling a bit guilty about it."

"What do you mean?"

"When he took me on, things were a lot different. The market hall was much busier, and so were we. He needed another pair of hands to cope with the demand. Now, there's not enough customers to warrant two of us working there. I reckon he'd like to let me go, but he's such a nice guy I don't think he can bring himself to do it.

I'd offer to leave but I'm only just managing to cover the rent as it is, so I can't afford to." She sighed. "Looks like I might have to, though."

"If Cutter doesn't come back, you mean?"

"Either way. I reckon the stall's days are numbered."

"Can you tell me about the last time you saw Cutter?"

"As he was leaving, he said he'd be late in the next day because he had the plumber coming around in the morning, to sort out his loo, which wasn't flushing properly. He said he should be in by lunchtime, but I never saw him again after that."

That rang true because I had seen a business card, for a plumber, stuck to Cutter's fridge.

"Have you spoken to Cutter's sister, Jill?"

"Yeah, she's adamant that Cutter wouldn't have deliberately disappeared."

"I agree."

"She mentioned that he'd been seeing someone recently."

"You mean Sarah." Rose scowled.

"I take it you didn't approve?"

She hesitated. "It was none of my business."

"But—?"

"Cutter is a really great guy, but he's been lonely for a long time, so when Sarah showed an interest in him, he was thrilled. I was really pleased for him. At first."

"What changed?"

"I just got the feeling she was using him. Cutter wasn't one for eating out, but Sarah soon had him taking her out two or three nights a week, and it was always somewhere expensive. Then, there were the presents. She'd come around here at least once a week, dropping hints about something she'd seen in the shops: a dress, a pair of earrings, whatever. Course, she knew Cutter would offer to buy them for her."

"How long did the relationship last?"

"Not long. A few weeks. Couple of months, maybe."

"Why did it finish?"

"No idea. I came into work one morning and I could tell something wasn't right. He fobbed me off at first when I asked what was wrong, but in the end, he told me that Sarah had dumped him. Good riddance if you ask me, but that's not how he saw it."

"How long was this before he went missing?"

"A couple of weeks, maybe. You don't think this is all because of that stupid woman, do you?"

"I don't know, but I think I need to talk to her. Which stall does she work on?"

"Suck It Up."

"Sorry?"

"That's where she works. They sell all kinds of spare parts for vacuums. It's at the far side of the market hall, next to the stall selling vinyl records."

"Okay, well thanks for the tea. I'll go and see if Sarah will talk to me."

"I hope Cutter is okay."

Chapter 17

The man behind the counter at the Suck It Up stall was red in the face, and he appeared to be having some kind of altercation with a woman, who was brandishing what looked like a suction hose.

"I want my money back, then," she demanded.

"Gladly." The man took the suction hose from her, opened the till, counted out some cash and handed it to her. "There you go."

"I won't be shopping here again."

"Is that a promise?"

"Rude." The woman stomped away.

Only then, did the man spot me standing there.

"Sorry about that."

"She seemed upset."

"I shouldn't talk about customers, but that woman is crazy. She came in at the weekend and bought this length of suction hose. Then she turns up this morning and complains that it won't suck up the hairs from her carpet. It shouldn't have been necessary, but I had to try and explain that the hose needed to be attached to a vacuum cleaner. Then she practically lost her mind and accused me of selling goods under false pretences."

"Wow!"

"My thoughts, exactly. Anyway, sorry again. What can I get for you?"

I handed him my card. "I'm looking for Sarah."

"What's she done?"

"Nothing as far as I know. I just need to talk to her."

"She doesn't work here anymore. She quit a while back. Is it something I can help with?"

"I've been hired to find Lorne Mower."

"Cutter? I heard he was missing."

"I believe he and Sarah were in a relationship for a while."

"That's right, but it didn't last long, and it was all over before he went missing."

"Why did she quit?"

"She didn't give a reason and, to be honest, I didn't ask. She was more trouble than she was worth."

"Care to elaborate on that?"

"It's not like she stole from me or anything, but her timekeeping left a lot to be desired and she'd often go AWOL during the course of the day. I'd be busy serving a customer and when I looked around, Sarah would be missing. Truth be told, she spent more time at other people's stalls than she did at mine. Just chatting and stuff."

"Is that how she and Cutter got together?"

"I guess so."

"Do you happen to have her address?"

"I do, but I'm not sure I—"

"I only want to talk to her. That's all."

"Okay, but you didn't get it from me." He scribbled the address on a scrap of paper and handed it to me.

"Thanks."

"No problem. Good luck with finding Cutter."

Sarah's timing for leaving her job, coming as it did so close to Cutters' disappearance, struck me as odd. I would definitely need to speak to her. And, after hearing what Rose had said about Cutter's cowboy friends, Tex and Hank (or whatever their real names were), I decided that it might be an idea to meet all of the members of Washbridge Cowboy Appreciation Society.

I gave Sam Rich a call.

"Jill, any news?"

"Nothing yet. How often does the Washbridge Cowboy Appreciation Society meet?"

"Every other Friday. The next meeting is the day after tomorrow. Why?"

"I think it might be an idea if I was to attend that meeting. I'd like to talk to some of your members."

"You can't possibly think that any of them had anything to do with Cutters' disappearance."

"I just think it's important not to leave any stone unturned. Ideally, though, I'd rather they didn't know I was a private investigator because that might put them on their guard. Could I present myself as a new member?"

"I don't think that would work."

"Why not?"

"WCAS is a men-only club."

"Really? I didn't think that was allowed."

"It is, I can assure you. You see the problem."

"Yes, but I think I might have a way around it."

"What's that?"

"I'll get my associate, Bruce, to attend the club if that's okay?"

"Sure. We meet at Richmond Hall on Bonny Street. The meeting starts at seven-thirty but tell him to be there at seven o'clock. That will give me chance to brief him before I introduce him to the other members."

"Excellent."

***

I was on my way back to the office when I received a phone call from an excited Pearl.

"Jill, can you come over here?"

"What's up?"

"Come over and we'll tell you."

The twins had left one of their assistants in charge of the counter, and they were seated at a table by the window. Both of them had huge grins and I didn't really need them to tell me why.

"You got the loan."

"We did!" Amber screamed.

"It's all systems go." Pearl beamed.

"That's brilliant news, girls, I'm really pleased for you. What happens next?"

"The design is already finalised. You've seen it, haven't you?"

"Yeah, it looked great."

"Next we have to talk to the builders to see when they can schedule the work."

"How long will it take once they start?"

"At least a couple of months."

"As long as that? What will you do while the work is being carried out? Will you be able to keep this place open?"

"We discussed this with the builder," Pearl said. "It might be possible to do it that way, but there would be so much disruption, we don't think the customers would put up with it."

"Plus, it would mean it would take even longer," Amber chipped in. "So, we decided that we'll close for the duration of the work being carried out."

"That's going to mean a big hit on your takings."

"We realised that, so we factored it into our calculations before we approached the bank."

"Sounds like you've thought of everything."

"We hope so," Amber said.

"What will you do while this place is closed? Become ladies of leisure?"

"No chance. We'll have plenty to do, planning the relaunch." Pearl's excitement was palpable.

"I'm genuinely excited for you guys."

"Thanks, Jill. It's all a bit scary."

***

"It's happened again," Mrs V said.

"What has?"

"That parachute thing. I went into your office to get your cup and I couldn't get through the door because the room is full of parachute. How did that happen when you weren't even here?"

She might well ask.

"It must be faulty. Don't worry, I'll sort it out."

When I walked into my office I was met with a wall of white fabric.

"Winky, where are you?"

"Over here."

"Over where?"

"By your desk."

"What were you thinking?"

"It was an accident. I was practising my jump and I got carried away and pulled the ripcord."

"And you just thought you'd leave it like this?"

"I've been trying to get it back into the pack, but I don't have the knack."

While we'd been talking, I'd slowly edged my way under the parachute, towards my desk. That's where I found Winky, holding the empty parachute case.

"There you are."

"Can you help me to put it back in?" he asked, somewhat sheepishly.

"I will, but then I'm confiscating the parachute."

"How am I supposed to practise my jumps if you do that?"

"You'll just have to improvise."

"How?"

"I don't care. You'll think of something. Agreed?"

"I suppose so."

In his efforts to repack the parachute, he'd got it into such a mess that it took even longer to repack it the second time, and when I'd finished, it was time for me to be heading home.

Mrs V eyed the pack on my back. "I'm glad to see you're taking that thing home with you."

"I thought it was for the best."

"What's in the backpack?" Jack said.

"A parachute."

"Very funny."

"It's true."

"And I suppose this is the ripcord."

"Don't!" I managed to pull away just in time. "I've spent most of the day repacking this stupid thing."

"You're serious, aren't you? It really is a parachute."

"Yes, it is."

"Why have you brought it home with you?"

"Because Winky kept deploying it in the office. I've barely got a scrap of work done today because I've spent all my time repacking this thing. Mrs V was not impressed."

"I can't wait to hear how you explained away the parachute."

"I told her that Sam Rich had lent it to me because I was thinking of doing a jump."

"You're not, are you?"

"Of course not. Anyone who jumps out of an aeroplane needs their head examining."

"Peter told me that he'd done it once, but he said he wouldn't do it again."

"Did he tell you why?"

"No, I got the impression he didn't want to talk about it."

"I'm not surprised. He jumped piggyback with an instructor, but their chute didn't open."

"How is he still alive?"

"Because, luckily for him, his wife's sister is a witch."

"You saved him?"

"Only just. I was still very much a novice witch at the time, but I managed to save him by making them land on a haystack."

"And he doesn't know it was you who saved him?"

"Of course not. How could he?"

"Wow!"

Just then, Florence came rushing into the hallway. "What's that, Mummy?"

"It's—err—just books for my work."

I didn't tell her what it really was because, knowing

Florence, she'd strap it to her back, and try jumping out of the bedroom window.

"Books are boring."

"What did you do at CASS today?"

"Make smells."

I glanced at Jack. "Has she caught Jay's tummy bug?"

Jack laughed. "No, she's fine. I think you'd better tell Mummy about the smells you made, pumpkin."

"We had to cast a spell to make a smell like a fruit. I did a strawberry smell."

"Right. Why?"

"Don't know. Mr Blossomgone didn't tell us why we had to do it."

"Talking of Jay, how is he?"

"He's okay. I'm going to play hide and seek with him now." She shot back upstairs.

Jay joined us at the dinner table, and he certainly looked much better than the last time I'd seen him. His appetite had definitely returned because he put away more chicken nuggets than the rest of us combined.

"You're looking much better, Jay," I said.

"I feel better. These chicken nuggets are yummy."

He reached for yet another one, but I tapped the top of his hand with my fork.

"I think you've had enough, or you might be sick again."

"It was just a bug."

"Even so, I don't think you should eat any more."

"Okay." He had clearly taken pouting lessons from Florence.

Chapter 18

I was beginning to think I was losing my mind. I was sure I'd picked up the Chococandy Pops box, but when I poured out the cereal, it smelled like strawberries. Confused, I checked again, and it was definitely a Chococandy Pops box.

It was only when Florence giggled that the penny dropped.

"Did you do that, Florence?"

"What, Mummy?" she said, as though butter wouldn't melt.

Jack began to laugh.

"Were you in on this too?"

"I don't know what you're talking about."

"You two must think I just fell out of the stupid tree. I know you've cast a spell to make my Chococandy pops smell like strawberries, and I'd like you to reverse the spell now, please."

"Can't." She shrugged. "Mr Blossomgone didn't show us how to reverse the spell. He said he would do that on Friday. Sorry."

She didn't look very sorry.

And so it was that I ended up eating strawberry Chococandy pops for breakfast. To my surprise, they actually tasted really nice, but I wasn't about to let those two know that.

"She's getting to be a proper little madam," I said after Florence had left the table.

"You have to admit it was funny." Jack grinned.

"I wonder if you'll think so when I make your muesli smell of garlic tomorrow."

"You wouldn't."

"Don't count on it."

Clearly eager to change the subject, Jack said, "How are your cases going at the moment?"

"Not great if I'm honest. I'm no nearer finding the missing chickens or Cutter.

"Who's Cutter?"

"The missing man I'm trying to find."

"What kind of name is Cutter?"

"His real name is Lorne Mower."

"You're having me on." Jack laughed.

"I'm not, honestly."

"Do you ever get to work with anyone who doesn't have a ridiculous name?"

"Not often. Any idea where I can get a cowboy outfit from?"

"That's a bit random, isn't it? Have we been invited to a fancy dress party?"

"No. Cutter is a member of WCAS, which stands for the Washbridge Cowboy Appreciation Society. I'm going undercover there on Friday, to see if I can get any leads."

"I'm jealous. I'd love to dress up as a cowboy."

"The breakfast table isn't the time to discuss your fetishes."

"I'm serious. I used to love playing cowboys when I was a kid."

"I can't say I share your enthusiasm. I'm not looking forward to rubbing shoulders with a bunch of men playing cowboys."

"There'll be women there too, won't there?"

"It's a men-only club."

"Why don't you let me do it, then? I'm sure Brad would

let me have a half-day holiday."

"No, it has to be me."

"Why? I've worked on cases with you before."

"That was just surveillance. This time, I need to get them talking to me."

"Have you forgotten I used to be a copper? I'm used to interrogating people."

"That's just the point. This isn't an interrogation; it requires a much more subtle approach."

"And obviously subtle is your middle name."

"We're digressing. Do you know where I can hire a cowboy outfit?"

"Can't you just magic yourself one?"

"I thought about that, but my idea of what a cowboy would wear might be very different to what these guys wear. It's important that it's authentic, so I don't raise any suspicions before I start."

"Don't you think the fact that you're a woman might do that anyway?"

"I'm not stupid. I'll use magic to change myself into a man."

"Who?"

"*Who* what?"

"Which man will you change into?"

His question reminded me of the trouble I'd got myself into when I'd used the 'doppelganger' spell to turn myself into Portia Parkspirit. After that close call, there would be no more modelling myself on random strangers; it was too dodgy.

"I'll probably change into a doppelganger of you."

"Because I'm so good looking, obviously."

"Something like that."

"Can I try it on?"

"You want to try on the cowboy outfit?"

"Yeah."

"On a scale of nought to sad, that's tragic."

"Can I?"

"I suppose so, but I have to find a costume first." I took out my phone and did a search on cowboy costumes in Washbridge. Much to my surprise, it threw up a link to Cowboy Costume Rentals. "This looks promising. It even says they are official suppliers to WCAS."

"Where are they?"

"On Charade Parade, wherever that is."

"That's the same street where Ten-Pin Supplies is based. Just off Turner Street. Funny I've never noticed it."

***

I'd talked to the neighbours on either side of Francesca Artichoke, neither of whom had seen or heard anything suspicious. My last hope was the neighbour whose house backed onto Francesca's property.

The houses on this tree-lined avenue were much grander than those on the street where Francesca lived. I doubt you would have seen much change from a million pounds for any of them. The house behind Francesca's was so large that it also backed onto Jason's property. The house nameplate read 'Cuthinda'. I was just about to press the doorbell when one of the windows on the first floor opened, and a man with an impressive moustache looked down at me.

"Hello, there, pretty lady. What brings you to my humble abode?"

"I—err—"

"Wait right there. I'll be down in the blink of an eye."

I'd only seen the guy for a few seconds, but it was long enough to know that he was a sleazeball.

The door opened, and the man stepped outside. Flushed from the exertion of hurrying down the stairs, he ran his fingers through what was clearly a toupee.

"Hello again. You look even more beautiful close up. How can I help you today?"

It was at moments like this that I regretted not carrying a vomit bag with me.

"My name is Jill Maxwell and I'm a—"

"Don't tell me. Let me guess, Jill." He slobbered. "Makeup. Am I right?"

"Sorry?"

"Do you have one of those catalogue thingies?"

"No, nothing like that. I'm a—"

"Who's this, Cuthbert?" A woman appeared behind me, weighed down with designer brand carrier bags.

"This is Jill, dearest. She has a makeup catalogue for you, Lucinda."

"You're wasting your time," the woman said. "I only buy Chanel."

"I'm not here to sell you makeup."

"Then what do you want?"

"I'm a private investigator."

She turned to her husband. "Why did you say she was selling makeup?"

"I must have misunderstood." He shrugged.

"I have to put these bags down. You'd better come in."

"Thanks." I followed the woman inside while keeping one eye on her husband who was behind me.

The woman led the way into a huge lounge where she deposited the carrier bags onto the coffee table.

"A private investigator, you say. What do you want from us?"

"I've been hired by your neighbour; the one who lives to the rear of your property."

"The funny little man who wears those awful clothes?"

"No, the other one. Francesca Artichoke. She has hired me to find her chickens."

At that, the two of them exchanged a glance and the atmosphere in the room changed.

"We don't know anything about chickens," Lucinda said. "Do we, Cuthbert?"

"Nothing at all. Not a thing. Nothing."

"I just wondered if you might have heard or seen anything unusual?"

"Absolutely not," Lucinda insisted. "Everything has been perfectly normal around here."

"More normal than usual," Cuthbert said.

My *something-doesn't-smell-right-ometer* was sounding an alarm, so I decided to press them further. "Are you aware that Ms Artichoke keeps livestock in her back garden?"

"We had no idea, did we, Cuthbert?"

"What? No, absolutely none. No idea whatsoever."

"So, you didn't hear the rooster in the mornings?"

"Definitely not, but then Cuthbert and I are both deep sleepers." She glanced at her watch. "Is that the time? You really must excuse us because Cuthbert and I have been invited out for lunch."

"Have we, dear?" It was clearly the first he'd heard of it.

"Yes, you remember. With the Forsyth-Masons."

"Oh, right, yes. Of course. The Forsyth-Masons. Such

lovely people."

"Show this young lady out, would you, Cuthbert."

"Yes, dear. This way please, Jill."

He ushered me to the door and sent me on my way without so much as a goodbye, leaving me in no doubt that my mention of the missing chickens had struck a nerve. Their whole demeanour had changed from that moment on. Instead of leaving, I scurried around the side of the house, and stood to one side of the largest of the lounge windows. After casting the 'listen' spell, I waited for Cuthbert to rejoin his wife.

"I don't like it," Lucinda said.

"There's nothing to worry about, popsicle."

"Didn't you hear what she said? She's a private investigator. What if she knows about Rankin?"

"How can she? And even if she does, what can he tell her?"

"You know what an idiot that man is. Give him a call and warn him about her. Tell him if she comes sniffing around, he's to say nothing."

"Okay, I'll call him later."

"No, you have to do it now. I'm going to take these bags upstairs and when I come back down, I expect you to have spoken with him. Okay?"

"Okay, dear."

After Lucinda had left the room, Cuthbert made a phone call.

"Rankin? It's me. Cuthbert. Cuthbert Justanut. Listen, this is important. A woman, named Jill Maxwell, just came around to our house. She said she was a private investigator and that she has been hired to find that rooster. Of course I'm worried and so is Lucinda. She told me to warn you. Look, Michael, I just want to be sure that if she should track you down, you won't say anything that might lead her back to us. Right. Good. Okay, bye."

Interesting. Very interesting.

***

Before heading into the office, I decided to call in at Cowboy Costume Rentals. First, though, I found a deserted alley where I used the 'doppelganger' spell to turn myself into Jack.

I took a right turn off Turner Street onto Charade Parade. Two doors down from Ten-Pin Supplies was Cowboy Costume Rentals. I could see how Jack hadn't noticed the shop because the sign was tiny, and there was nothing in the window to indicate what was sold inside.

I expected the staff to be dressed in cowboy attire, but the only person in the shop was a middle-aged man who was wearing flares, a tank top and platform shoes.

"Howdy, partner," he greeted me. "I'm Grant."

"Err, howdy."

He must have noticed my puzzled expression because he went on to say, "You're probably wondering why I'm dressed like this. I'm taking part in Sponsor Seventies, it's on behalf of a local children's charity." He pointed to a collection box on the counter.

"Right." I took a couple of pound coins out of my pocket and dropped them in the box.

"Thanks. I honestly don't know how people used to wear this stuff back in the seventies, particularly the shoes. They're killing me. Still, it's for a good cause. Now, how can I help you, sir?"

"I'd like to hire a cowboy outfit."

"Then you're in the right place. We have lots to choose from as you can see. Did you have anything in particular in mind?"

"Not really, but it must be authentic."

"You need have no worries on that score." He pointed to a small sign on the wall behind him. "We're approved by WCAS."

"*WCAS?*"

"Washbridge Cowboy Appreciation Society. If you're interested in cowboys, you should really consider checking them out. Their next meeting is tomorrow, I believe."

"I might do that."

"Would you like any help with choosing your outfit or would you prefer to do it alone?"

"I think I'll take a look by myself first, but I'll give you a shout if I need any help with anything."

"Groovy, man."

Thirty minutes later, I was looking at myself/Jack in the mirror of the changing room. Although I say it myself, I was rocking the cowboy look, with my Stetson, waistcoat over a blue shirt, jeans and boots. Satisfied that I looked the part, I stepped out of the changing room and called to Grant, to ask for his opinion.

After looking me up and down, he said, "Excellent choices. May I just make a couple of suggestions?"

"Sure."

"A belt and buckle would finish off the look nicely."

"Agreed. Which would you recommend?"

After he had picked out a belt and buckle, I changed back into my own clothes and then went to the counter to find out what the damage was.

"Do you want to return them on Friday or Saturday?"

"What would it cost?"

"If you return them by five o'clock tomorrow, the total is one-hundred and twenty pounds. If you keep them longer than that, it will cost you another eighty-five pounds per day."

"I'll get them back to you by five tomorrow. Definitely."

Chapter 19

Mrs V eyed the three carrier bags suspiciously, but she was too diplomatic to ask about their contents. Winky had no such reservations.

"Cowboy Costumes? What the actual heck?"

"None of your business."

"Give us a look." Before I could stop him, he'd grabbed the hat and put it on his head.

"Take that off. If there are cat hairs all over it when I return it to the shop, they'll impose a surcharge."

"Do you think it suits me? I've always fancied myself as a bit of a cowboy."

"No arguments from me there." I snatched the hat off his head. "Don't take anything else out of these bags."

"Are these for some kind of kinky bedroom games?"

"What? No, don't be so disgusting. I need them to go undercover on the missing person case I'm working on."

"Those trousers will never fit you. They're miles too big."

"I won't be going there as myself. It's a men-only club, so I'll change myself into Jack."

"Can I come with you?"

"Definitely not."

"Go on. It sounds like fun. I could wear a cowboy outfit."

"You're not coming with me and that's final."

"Spoilsport."

My phone rang with a call from Kathy.

"Jill, I'm just finalising the booking for Wonder World, and I wanted to make sure Florence is still coming with us."

"Yes, please. She's really looking forward to it."

"What about you and Jack? Why don't you come too? You could both do with a break."

"It's impossible, Kathy. We've both got commitments we can't get out of."

"Fair enough. I'll get it booked."

"Let me know how much I owe you."

"Don't be daft. This is on us."

"I can't let you do that."

"You don't have any choice. If I want to spoil my niece, I'm going to do it."

"Okay, thanks, I really do appreciate it."

"We're taking the kids to the Norfolk Broads this weekend. Are you three doing anything exciting?"

"Clearing out the spare bedroom."

"Sounds like fun."

***

It was obvious that Francesca Artichoke's neighbours, the lecherous Cuthbert and his wife, Lucinda, were somehow involved with the missing chickens. As soon as I'd left their house, Cuthbert had called someone called Michael Rankin, to warn him that I'd been hired to find out what had happened to the missing poultry.

Tracking down Michael Rankin turned out to be much easier than I'd expected. A single internet search revealed that he was a fellow private investigator based in nearby West Chipping.

I gave him a call.

"Rankin PI speaking. How can I help?"

"Hello, Mr Rankin, my name is Julie Poole. I think my

husband might be cheating, but I need proof. Is that something you can help with?"

"Absolutely, Julie. Is it okay to call you Julie?"

"Yeah, that's fine."

"Well, Julie, my speciality is tracking down unfaithful partners, so I'm sure I'll be able to help."

"Great. Could I come and talk to you in your office? I don't really like to do it over the phone."

"No problem at all. When would suit you?"

"The sooner the better."

"I'm free all afternoon if you can get here today."

"Absolutely. I can be with you in under an hour."

"Great. Do you have my address?"

"Yes, I got it from your web site."

"Okay, I'll see you shortly."

You sure will.

I thought the building in which my office was located was run down until I found the building that housed the offices of Michael Rankin PI. I had to double-check the address because from the outside, the building looked derelict. As I stepped into what had once been the lobby, a small creature dashed across the floor. On the wall, just inside the door, was a board, which listed all of the occupants of the building. There was now just the one: Michael Rankin PI, who was located on the third floor. There was an 'out of order' notice stuck to the lift door, not that I would have risked using it anyway. The stairways were dirty and smelly. On the frosted glass in the door, were the words: **Michael Rankin – Washbridge's Premier Private Investigator**.

I don't think so.

I knocked on the glass, then tried the handle. The door opened into a small office which contained a desk and chair, a filing cabinet and a well-worn armchair. I was just about to call out when a voice came from behind the only other door in the room.

"I'm in the loo. I'll be out in a couple of ticks."

Lovely.

"Take a seat."

After a closer examination of the armchair, I elected to remain standing. After today, I would never again complain about my office, which was palatial compared to this dump. A couple of minutes later, the toilet flushed, the door opened, and out stepped Michael Rankin. The man was tiny with a fat nose and the eyes of a serial killer.

"Nice to meet you, Julie. I find it hard to believe that your husband would cheat on someone as beautiful as you," said the sleazy serial killer wannabe.

"Actually, my name isn't really Julie Poole."

"I understand. A lot of my clients prefer not to use their real names until I've gained their trust. Won't you take a seat?"

"I'd prefer to stand. My real name is Jill Maxwell, and I'm in the same line of business as you."

"I've heard of you." His smile dissolved. "What do you want?"

"I'd like to talk about the work you did for two of your clients recently. A couple by the name of Cuthbert and Lucinda."

"You know I can't do that. It's privileged information."

"Normally, I'd agree with you, but I'm not sure the PI code of conduct covers theft."

"I have no idea what you're talking about."

"Maybe this will jog your memory: Chickens."

His body language told me everything I needed to know.

"I didn't take them."

"You're a liar, and not even a good one."

"It's true. Look, I admit I took the job. I'm not proud of it, but times are hard. I'm three months behind on the rent for this place."

"That's no excuse. Where are the chickens? What did you do with them?"

"If you won't sit down in here, will you at least come with me to the coffee shop around the corner, and we can talk there?"

Call me a softie, but I was actually beginning to feel sorry for this pathetic little guy.

"Okay, but I want to know everything."

The coffee shop was called Joffe Coffee, and was a bit of a dump, but still several notches up from Rankin's office. At least the seats didn't look like something had crawled onto them and died. To give him his due, Rankin offered to buy the drinks, but the guy clearly didn't have two pennies to rub together, so I got them.

"Thanks for the drink." He took a sip of the cappuccino.

"Okay, spill the beans."

"Cuthbert asked me to visit him at his house. He wouldn't say what it was about over the phone, but when I got there—by the way, have you seen their pad?"

"I have."

"When I got there, I thought my luck had changed for the better, and that I was in for a big payday. I assumed his wife was playing away and that he wanted me to follow her. I do a lot of that sort of work, do you?"

"Some."

"Anyway, I was wrong. He was unhappy with the neighbour who lived at the property that backed onto his house. He told me that their rooster was driving him and his wife crazy. I assumed he wanted me to get proof that his neighbour was keeping chickens, so that he could report her to the local authority, but then he said he wanted me to get rid of the rooster."

"What did he mean by *get rid of*?"

"He didn't specify. He just wanted that rooster gone by any means."

"So, you agreed to steal and kill the rooster?"

"Hang on. I'm no animal killer."

"So, what did you do with it? And why did you take all the chickens? Don't tell me you didn't know which one was the rooster?"

"I told him I wouldn't do it at first."

"But?"

"But then he told me how much he was prepared to pay. I mean, it was silly money. More than I'd made in the previous month."

"So, what did you do with the chickens?"

"I didn't do anything with them. Oh, and by the way, I do know the difference between a chicken and a rooster."

"What do you mean you didn't take them?"

"Exactly what I said. I went over there under the cover of darkness, to grab the rooster, but when I got there, the chickens had gone."

"Gone? What do you mean *gone*?"

"I mean gone. Disappeared into thin air. There were a few tiny eggs on the ground, but no sign of chickens."

"You're lying."

"Why would I? I've already admitted I took the job and that I was going to take the rooster."

"Have you killed them?"

"You're not listening to me. When I got there, they'd already gone."

"If that's true, what did you tell Cuthbert?"

"I—err—"

"Well?"

"I wasn't going to tell him the truth, was I? If I'd said the chickens had already gone, he might not have paid me, so I just told him that the rooster wouldn't cause him any more problems."

"And he paid you?"

"Yeah."

Much as I despised this little man, my gut told me that he was being truthful. So, if he hadn't taken the chickens, who had?

***

An excitable Jack met me at the door.

"Is that it?" He eyed up the carrier bags.

"If you mean *my* cowboy outfit, then yes."

"Let me try it on." He tried to grab the bags, but I held on tight to them.

"No."

"Come on, Jill, you're borrowing my body. The least you can do is let me try on the outfit."

"You make me sound like a Triffid."

"Come on, please."

"Say pretty please."

"Pretty please."

"Pretty please with sugar on top."

"Give them here."

This time I let him take the bags.

"What about dinner?" I said.

"It's your turn to make it."

"Are you sure?"

"Positive."

"Where's Florence?"

"Upstairs, making smells. She learned some new ones at CASS today." And with that, he headed upstairs.

"Why is Daddy wearing that funny costume?" Florence asked over dinner.

"Don't you like it?" Jack tipped his hat.

"You look silly."

"Don't you dare get any sauce on that costume." I shot him a look.

"I should check out that cowboy club. I've been looking for a new hobby for a while."

"We can't afford for you to have any more hobbies. Your ten-pin bowling costs us a small fortune." Suddenly, an unexpected smell assaulted my senses.

"Florence Maxwell, why does my steak and kidney pie smell of garlic?"

"Don't know." She giggled.

"I think you do. I don't want any more smells at this table, please."

She pushed her empty plate away. "Can I go outside and play, please?"

"Yes, and please take your smells with you."

"How is your other case going?" Jack asked. "Have you tracked down those chickens yet?"

"No, and I'm beginning to think I never will." I told him about my visit to see Michael Rankin.

"Poor guy."

"Poor? He was going to steal the rooster and do who knows what to it."

"From what you've said, it sounds like he was desperate."

"That's no excuse."

"Don't you have any more leads?"

"None. I might pay another visit to that Jason character. There was something seriously weird about him."

Chapter 20

It was the next morning, and Jack was in my bad books.

"You can barely see it," he said.

"I told you not to wear it while you were eating your dinner. If they make me pay a surcharge when I return it, you'll have to stump up."

"I'm sorry, but you have to admit I rocked that outfit. When is your meeting with the cowboys?"

"This afternoon. I'm just hoping I get away early enough to return the outfit before the shop closes at five, otherwise I'll have to pay for another day."

Jack scooped up a spoonful of muesli but then stopped short of his mouth and sniffed at the sawdust.

"Florence." He glared at her.

"What, Daddy?"

I had to hand it to her; she had that innocent look off to a tee.

"Why does my muesli smell of liquorice?"

"Maybe it's a new kind."

If I'm honest, I thought it was no more than Jack deserved for spilling sauce on my cowboy costume, but I was conscious that we had to present a united front when it came to Florence.

"That's it, Florence," I said. "If you cast any more smell spells at the table, I'll tell Auntie Kathy that you can't go to Wonder World."

"No! I want to go."

"No more smell spells, then. Okay?"

"Okay."

***

My visit to WCAS wasn't until the afternoon, so after ringing Mrs V to check if there were any messages (there weren't), I paid another visit to the house of Francesca's weird neighbour, Jason. On my previous visit, he'd refused to let me in. This time, I intended to get inside to take a look around, with or without his permission.

As luck would have it, he was just leaving his house as I arrived, so I hid behind a tree and watched him walk away. Halfway down the road, he took a seat at the bus stop, and five minutes later he boarded a number thirty-two bus to Washbridge town centre.

With the coast clear, I magicked myself inside his house. I was expecting weird, and I wasn't disappointed. The walls in the hallway were painted bright yellow, and were so bright, I regretted not bringing my sunglasses. Hanging on the walls were a series of framed photographs, all of frogs. Or toads. I'm still not sure how to tell the difference. The front room was empty, and by that, I mean completely empty: no carpet, furniture—nothing. The kitchen, with dishes on the drainer and clothes on the airer, did at least look like someone lived there. The fridge contained five bottles of milk and three packs of sliced ham—nothing else. Moving upstairs, the walls on the landing were yellow to match those in the hallway, with more framed photographs of frogs/toads. The bathroom, which was small and surprisingly clean, had a pleasant pine aroma. The bedroom, on the front of the house, contained a large four-poster bed, which looked totally out of place. The second bedroom, at the rear, was much smaller. From the window in that room, I had a good view of Francesca Artichoke's back garden: The two sheep appeared to be dozing, and the goat was worrying a water barrel. I was just about to leave the bedroom and check the bathroom when I noticed a carrier bag in the corner of the room. That's when I heard the door open downstairs. I'd expected Jason to be gone for much longer, but that didn't matter now because, after what I'd just seen in the carrier bag, that man had a lot of explaining to do.

From the top of the stairs, I watched Jason head towards the kitchen. I recognised the bag in his hand, which was from a shop not much more than a half mile down the road. No wonder he hadn't been gone long; the lazy so and so had taken a bus when it would have taken less than twenty minutes to walk there and back.

What do you mean, I can talk? Obviously, I would prefer to walk more often than I do, but, in my line of work, time is money.

A couple of the stairs creaked as I made my way down, but Jason obviously hadn't heard me because he was busy unpacking his purchases, which as far as I could make out consisted of more ham and milk.

"You really do like ham, don't you, Jason?"

Shocked, he stumbled backwards and almost fell, but managed to grab hold of the table.

"What are you doing in here? How did you get in?"

"That would be telling."

"I'll, I'll, I'll call the police."

"Be my guest."

"I mean it. I will."

"Okay, and when they arrive, you can explain why you stole and killed your neighbour's chickens."

"I didn't. I haven't killed anything."

"I don't believe you."

"Get out."

"No."

"Please."

"Not until you've explained why you have a bag full of feathers upstairs."

"What?"

"There's no point in playing innocent, Jason."

"They, they—err—they aren't—"

"Come with me."

"No, I don't want to."

He tried to pull away, but I grabbed his wrist and led him up the stairs into the smaller of the two bedrooms.

"There!" I pointed to the carrier bag. "The game is up."

"Pillow."

"What?"

"Pillow."

"What are you talking about?"

"The feathers came out of my pillow. It split open."

"You're lying."

"I'll show you." He pointed to the bed, which I now realised was minus one pillow. Then, he opened the wardrobe and retrieved a rather limp looking pillow, which had clearly split open along one edge.

Could he be telling the truth? I took a closer look at the feathers, and realised that, although I'm no expert on the subject, they didn't look an awful lot like chicken's feathers.

"Why did you keep the feathers?"

"I'm going to get my sister to mend the pillow, but she's on holiday."

Oh bum! I was beginning to realise I'd got this badly wrong. Jason was still in shock, but when he got over that, he would be justified in calling the police and having me arrested for breaking and entering. Assault too, possibly.

I had only two options: apologise profusely and hope that Jason decided not to press charges. Or play it safe and cast the 'forget' spell, so that he would remember nothing of my uninvited visit. It took only a few seconds to decide to play safe and go with the second option. When I left the house, Jason was sitting on the bed, looking a little dazed.

That had not been my finest hour. I'd accused an innocent man on the flimsiest of evidence. What had I been thinking? The man might be a little eccentric, but was he really likely to have held onto chicken feathers as some kind of trophy? They didn't even look like chicken feathers. Conclusion: I'm an idiot.

There's no need for you lot to agree, thank you.

***

"Are you okay, Jill?" Mrs V said. "You're looking a little peaky."

"I'm fine, but a cup of tea would be nice."

"Coming right up."

I was sipping my tea, and still feeling pretty low when Winky jumped onto my desk and asked me what was wrong.

"It's nothing really. I'm just not getting anywhere with any of my cases."

"So, what's new?"

"Every lead I've followed up so far has led nowhere, especially on the missing chicken case. I think I'm going to have to admit defeat on that one and tell the client that I can't help."

"Did you see today's Bugle?"

"You know I don't read that rag."

"You should take a look at today's edition. I was checking an article on my old buddy, Gary the Goat, and I saw it."

"Saw what?"

"Move out of the way, and I'll show you." He grabbed the mouse and brought up the online version of The Bugle. "Look, that's Gary."

The main headline of The Bugle was about a cat called Gary who had to be rescued from a tree by the fire service.

"Why would The Bugle run a story of a cat getting stuck up a tree as their main headline?"

"It was obviously a slow news day. Here's the best part, though, Gary wasn't stuck."

"He looks pretty stuck to me."

"Why do you think he's called the goat?"

"Because he looks like one?"

"It's G-O-A-T."

"Spelling the word doesn't make it any clearer."

"You're hopeless. It stands for Greatest Of All Time. Gary is the best tree climber in the business."

"That's not much good if he can't get back down."

"He can. That's the whole point. He could have got down from there any time he wanted to."

"So why didn't he?"

"Because he thrives on publicity. He loves to be in the limelight. That's why he acts like he's stuck. He knows that way they'll call out the fire brigade and if he's lucky, he'll get into the newspapers."

"This is all very fascinating, but I don't see—"

"Hold on, I'll show you." He scrolled down the page

until he came to another headline that read, "My Chickens Are Missing.

"Move over." I nudged him to one side and then clicked on the headline.

The story was about a woman called Paula Featherstone whose chickens had disappeared from her garden overnight. The article included a photograph of the woman, who looked quite distressed, staring at an empty chicken coop. According to the article, Paula had been in touch with the police, but they'd said they were unable to spare any of their limited resources on a case of that nature. That's why she was appealing to members of the public to come forward if they had any information that might help to find her chickens.

"Bit of a coincidence, don't you think?" Winky said.

"Yeah, I'll give her a call."

I phoned the landline number mentioned in the newspaper article and a woman answered on the first ring.

"Is that Paula Featherstone?"

"She isn't here at the moment."

"Oh. I'm calling about the article in The Bugle."

"Her father has taken ill, so I'm housesitting for her until she gets back. I don't know when that's likely to be."

"Is there any way I can contact her? Do you have a mobile phone number for her?"

"I'm afraid not. And besides, she probably won't want to be disturbed just now because her father is quite ill. Can it wait until she gets back?"

"Sure."

I gave the woman my name and phone number and she promised she would pass them onto Paula when she returned.

"No joy, I take it?" Winky said.

"Nah. Yet another dead end."

Chapter 21

Mrs V had nipped out to pick up a sandwich for her lunch, so I took the opportunity to change myself into a Jack lookalike, and to try on the cowboy outfit.

"Very authentic," Winky nodded his approval. "I like the way you even have a blood stain on the chest."

"That was Jack and his stupid ketchup."

Just then, the door opened, and Mrs V walked in. "I forgot my purse, so I—" She stopped dead in her tracks and did a doubletake. "Jack? I didn't realise you were here."

"Hi, Mrs V, I just stopped by to have a quick word with Jill."

She glanced around the office. "Where is she?"

"She's—err—just gone down the corridor to see Talbot."

"Right." She looked me up and down. "Pardon me for asking, but why are you wearing a cowboy outfit?"

Out of the corner of my eye, I could see Winky was doing his best to stifle a laugh.

"Err, it's for the promotion they're running at the record shop today. Country and Western."

"Right."

"Anyway, I'd better get back there, or they'll be sending out the search party for me."

"Do you want me to give Jill a message?"

"No, it's okay. I managed to catch her before she nipped up the corridor." I hurried past her. "It was nice to see you, Mrs V."

I got a few strange looks as I walked through the streets of Washbridge to Richmond Hall on Bonny Street. That didn't bother me nearly as much as the crippling pain I was getting from the boots, which were rubbing the back of my feet red raw. Richmond Hall was a social and snooker club, with snooker tables on the ground floor, and the social club upstairs. As I made my way to the staircase, I half-expected to be on the receiving end of wise cracks from the men playing snooker, but they didn't so much as blink an eye. Clearly, they were used to seeing cowboys passing by.

Upstairs, was a single large room with a bar at one end. I had arrived ten minutes early, but there were already several cowboys in the room, most of them gathered around the bar. One of them spotted me and waved for me to join them. He was wearing a very distinctive white cowboy's outfit.

"Howdy, partner." He raised his hat by way of a greeting.

"Howdy." I returned the gesture, even though I did feel a little self-conscious.

"Haven't seen you around these parts before."

"No, this is my first time. I'm new to the area."

"New members are always welcome. I'm Billy, not really a kid, though." He laughed.

Oh bum! I should have decided upon a name before I got there.

"I'm Bill. Buffalo Bill."

"I like it." He was a big guy, so when he slapped me on the back, he almost knocked me over. "Let me introduce you to these two reprobates." He nodded to the two men who were chugging their beer. "This here is Hank. And that's Tex. They're brothers. Guys, this here is Buffalo Bill."

"Great to meet you, err—do you prefer Buffalo or Bill?"

"Bill is fine."

"Welcome to WCAS," Tex said.

"Yeah, good to have you on board." Hank nodded.

"We're two of the founding members," Tex said. "Everyone calls us Tank."

"Sorry?"

"Tex and Hank mixed together makes Tank, get it?"

"Right, yeah. That's very good." And even sadder than I would have believed possible.

"New guy in town?" said a familiar voice behind me.

I turned around to find Sam Rich standing there.

"This here is Buffalo Bill," Tex said.

"Good to meet you." Sam shook my hand. "Do you think I could have a word in private?"

"Of course."

"Don't take any shooting tips from him," Hank shouted after us. "He couldn't hit a barn door at ten paces."

Once we were in a quiet corner of the room, Sam said, "Bruce?"

"At your service."

"Has Jill briefed you?"

"She has."

"Good. Your outfit is spot on, by the way. Do you need anything from me?"

"No, I don't think so. I'll just mingle and see what I manage to pick up."

"Okay, good luck."

Over the next ten minutes, the place filled up with cowboys of all ages. I hadn't known what to expect of the gathering, but it turned out to be little more than a talking shop where these overgrown kids discussed all things cowboy. Except for one group of four seated near the bar, who were busy analysing the England football team's defeat the previous night. I made it my business to chat to as many of the cowboys as possible, but my main focus was the dynamic duo, better known as Tank. I wanted to try and talk to them separately, and I saw my opportunity when Tex disappeared in the direction of the toilets.

"Hey, Hank."

"Hi, Bill, what do you think of our little club?"

"I really like it. There are some great guys here."

"Think you'll come again?"

"You bet. If the missus let's me." I laughed.

"I know what you mean. My Marlene hates all this, but like I always tell her, at least she knows I'm not chatting up other women while I'm here."

"True." I made a show of looking around the room. "I was hoping to see an old buddy of mine, but it doesn't look like he's here."

"Who's that?"

"Lorne Mower."

"Cutter?"

"Yeah, he was the one who told me about this place."

"He hasn't been here for a couple of weeks."

"Is that usual?"

"No, he hardly ever misses a meet. That stuck-up assistant of his reckons he's gone missing. Apparently, no one has seen him for a couple of weeks."

"Do you mean Rose?"

"Yeah. I don't think she likes me or Tex."

"How was Cutter the last time you saw him?"

"He was his usual miserable self. You know how he is. He'll be back just like a bad penny."

"What are you two plotting?" Tex appeared at Hank's side, which thwarted my plan to try and get him by himself next.

"Bill was asking about Cutter."

"Where has the miserable sod got to? I haven't seen him in an age."

"That's what Hank and I were discussing," I said. "Rose reckons no one has seen him for weeks."

"He probably took off somewhere with that new woman of his."

"Nah," Hank said. "Sarah dumped him."

"Did she? No one tells me anything. Weird woman that. Do you know her, Bill?"

"No, I've never met her."

"Wouldn't surprise me if she had bumped off Cutter, sawn him into a dozen pieces and thrown him into the river."

"You can't go around saying stuff like that," Hank said.

"Why not? You know what she's like. There's something of the night about that woman."

"Tex, when was the last time you saw Cutter?"

"I'm not sure. It would have been here, I reckon. Must be a couple of weeks ago."

"And he didn't say anything about going away?"

"Nah, if I remember rightly, he was talking about some new spurs he was thinking of buying."

"Everybody!" A man wearing a ten-gallon hat took to the small stage. "It's time for this week's raffle draw."

A little earlier I'd been cornered by an eager cowboy, by the name of Matt D, who had persuaded me to buy a ticket for the exorbitant price of five pounds.

"And the winner is number thirty-seven."

"That's mine." I stared in disbelief at the winning ticket. I'd never won a raffle in my life so was really excited until I saw the prize.

"You're a lucky son of a gun." Tex slapped me on the back and almost sent me tumbling. "I've been trying to win this here raffle for six years without so much as a sniff."

"It's a saddle," I said, somewhat redundantly. "It's heavy."

"Don't worry if it's the wrong size," Matt D said. "Jimmy at Washbridge Saddles said he'd swap it."

"That's—err—great, thanks."

I came away with little or no information that would help my investigation into Cutter's disappearance. On the bright side, though, I did have a handsome new saddle. The meeting had gone on much longer than I'd expected, which meant I only had a few minutes to get the costume back to the rental shop before they closed. If I didn't make it, I'd be charged for another twenty-four hours.

I was halfway down Turner Street and about to turn onto Charade Parade when a familiar voice stopped me dead in my tracks.

"Jack?"

Oh bum, bum and triple bum!

"Peter. Hi."

"Why are you dressed like that? And is that a saddle you're carrying?"

"Yes, it is."

"Don't tell me. Let me guess. You've lost your horse." He laughed.

"Very funny. Jill and I went to a fancy-dress party last

night and I'm just returning my costume."

"I love a good fancy dress party and I know Kathy does. How come we didn't get an invite?"

"It was a charity thing. Ex policemen only, I'm afraid."

"Have you got time for a quick drink? It's ages since you and I had a chat."

"I'd love to, but I have to get this costume back before the shop closes." I began to edge away. "See you."

"Hold on a second." Before I could stop him, he'd taken out his phone and snapped a photo of me. "Kathy is going to love this."

Somehow, I managed to get to the costume shop just as the owner was about to lock up.

"Wait. I've brought back your costume."

"You're too late. You'll have to bring it back tomorrow."

"Please, I ran all the way."

"Is that the new Karlita saddle?"

"Err, I—err—"

"It is, isn't it? I was going to order one, but the waiting list is three months."

"I might see my way to letting you buy this one from me."

"Really? Would you do that?"

"I might."

"I can't afford to pay silly prices."

"Tell you what, let me in, and you can have the saddle at list price. If—"

"If what?"

"You don't charge me for the hire of the costume."

"Deal." I handed him the saddle and then hurried into the changing room. Moments later, I emerged and gave him back the costume.

After he'd paid me for the saddle, I took my leave. Once outside, I found a quiet alleyway and reversed the 'doppelganger' spell. It was nice to be myself again.

"I've just had the weirdest phone call," Jack said when I walked through the door. "Kathy wanted to know what fancy-dress costume you'd worn and asked me to send her a photo. I told her I had no idea what she was talking about, but she didn't believe me. She said it must have been something pretty awful for you to have forbidden me to share it with her. Care to explain?"

"I bumped into Peter in town while I was still dressed as a cowboy."

"If he saw you, how come Kathy was asking about your costume."

"Because when Peter saw me, I wasn't me, I was you."

"I can feel a headache coming on."

"I told you I was going to have to change myself into you because the Washbridge Cowboy Appreciation Society is open to men only."

"How did it go? Did you make a breakthrough?"

"No, but I did win a very handsome saddle."

Chapter 22

Despite my best efforts, the last week had been a complete bust, so on Saturday morning, I told Jack I was going to have to work that day.

"Oh no you don't. I know what you're up to."

"What are you talking about?"

"You're just trying to get out of tidying the spare bedroom."

"I'd forgotten all about that."

"Of course you had."

"It'll take ages."

"No, it won't. Not if we both get stuck in. It'll be fun."

"Your idea of fun and mine don't even share the same post code."

"I thought we could make a start on it while Florence is at her dancing class."

"Why don't you do it by yourself? You're so much better at tidying than I am."

"You promised, Mummy," Daddy's little girl chimed in. "Jay is looking forward to having a room of his own. He'll be upset if you don't do it."

"Fine, I can see it's three onto one again. But, as soon as we've done, I'm putting my feet up with a glass of wine and a box of chocolates."

"We don't have any chocolates," Jack said.

"Maybe not right now, but you're going to buy me a box for helping to tidy the spare room."

Jack was taking Florence to her dance class when Kathy rang.

"You know how much I love fancy dress," she said.

"Why didn't you invite me to come with you and Jack?"

"We couldn't. It was an invitation only do."

"What did you go dressed as? Jack wouldn't tell me."

"I went as a witch."

"A *witch*? How boring."

"Witches are *not* boring."

"You should have gone as a clown." She laughed. "Oh, sorry, I forgot that you're scared of them."

"I am not afraid of clowns."

"Not much."

"Did you want something, Kathy, because I'm in the middle of tidying our spare room."

"When you say *you're* doing it, I assume what you mean is that Jack is doing all the work while you stand around supervising."

"Goodbye, Kathy."

The cheek of the woman.

Jack came through the door. "Who was that?"

"Just Kathy."

"I thought you might have made a start on the spare room while I was gone."

"I would have done, but Kathy rang me, and you know what she's like."

"Come on, then." He headed for the stairs. "The sooner we make a start, the sooner we'll finish."

"I thought we might have a cup of tea and a biscuit first."

"We can have those when we take a break."

"When will that be?"

"Eleven o'clock."

"Eleven? That's over an hour away."

"Come on, Jill."

"Why did I marry a slave driver?" The room was so full of junk that I could barely get the door open. "Most of this stuff is yours."

"No, it isn't." Jack squeezed past me. "There's as much of your junk in here as there is of mine."

Before I could respond, I felt something strange under my foot, accompanied by a crunching sound. "What's that?" I took a step back.

Jack stooped down to get a better look. "So, that's what you did with them."

"Did with *what*?"

"All those boxes of that awful cereal you bought." He picked up one of the shrunken boxes. "You shrank them."

"It was the only way to get them in here." I got down on all fours to get a better look. "Hang on, over half of these boxes are empty."

"Don't look at me. I wouldn't touch that stuff if you gave me a million pounds."

"Then who—?"

The truth struck us both at the same instant.

"Jay!" we said in unison.

"No wonder he was so sick." Jack laughed.

"It isn't funny."

"It is a bit."

"I'm going to have to have a word with that jelly monster before he helps himself to the rest."

"I don't think you need worry on that score. I doubt he ever wants to see another packet of that ChocoStrawberryToffee muck after what happened last time."

"Can we take a break now?"

"No, we've only been working for ten minutes. Why

don't you start over by the window and I'll take this side of the room."

"How am I supposed to get over there?"

"Climb."

"Not likely, I'll do myself an injury." I cast the 'levitate' spell and floated across the room.

How on earth did three people accumulate so much rubbish?

"Can I throw this away?" Jack held up a broomstick.

"No, you can't."

"Why not? It's not like you're ever going to use it. I can't even remember the last time you used the vacuum cleaner."

"Cheek. That's a souvenir from my tournament days. We really ought to have it mounted on a wall in the lounge."

"That wouldn't look weird. At all."

"What about these?" I held up a couple of bowling shirts.

"I'm not throwing away my bowling shirts."

"These are at least two sizes too small for you now."

"Rubbish. I haven't put on any weight since I bought those."

"Yeah, right." I scoffed.

"Throw them over here and I'll prove it."

"Have at it." I launched them across the room.

Talk about delusional.

Five minutes later, Jack had managed to struggle into the pink and green shirt (yes, you heard right: pink and green).

"See, it fits fine."

"Is that why you have only fastened two of the

buttons?"

"That's how they're supposed to be worn."

"You're so full of it. Why don't you stop holding your stomach in?"

"I'm not holding—" One of the two buttons that he'd managed to fasten flew off.

"I rest my case."

"They must have shrunk."

"Sure, that must be it."

"I'll go and make that cup of tea."

"Bring me a couple of custard creams, would you? And while you're down there, throw those shirts in the bin."

Jack shot me a look on his way out of the door.

"Has he gone?" The tiny voice came from somewhere beneath the clutter close to my feet.

"Who's there?"

One tiny hand appeared through the jumble, then another. Moments later, a tiny creature with big ears pulled himself clear of the junk.

"What are you up to?" the little creature demanded.

"Never mind that. Where did you come from?"

"Under there." He pointed to the pile of rubbish.

"I know that, but where did you come from before that?"

"Belvedere Street. Number twenty-four, I believe."

"Sorry, I'm a little confused. What—err—what are you?"

"I'm an untidy elf."

"What are you doing in my bedroom?"

"We live here."

"We?"

"Yeah, me and my pals."

"How many of you are there?"

"Let's see. There's me—I'm Wibbly, by the way, then there's Bibbly, Tibbly, Kibbly, Jibbly and Rib—err—"

"Ribbly?"

"No, Ribberson."

"Where are the others?"

"Under there somewhere. Hey, guys!" He put two fingers in his mouth and whistled.

Moments later, five small heads popped up.

"Who's that?" the elf wearing the tartan waistcoat asked.

Wibbly shrugged. "She hasn't introduced herself."

"I'm Jill Maxwell and this is my house, and you still haven't told me what you're doing here."

"I would have thought that was obvious," Wibbly said. "We go where the untidy is, and it doesn't get any better than this."

"It isn't that bad in here."

"Yeah, right." Wibbly scoffed. "Did you hear that, lads? She says it isn't untidy in here."

"Alright, I admit we have neglected this room a little."

"A little." The elf with the sparkly hat rolled his eyes.

"Okay, okay, so it's a mess, but it won't be after we've finished."

"Hold on," Wibbly said. "What are you planning to do?"

"We're having a clear-out, so that we can use this room as a bedroom."

"What about us?"

"What about you?"

"Where are we supposed to live? We won't be able to stay here if you tidy the room."

"That's not my problem. You shouldn't have been here in the first place."

"How very inconsiderate. Come on, guys, it's time we left. We're clearly not wanted here."

And without another word, they made their way out of the open window.

"Who were you talking to?" Jack said when he returned with the tea and biscuits.

"Wibbly, Bibbly, Tibbly, Kibbly, Jibbly and Ribberson."

"Who?"

"They're untidy elves who have been living here, apparently."

"In our spare bedroom?"

"Yeah, and they weren't very thrilled to learn we were going to clear out this room."

"Where are they now?" He passed me my drink and biscuits.

"They left in a huff. Where's the rest of my custard creams?"

"You said you wanted a couple. That's what you've got."

"You know very well that when I say a couple, I mean at least four."

"Tough. If you want any more, you'll have to go and get them yourself."

"And here was I, thinking you loved me."

"Your emotional blackmail isn't going to work either."

By the time Jack took a break to collect Florence from her dance class, we were beginning to make some progress. While he was gone, I took the opportunity to nip downstairs and grab a couple more custard creams. While I was down there, Jay came bouncing down the stairs into the kitchen.

"Is Florence back yet?" he asked.

"She'll be back in a minute. Her dad has just gone to get her."

"Goody!" Jay clapped. "We're going to play space school."

"Right? I'm glad I've seen you, Jay because there's something I want to ask you."

"What?"

"I was just thinking about the other day when you were poorly."

"My tummy hurt." He rubbed it for effect. "And I was sick."

"I remember. What do you think caused that?"

"Don't know." He shrugged. "Probably germs."

"Or Chococandy Pops."

He blushed from his head to his toes and stammered, "I—err—I—"

"I know you ate them, Jay, so there's no point denying it."

"I'm sorry. They were so tiny that I didn't think they were yours."

"Who did you think they belonged to?"

"Don't know." He shrugged.

"Normally, I'd punish you, but I think you've suffered enough already. You mustn't eat any more of them, though."

"I won't. I never want to see another Chococandy Pop as long as I live."

"Jay!" Florence came charging into the room. "Let's go and play space school."

The two of them rushed upstairs.

"What's all this space school stuff about?" I asked Jack.

"Your guess is as good as mine." He spotted the open packet of biscuits. "Have you had some more of them?"

"Only because you shortchanged me the first time."

"At least we've nearly finished the bedroom. I'll take the rubbish we're throwing out to the council tip this afternoon."

"It's okay, I'll do that."

"How come you're volunteering? You hate going to the tip."

"There's somewhere else I have to go, so I can drop the rubbish off on my way past."

"Where do you have to go?"

"That would be telling."

***

"Jill!" Deli came hurrying over and gave me a big hug. "How lovely to see you again."

"Hi." I managed to break free from her bear hug. "I thought I might take you up on that free offer."

"The leeches?"

"Err, yeah. Are you still doing it?"

"Of course. It's been a roaring success. Most of the people who had the free trial have signed up for a course of treatment."

"After I spoke to you, I did some research on leech therapy, but all I could find was information about leeches being used by the medical profession for joint disease or bad circulation."

"That's right, but the leeches we use are not the same leeches."

"I didn't realise there was more than one kind."
"Neither did I but there are thousands, apparently."
"Does it hurt?"
"Not at all. You'll barely feel a thing, I promise. Come with me."
I was already starting to have second thoughts, but it was too late now. Deli led the way to the far corner of the salon where there were a number of small booths.
"Take a seat in here, Jill, and I'll go and get the hungry little lads."
"Maybe this wasn't such a good idea."
"Rubbish. It'll do you the world of good. Now, slip your dress off and I'll be back in two ticks."
What on earth had I been thinking? Was I really going to let Deli cover me in small bloodsucking creatures? Apparently, I was, so I did as she asked and removed my dress. Moments later, Deli returned carrying a large glass jar.
"They're horrible." I instinctively took a couple of steps back at the sight of the loathsome little creatures.
"Don't be silly." She put the jar on the small table and then got me to lie on my front on the couch. "These little darlings are just adorable. Now, stay perfectly still."
Moments later, I felt something small and slimy on the top of my back.
"That feels horrible," I shuddered.
"Keep still, Jill."
Over the next couple of minutes, she placed several more of the slimy horrible creatures on my back.
"How many more are there?"
"That's it. All done. I'll be back in a little while."
"Hang on. You're not going to leave me alone with

these things, are you?"

"You'll be fine. Just try to relax. Have a little nap if you like."

"Sleep? Are you kidding? How long do I have to keep them on my back?"

"Not long. I'll be back in about thirty minutes."

"Thirty—"

It was too late; she'd already left the room.

Coming to the salon had been a big mistake, but there was nothing I could do now except suck it up and wait until it was over.

"This one is yummy," said a tiny voice.

"Yeah, really tasty."

I jumped up off the couch.

"Who said that?"

"What are you doing? You're going to knock us off."

I glanced in the full-length mirror at the leeches on my back.

"Did one of you lot say that?" I said.

"I don't see anyone else in here, do you?" One of the leeches released its grip on my back and fell to the floor. Then, to my amazement, it transformed into a man. Or to be precise, into a vampire.

"What's going on?" I demanded. "Get these others off my back."

"Come on, guys, we're wasting our time with this one. She's a witch."

Within a matter of seconds, the other leeches had transformed into vampires. The booth was only tiny, and certainly wasn't designed to accommodate the six of us.

"What's your game?" I said.

"What does it look like?"

"It looks like you're masquerading as leeches in order to suck human blood."

"We're not doing anyone any harm."

"I'm pretty sure the rogue retrievers would disagree."

"Hey, there's no need to get them involved."

"Why do this, anyway? It can't possibly be worth it for the amount of blood that each of you can extract."

"Needs must. All our regular suppliers have been closed down."

"There's plenty of synthetic blood to be had."

"Did you hear her, guys?" He scoffed. "Synthetic just doesn't do it."

"This has to stop."

"Why? You said yourself that we're only taking really small amounts of blood. The humans don't seem to mind. The woman who owns this place has got them convinced that it's doing them good."

"I don't care. It isn't right, and if you don't shut this operation down within the next twenty-four hours, I guarantee that you will receive a visit from Daze and Blaze who are personal friends of mine."

"Not those two. Please."

"You know what you have to do, then. I'll be checking up on you."

"How's it going in there, Jill?" Deli called through the door.

"Great, but I think I'm done now." I turned to the vampires. "Quick, get back in that jar."

Deli stared in disbelief at the leeches in the jar. "I thought you couldn't stand the sight of them. How did you manage to get them off your back and into the jar?"

"I had a quiet word in their shell-likes, and they jumped

back in the jar themselves."

"You did what—oh, you're such a joker. So, be honest, do you feel better for that?"

"I honestly think I do."

"What did I tell you? Shall I book you another appointment?"

"Not right now, but I'll definitely check in with you later in the week."

"Great!

Chapter 23

The next morning, there were four of us seated at the breakfast table: me, Jack, Florence and Jay. I was saddened to see Jay tucking into a bowl of muesli, and I felt it my duty to try and stop him joining my husband and daughter on the dark side.

"Are you sure you wouldn't prefer Chococandy Pops, Jay?" I held out the cereal box.

"No, thanks." He couldn't even bring himself to look at the box. "I never want to eat any of those again."

"I know that the last time you ate them they gave you an upset tummy, but that's only because you ate half a ton of them."

"I'm going to stick with the muesli."

"Another convert to healthy eating." Jack couldn't have looked any smugger if he'd tried. "Welcome aboard, Jay."

Another lost cause.

Five minutes later, I'd finished my delicious, healthy cereal. "I'm going to head out. I'm not sure what time I'll be back."

"Do you really have to work today?" Jack said. "It is Sunday."

"I don't have any choice. I'm going to lose a day tomorrow because I have the shoot for the Droza ad, so I need to make up the time."

"It's not like you're on the clock. It is your own business."

"I realise that, but these cases aren't going to investigate themselves."

"Are you still looking for those chickens?"

"I am, but that's not what I'll be working on today. I'm

going to speak to Cutter's ex-girlfriend."

"The guy who has disappeared?"

"Yeah, she lives in Bottom Wash."

"You need to be careful over there." Jack frowned. "You know what kind of reputation that area has."

"I know, and I will be."

"Will you be back for lunch?"

"I'm not sure. I'll let you know." I walked around the table and kissed Florence on the top of her head. "Have a nice day, sweetie."

"Bye, Mummy."

***

A few of the people I'd spoken to about Cutter had mentioned Sarah, his lady friend. And, perhaps more significantly, none of them had had a good word to say about her. Cutter's assistant, Rose, had told me that she thought Sarah had been using Cutter, getting him to buy her presents he could ill afford. The owner of Suck It Up, the stall where Sarah had worked, had been glad to see the back of her because she'd spent too much time talking to people on the other stalls. Tex and Hank, from WCAS, weren't exactly enamoured with Sarah; in fact, Tex had said there was something of the night about her.

Bottom Wash had a bad reputation, and for very good reason. The whole area was run down and in dire need of rejuvenation. According to Jack, the number of crime incidents was five times that of any other area of Washbridge.

Sarah lived in a mid-terrace house on a street where at least one third of the properties were boarded up; two of them had been burnt out. As I drove down the road, looking for her house number, I began to question the wisdom of leaving my car there. But then I spotted what looked like a brand-new BMW parked halfway down the road. That vehicle was worth at least four times what my car was, so maybe it would be okay to park there. It was only when I got closer to the BMW that I realised it was parked outside house number forty-three, which was the address I had for Sarah.

I parked next to the BMW, and I'd just stepped onto the pavement when a young man on an e-scooter came flying past me at the speed of light.

"Hey, idiot, you could have killed me."

His only response was to shoot me the finger.

The house had a doorbell, but it was hanging off the wall by a single frayed wire, so I ignored it, and instead knocked on the door.

"Who is it?" The woman's voice came from inside the house.

"Sarah?"

"I asked who you are."

"Do you think you could open the door?"

"Not until you tell me who you are."

"My name is Jill Maxwell. I'd like to talk to you about Cutter."

"You the police?"

"No, I'm a private investigator."

She fell silent and I was beginning to wonder if she'd done a runner out the back when the door opened. The woman standing there was dressed from head-to-toe in what were clearly designer clothes, which were in stark contrast to this squalid property.

"You're lucky to catch me in." She beckoned me inside. "I don't spend much time here these days."

"Oh?"

"I'm going to put the place on the market when I get around to it."

She led the way down a hallway, which looked like it had not seen a vacuum or duster since the turn of the century, through to the kitchen which wasn't much better. She gestured for me to take a seat at the kitchen table, but she remained standing. I couldn't make my mind up if she'd done that in an attempt to establish some kind of dominance over me, or because she didn't want to sully her outfit. Most likely the latter.

"Who hired you?"

"Sam Rich. Do you know him?"

"He's one of those cowboy weirdos, isn't he?"

"He's a member of WCAS, yeah."

"They're like big kids that lot." She rolled her eyes. "Walking around dressed as cowboys. What's that all about?"

"You knew Cutter was a member, I assume."

"Course I did. Told him what I thought about it too, didn't I?"

"Do you have any idea where he might be?"

"How would I know?"

"You and he were an item for a while, weren't you?"

"We went out a few times if that's what you mean, but I'm not sure I'd call us an *item*. He wasn't really my type."

"*Wasn't*?"

"I meant *isn't* my type. He's a bit wet if you know what I mean."

"When was the last time you saw him?"

"A couple of weeks ago, maybe."

"Do you remember where specifically?"

"He took me to that new Greek restaurant down near the river."

"I've seen that place. It looks expensive."

"Yeah, well, it's not all that. Took them ages to refill my wine glass."

"And that was definitely the last time you saw him? Are you sure about that?"

"Yeah, I told him that I didn't want to see him anymore."

"How did he take it?"

"Not sure. He seemed alright about it."

"Did you leave together?"

"Nah, I left him to get the bill and I went and got a taxi."

"Did he say anything that night that might have suggested he was depressed?"

"Not really. He spent most of the time talking about a new cowboy costume he'd bought. That's why I decided to dump him." She glanced at her phone and said, "I'll have to go. I've got an important meeting in twenty minutes."

"Okay, well, thanks for your time." I handed her a card. "Call me if you think of anything else, would you?"

"Sure." She stuffed it in her pocket without so much as a glance at it, and then ushered me out of the house.

Without another word, she jumped into the BMW and set off up the road. On a whim, I hopped into my car and followed her. She headed for Washbridge city centre and turned into one of the multi-storey car parks. I followed her inside, waited until she'd parked, then drove to the next level, so she wouldn't spot me. I thought she was going to take the lift, but she walked straight past it and began to descend the stairs. Out on the street, she took a left towards the high street. Her destination turned out to be a travel agents called Global Exclusive.

If I'd followed her inside, she would have clocked me for sure, so I used the 'doppelganger' spell to make myself look like Kathy. Sarah had taken a seat at one of the desks and was already deep in discussion with one of the assistants. Fortunately, there were several racks of brochures quite close to where she was seated, so I began to look through them, while using the 'listen' spell to overhear their conversation.

"How long does it last?" Sarah asked the assistant.

"The Magna World Cruise lasts one-hundred and sixty-eight nights."

"And how much is that?"

"Fares start at eighty-three thousand pounds."

Eighty-three grand? I almost choked when I heard that.

"I would want a suite."

"In that case, you'd be looking at closer to two-hundred thousand."

I was waiting for Sarah's response when someone tapped me on the shoulder. I spun around to find one of the other assistants standing behind me. I was just about to tell her that I didn't require any help when she said, "Kathy? I haven't seen you for ages."

Oh bum!

"Oh, hi." I had no idea who this woman was.

"How's the family?"

"Fine, thanks."

"How old are the kids now?"

My mind went blank, and I couldn't remember how old they were.

"I've lost track." I laughed.

"Still a joker." She laughed. "I suppose you heard about me and Ray?"

"I—err—yeah, I'm sorry about that."

"*Sorry*? We got married."

"Yeah, I meant I was sorry that I've not been in touch before."

"That's okay. You must be busy with the shops. How many do you have now?"

"Too many. There aren't enough hours in the day."

"I bet. We must get together soon: you and Pete, me and Ray."

"Absolutely. I'll give you a call."

"Promise?"

"Cross my heart."

"Were you thinking of booking a cruise?" She gestured to the brochure that I'd been flicking through.

"No, just wishful thinking. Do people really pay these prices?"

"Yeah, there's more demand than there are places."

"Unbelievable."

"I'll have to go, Kathy. I think that guy needs some help."

"No problem. Nice to see you again."

Phew, I'd somehow managed to get away with it, but when I turned around, Sarah had disappeared. I hurried out of the shop to see her in the distance. I expected her to return to the car park, but she was headed in the opposite direction. Keeping my distance, I followed her for several minutes until she entered The Jewel, one of the newest, and most expensive hotels in Washbridge. Through the windows, I watched as she bypassed the reception desk and headed straight for the bank of lifts. After swiping her card, she boarded the lift.

Sarah didn't appear to know (or care) what had happened to Cutter, and she'd told me that they had actually split up. One thing bothered me, and that was how someone, who had been working as an assistant on a market stall until recently, could afford designer clothes, a brand-new BMW and a luxury world cruise. She also appeared to be staying at one of the most expensive hotels in the city. Something just didn't smell right.

***

"Two hundred grand?" Jack said. "Do people really pay that kind of money for a cruise?"

"Apparently, they're queuing up to book them."

"How the other half live."

"I nearly came a cropper in the travel agent. One of the assistants in there knows Kathy."

"So?"

"I'd made myself look like Kathy so the woman I was following wouldn't clock me."

"Oh dear. What happened?"

"I did what I do best."

"Lied?"

"No, I called upon my world renowned thespian skills and played the part of Kathy."

"Did you get away with it?"

"Just about."

Florence came running into the lounge, dressed in her PJs.

"You're supposed to be fast asleep in bed, young lady," I said.

"I was having a nightmare."

"Come here and have a hug." I wrapped my arms around her. "What was it about?"

"I dreamt a big pile of toilet rolls fell on my head."

With that, she pulled away and dissolved into laughter. Jack joined in.

"You put her up to this, didn't you?"

"Sorry," he said. "I was telling her that you're going to be shooting another commercial tomorrow."

"Will you get covered in toilet rolls again, Mummy?"

"I sincerely hope not."

Chapter 24

It was Monday morning, and I had left home a little earlier than usual because I wanted to drop in at the office before going to the Droza ad shoot. By the time I got to Washbridge, I was beginning to regret my decision not to have a drink before I left the house, so I nipped into The Corner Coffee Shop—the one that wasn't on the corner. Marcy, who was behind the counter, was the only person in the shop.

"Good morning, Marcy."

"Hi."

"It's quiet in here."

"The lull before the storm. The early morning rush will be starting anytime now. What can I get for you?"

"Just a caramel latte, please. Can I get it to go?"

"Sure. Anything to eat?"

"I shouldn't."

"I can definitely recommend the chocolate twists." She wiped her lips. "I've just finished one."

"Go on, then."

What? Acting is very demanding, so I obviously needed to up my calorie intake.

"Is that chocolate on your lips?" Mrs V said.

"What? No, it must be toothpaste."

"Brown toothpaste?"

"I'd run out of mine, so I had to use Jack's. It's probably organic."

"Hmm. Will you be in all day today?"

"No, I'll be leaving shortly because I have the ad shoot."

"For the toilet rolls?"

"*Premium* toilet rolls."

"Right." She chuckled.

"I still think you should take me with you," Winky said. "I'd be the making of that advert."

"I'm not taking you and that's final."

"What's the plot of this one?"

"I haven't seen a script, but I've been assured that it won't involve me being buried under a mountain of toilet rolls."

"Just take care. I don't want you getting injured."

"Since when did you care about my wellbeing?"

"I need you fit and well so you can drive me to the parachute jump."

"I should have known."

I took a seat at my desk and updated my notes on the Cutter case and the missing chickens' case. Neither of them made for good reading.

"Have you found those chickens yet?" Winky jumped on my desk.

"No, and I don't think I'm going to. I've spoken to all of the neighbours and none of them saw or heard a thing. How does someone steal a load of chickens without someone seeing something?"

"If it's any consolation to your client, she isn't the only one to lose her chickens."

"I know. You already told me about Paula Featherstone."

"I don't mean her."

"Who then?"

"I was scrolling through TikCat last night and came across a guy bemoaning the fact that his chickens had been nicked from his garden."

"Can I see it?"

"If I can find it." He took out his phone and began scrolling. "Here it is."

The man in the video was talking to the camera from what was obviously his back garden. Behind him was a chicken coop, not unlike the one belonging to Francesca Artichoke. His mouth was moving but I couldn't hear a word he was saying.

"The sound doesn't work."

"You need to press unmute." Winky rolled his eye. "Sheesh, you and technology."

I unmuted, then restarted the video, and listened as the man told his story, *"When I went to bed last night, the girls were all fine. I slept in this morning, which I thought was strange, but then I realised Tommy hadn't crowed. Tommy always crows at about six o'clock, so I thought maybe he was ill. But then when I came out to check on him, I found this."* He pointed to the coop. *"Empty. Tommy and all the girls had gone. All that was left was these."*

It took me a moment to realise what he was holding: half a dozen miniature eggs, about one tenth the size of a normal egg. The man continued, *"If anyone knows where my babies are, please reply in the comments. I can't bear the thought that I'll never see them again."*

"When was that video posted?" I asked Winky.

"About a month ago."

"Do you reckon he found his chickens?"

"I doubt it, or he would have updated his original post. Did you see those eggs?"

"Yeah, they were tiny. They can't have come from his chickens."

"Where else would they have come from?"

"That's what I'd like to know. Anyway, I have to go, and I need you to do me a favour."

"What's it worth?"

"It's worth taking you to your parachute jump."

"Okay, what do you need?"

"I want you to search through every social media channel and see if you can find any more reports of people having their chickens stolen."

"And if I find any?"

"Bookmark them so I can check them out when I'm back."

"No problem. I'll get straight on it."

***

The address I'd been given for the ad shoot was an abandoned airfield on the outskirts of West Chipping. Thanks to three different sets of roadworks, I arrived there with only a few minutes to spare. At first, I thought maybe I'd gone to the wrong place because the airfield appeared to be deserted, but then I saw someone in the distance, next to an old aircraft hangar, waving furiously at me. As I drove towards the hangar, I realised it was Freda, the woman who had directed the first advert. After parking my car at the side of the hangar, I hurried to greet her.

"Jill, how lovely to see you again. I was so glad when Talbot told me you'd agreed to take part in the sequel."

"How could I refuse?"

"Come inside. Moo is already here." She pointed to a small portacabin; one of the portacabin doors opened and Moo stepped out.

"Jill, darling, how wonderful to be working with you again." He came over and air-kissed me.

"Hi, Moo."

"I actually go by Tristan now. I felt it was time to leave Moo behind."

"Right."

Apparently, young Tristan had turned into a proper little luvvie since last we'd worked together.

"I only took this job for Freda," he said. "My agent's phone has been ringing off the hook since the last one aired, but I imagine you know how that feels."

"I—err—"

"So many juicy parts. It's difficult to choose, but I'm erring towards the stage. I've just signed up to play Romeo."

"In Romeo and Juliet?"

"No, as in Romeo Wasn't Built In A Day."

"Right?"

"Who's your agent, Jill?"

"I don't really have one. Talbot Bottle set me up with these jobs."

"That amateur? Really, that simply won't do. You need to find yourself a real agent." He took a card from his pocket and handed it to me.

"Rocky Roll?"

"The man is the best. I've never seen anyone negotiate like Rocky. Give him a call and tell him I said you should contact him."

"Right, thanks."

"We really should be making a start," Freda said. "You'd better go and put your costume on, Jill."

"*Costume*?"

"Oh yes." She grinned, somewhat disconcertingly. "I'd forgotten that you haven't seen the script yet. You'll love it."

"Where do I get changed?"

"Your costume is in the portacabin."

"Okay." It was with some trepidation that I made my way into the changing room. And, as it turned out, with good cause. "What? You can't be serious!"

"Fabulous!" Freda gushed. "You look amazing."

"I can barely breathe in here."

"You'll be fine. The shoot shouldn't take more than an hour."

"An hour?"

"Two max."

"What shall I call her?" Tristan asked.

"I hadn't really thought about that." Freda looked me up and down. "How about Willow? What do you think, Jill?"

I would dearly have loved to tell her what I really thought, but I figured that the sooner we started the shoot, the sooner I would be able to get out of this stupid cat costume. The only thing that could have made this worse was if Winky had been there to see me.

"Okay, follow me, you two."

Freda led Tristan and me out of the hangar, around the side and to the rear of the building.

"You look amazing, Jill," Tristan said.

I couldn't make my mind up if he was being sincere or if he was having a laugh at my expense. Either way, I had bigger problems because behind the hangar were five giant-sized toilet rolls lined up on the tarmac, each one as tall as me.

"What the—?"

"Time for you to see the script, I think." Freda handed it to me. "It was headed Hide and Seek Kitty, and the plot was pretty simple.

"You want me to hide inside one of those things?"

"Yes, the one on the far right. Then Tristan, who has lost his little kitty, will look inside each toilet roll. By the time he reaches the final one, he's beginning to lose hope, but then you jump out and surprise him."

"That's it?"

"Amazing!" Tristan gushed. "How would you like me to play it? Should I cry?"

"No need for tears," Freda said. "But maybe you could look a little more distressed after you check each of the toilet rolls."

"No problem." Tristan was clearly keen to get started.

"I have a question." I raised my paw.

"Yes, Jill. Or should I call you Willow?"

Freda and Tristan laughed, making me want to give them both a slap.

"How on earth do I get inside there?"

"That's the clever part. If you go around the back of the toilet roll, you'll find some steps built into it. Okay? Right, off you pop, Willow."

I don't have a lot of experience of climbing giant toilet rolls, and the task wasn't made any easier by having to wear the stupid cat costume because the tail kept getting tangled up in my legs. Eventually, though, I made it to the top of the toilet roll at the end of the line.

"What now?"

"There are more steps inside. Climb down until you are out of sight."

Once I was inside, I looked up. This must be what it feels like to be standing at the bottom of a well.

"Are you okay in there, Willow?"

"Fine."

"Okay, I'll call action in a minute. Stay hidden inside until you hear the bell."

"Did you say bell?"

"That's right. When Tristan is about to approach the final toilet roll, I'll ring the bell. That will be your cue to climb back up the steps to surprise him. Okay?"

"Sure."

"Right, let's get this show on the road. Ready, Tristan?"

"Ready."

"Okay, action."

While I waited inside the toilet roll, I tried to decide if this experience was better or worse than the first ad shoot. It was a close call. Time passed, and I began to wonder what was taking so long. The ad surely wouldn't last more than a couple of minutes and yet it must have been at least five minutes since Freda called action. I was tempted to call out or climb up to see what was happening, but I didn't want to ruin the take, so I sat tight.

After another five minutes, I had had enough. Something was clearly wrong, but no one had bothered to tell me, so I climbed up the steps and stood on top of the toilet roll. Freda and Tristan were standing together, deep in conversation.

"Hey, guys, what's going on?"

"Sorry, Jill, I realised the camera set-up was all wrong. We need to follow the action as Tristan goes from one toilet roll to the next, but we don't have a rail set up and there isn't time to get one now."

"Are we abandoning the shoot?"

"Definitely not. Rodney is going to get his Jeep. Jimmy will sit on top and film from there."

"Isn't that dangerous?"

"No, they'll only be driving at a snail's pace. Here they come now."

The vehicle came around the side of the hangar, with the cameraman kneeling on top.

"Do you want me to get back—" I stopped mid-sentence when I realised that the Jeep had suddenly speeded up. "What's he doing?"

Judging by Freda's expression, she was just as shocked as I was.

Jimmy, the cameraman lost his footing and fell off the Jeep which was now heading straight for the toilet roll that I was standing on.

"Stop!" I screamed at the Jeep.

Moments later, the Jeep hit the toilet roll, sending me plunging down inside the tube. The impact of the crash knocked it on its side, and it began to roll down the airstrip. I was being spun around like the inside of a washing machine. That seemed to go on for a lifetime before the toilet roll finally came to a halt. Bruised and dizzy, I managed to clamber out of one end.

"Jill, are you okay?"

Freda, Tristan and Rodney were running towards me.

"I'm okay." I wasn't really. "What happened?"

"I'm so sorry," Rodney said. "A wasp got into the Jeep. I was trying to swat it away and I lost control."

"How's Jimmy?" I asked.

"A bit bruised, but otherwise okay. What about you? Are you sure you're alright?"

"Yeah, but I don't think I'm up to doing another shoot today."

"There's no need," Freda said. "This turned out much better than we could ever have hoped."

"You shot the whole thing?"

"Yeah, Jimmy is the consummate professional. Even though he was injured, he managed to capture the whole thing. It's amazing."

Chapter 25

I'd started the day believing the new ad shoot couldn't possibly be any worse than the first one. I'd been wrong. The first time around, the only thing that had suffered was my pride. This time, I came away feeling like I'd been run over by a steamroller. The only consolation was that I had been assured my fee would be in my bank account the following week.

"Are you alright, Jill?" Mrs V said.

"Yeah, I'm fine."

"Are you sure? You look rather—err—dishevelled."

"I'm okay. Nothing a nice cup of tea won't put right."

"Coming right up."

"What happened to you?" Winky laughed.

"The ad shoot happened."

"That bad?"

"Worse. I had to dress up as a cat."

"That's outrageous. If they wanted a cat, they should have hired a real one. I told you I was available."

"You want to thank your lucky stars that it wasn't you." I told him about the setup for the ad shoot and how things hadn't exactly gone as planned.

"Let me make sure I've got this right." He grinned. "You fell into the centre of a giant toilet roll, and then rolled down the road. All while dressed as a cat."

"Pretty much, yeah."

"Amazing. When does the ad air? I can't wait to see it."

"I neither know nor care. I'm done with acting."

"*Acting*." He scoffed.

Mrs V came through and handed me my tea.

"Thanks, Mrs V. I meant to ask earlier if there had been

any calls while I was out?"

"Just a Mr Eli Phant who wondered if you might help him find his trunk. Do you want me to call him back for you?"

I glared at Winky who was smirking.

"No, I don't think I'll bother. Thanks for the tea."

I waited until she'd gone back through to her office, then gave Winky both barrels. "Mr Phant? Seriously? Don't you have anything better to do with your time?"

"What can I tell you? I was bored."

"You were supposed to be doing some work for me. I suppose you forgot about that."

"Well, that's where you're wrong. I had quite a productive morning."

"Did you find someone else whose chickens have gone missing?"

"Not just one. I found two people in the Washbridge area who have lost their chickens in the last six months."

"That can't be a coincidence."

"There's more. In both cases, the person mentioned finding tiny eggs after the chickens had been taken."

"That's just weird. Francesca Artichoke didn't say anything about tiny eggs. Let me check with her." I gave her a call, but I didn't really expect her to answer because she spent most of her time in court. But for once I was lucky.

"Francesca, it's Jill Maxwell."

"I'm just on my way into court, Jill. Can it wait?"

"Just one quick question. After the chickens disappeared, did you find any tiny eggs?"

"I did, actually. They were minute."

"You never mentioned it."

"I didn't think it was important because they couldn't have been chicken eggs. They were much too small. Sorry, I really do have to go."

"Okay, thanks."

Winky had been listening in to the call and asked, "What do you make of that?"

"I have no idea. I need to speak to the other people whose chickens disappeared. I don't suppose you managed to get their names and addresses, did you?"

"As it happens, I did."

"I'm impressed."

"Impressed enough to break open the salmon?"

"Go on, then."

"Red not pink."

"Obviously."

I decided to strike while the iron was hot, so I told Mrs V that I would be out for the rest of the day. Maybe, I would be able to find some common denominator between Francesca Artichoke and the other people whose chickens had disappeared. As I was walking to the car park, I received a call from Kathy.

"Hey, Jill, do you believe in doppelgangers?"

"*Doppelgangers*?"

"It's what they call someone who is a double of you."

"I'm not stupid; I know what a doppelganger is."

"So, do you believe in them?"

"Don't they say everyone has a doppelganger somewhere?"

"Do you remember Mary Short?"

"I don't think so."

"She used to work with me at Ever."

"Still not ringing any bells."

"She got married and is Mary Long now."

"Is that the long and short of it?" I laughed.

"I feel sorry for Jack having to put up with your stupid jokes."

"Your problem is that you don't recognise comedy gold when you hear it."

"Anyway, as I was saying, I bumped into her just now and, apparently, she works in a travel agent."

Oh bum! I had a horrible feeling I knew where this was headed.

"That's nice, but I don't really see—"

She asked me if I'd decided to book the cruise that I was looking at in her shop yesterday. I told her that I wasn't in her shop, but she swears it was me."

"That is weird."

"Do you think someone might be going around, impersonating me?"

"I wouldn't have thought so. It's probably just a case of mistaken identity. Anyway, I have to go because I have a hot lead on one of my cases."

"Before you go, remember the password: cheesehead."

"Why do I need a password?"

"If you bump into someone who looks like me, it might not actually be me. It might be my doppelganger. If you ask them for the password, and they don't say cheesehead, then you know it isn't me."

"O—kay."

Oh boy! What had I started?

***

The first name on Winky's list was a Mrs Harvington-Smythe who lived in Far Wash village. If we didn't have such a beautiful home in Middle Tweaking, I would have loved to live in Far Wash. The village, which had a duck pond on the green, was only about half the size of Middle Tweaking. Mrs Harvington-Smythe's property, which was located at the northern end of the village, was the largest house in Far Wash.

I hadn't called in advance, so I wasn't sure what kind of reception I would get, or even if she'd be at home. I needn't have worried because when she opened the door and I explained the purpose of my visit, she was only too keen to talk to me.

"Do come in. Can I get you a drink? I was just about to have a glass of wine."

"Not for me, thanks."

After pouring herself a generous glass of white wine, she took me through the house, and out into an enormous garden. We took a seat on cane chairs on the patio, which overlooked a beautifully manicured lawn, bordered by colourful flowerbeds.

"I'm hopeless with names," she said. "Did you say you were called Jane?"

"Jill."

"Right, sorry."

"This is an amazing garden, but I'm a little confused. Where did you keep the chickens? Surely, not out here?"

"Goodness, no. Reginald, that's my hubby, would have had a seizure. This garden is his pride and joy. I used to keep them on the allotment, which is a couple of miles up the road."

"Can I ask what made you decide to keep chickens?"

"I grew up on a farm. That was many years ago now, before I became a model. I always loved the chickens, so when we both retired, I managed to persuade Reginald to let me take a plot on the allotments, to keep some. It was all going swimmingly until the day they disappeared."

"Can you tell me about that day?"

"There's not much to tell, I'm afraid. I've always been an early riser, so I'd visit the allotment first thing, to check on my babies, and to collect the eggs. I do miss those eggs—they were delicious. Anyway, this particular day, I cycled to the allotment as usual, but when I got there, they'd vanished."

"What did you do?"

"I was in shock. I just couldn't believe they'd actually gone. I spent the best part of an hour searching the other plots, but to no avail."

"Did you lock the chickens in a coop?"

"Yes, I'd cycle over there in the evening and make sure they were all safely inside for the night, away from the foxes."

"Had someone broken into the coop?"

"No, it was still locked."

"How could that be?"

"I wish I knew."

"On the video you posted online, you mentioned something about tiny eggs?"

"That's right. The coop was empty except for half a dozen of them."

"Had you ever seen anything like them before?"

"No, never."

"Have you replaced the chickens?"

"Reginald encouraged me to, but I didn't have the heart.

I would always be worrying that the same thing might happen again. You mentioned that your client had the same thing happen to them?"

"That's right, in circumstances almost identical to yours."

"Do you have any idea who might be behind it?"

"Not at the moment, I'm afraid. I'm hoping that by talking to people who have experienced the same thing, I might find some connection."

After leaving Mrs Harvington-Smythe's, I headed for Grimly Lane, which was about as big a contrast to Far Wash, as you could have hoped to see. As soon as I'd knocked on the door of number twenty-seven, one of the windows on the upper floor flew open, and a man wearing a string vest, leaned out.

"Who are you? What do you want?"

"My name is Jill Maxwell. I was hoping to—"

"Did Big Tommy send you?"

"What? No, I—err—"

"You can tell him if he's got something to say to me, he can come and say it to my face because I'm not talking to his pet poodle."

I'd been called some things in my life, but never a pet poodle.

"I don't know Big Tommy, and he certainly didn't send me here."

"Are you here about that foot spa? We sold it last week."

"No, I was hoping to talk to you about your chickens."

"Is that supposed to be funny? Did Micky put you up to this? Or was it Moley?"

"No one put me up to this, I promise."

"What are you doing here, then?"

"Some chickens belonging to a friend of mine disappeared too."

"Really?"

"Yeah, and it's happened to a few other people. I'm just trying to figure out what's going on."

"Why didn't you say so before? Stay there. I'll put some trousers on and be down in a minute."

He was still fastening his trousers when he appeared at the door.

"What did you say your name was?"

"Jill Maxwell."

"Pleased to meet you, Jill." He offered his hand. "I'm Jack Mason, but everyone calls me Mase."

If I'm honest, I wasn't overkeen on the idea of shaking his hand, but I didn't want to alienate him, so I took one for the team.

"Nice to meet you, Mase."

"Come inside and I'll make us both a brew. How do you take it?"

"White, no sugar, please."

"Take a seat in the living room. I'll be back in two shakes of a ferret's tail."

The small living room was made to look even tinier by the two huge corner sofas that had somehow been wedged inside it. The only way to sit on one of them was to climb over the back, so that's what I did. While I waited for my host to return, I looked at the framed photos that adorned the walls; they were all of chickens.

When Mase returned, he passed both cups to me, and then climbed over the back of the sofa.

"You're probably wondering why I have such large sofas in this small room."

"They're very nice." Just insanely huge.

"They are. That's why I took them off my cousin Martin when he was going to throw them out. He insisted I take the pair or none at all."

"I was just admiring your photographs."

"I'm thinking of taking them down."

"Why would you do that?"

"I don't spend a lot of time in this room, but whenever I do, it always upsets me." I thought for a moment, that he was going to cry, but instead he forced a laugh. "Silly, eh?"

"Not at all. Are these photos of the chickens that went missing?"

"Some of them, yeah. People thought I kept them just for the cheap eggs, but that wasn't it. Don't get me wrong, that was a nice bonus, but I've loved chickens ever since I was a little kid. It was a dream come true when I was able to get some of my own. That one there is my favourite."

"That's a rooster, isn't it?"

"Yeah, I called him Freddy." He smiled. "He's a handsome guy, don't you think?"

"Err, yeah, I guess so." If roosters are your thing. "What's wrong with that thing on his head?"

"His comb? Nothing. It's just a bit droopy because of his age." He grinned. "He wasn't very popular with my neighbours."

"Do you think one of your neighbours might have taken the chickens?"

"Definitely not. They might have complained about them, but they know better than to cross me."

"Do you have any suspicions as to who did take them?"

"No idea. I still can't figure out how they could have taken them without me seeing or hearing anything. My bedroom is on the back of the house, so I should have heard something."

"But you didn't?"

"No, not a thing. I didn't know they'd gone until I realised that I hadn't heard Freddy that morning, so I went outside to check on him."

"Would it be possible to see where you kept them?"

"Sure. We'll go through the kitchen."

We both scaled the sofa, walked through the kitchen and out the back door, into a tiny garden. Unlike Francesca Artichoke and Mrs Harvington-Smythe, Mase didn't have a fancy chicken coop. Instead, he had converted a regular garden shed into a makeshift one. The shed/coop was surrounded by a tall, wire fence with a gate to allow access. The gate was secured by a padlock.

"How did the thieves get in there?" I asked.

"Beats me." He shrugged. "The padlock was still fastened.

"And you haven't repaired the fence since then?"

"No, it wasn't damaged."

"I don't get it."

"That makes two of us."

"Do you plan on replacing the chickens?"

"I can't afford to. It took me years to save the money to buy them in the first place. And, even then, I only managed it because the guy at Feathers And More did me a good deal. And besides, I couldn't bear the thought of it happening again."

I left Mase feeling quite sorry for the guy. Although the

others had been affected by the loss of their chickens, they hadn't felt it as badly as Mase seemed to have. The chickens had been his life and their loss had left him a shell of his former self.

No pun intended.

Chapter 26

Florence finished chewing on the muesli, then said, "Tell me the story again, Mummy."

"Yeah." Jack grinned. "Tell us one more time."

"I've told you everything there is to tell."

"How big were the toilet rolls?" Florence pushed.

"Way taller than me."

"When do you reckon they'll start showing the ad?" Jack asked.

"Never, I hope. Now, can we please change the subject? Florence, you never told me what you did at CASS yesterday."

"Nothing much."

"I'd still like to know."

"Just bolts."

"*Bolts*? What's that?"

"You know." She pointed with her middle finger. "Bolts."

"Hang on. Do you mean lightning bolts?"

"Yeah."

The 'lightning bolt' spell was one of the most dangerous spells available to witches and had the potential to be lethal. Surely, no one at CASS would have been reckless enough to allow a six-year-old kid to use it.

"What did you do exactly?"

"Zapped stuff."

"What kind of stuff?"

"Mainly trees."

"Were all the kids in your class doing it?"

"Nah, just me."

"What do you mean, *just you*?"

"I was the only one who did it. Can I go upstairs and play now?"

"No."

"I've finished my muesli."

"You can go in a minute. I need you to tell me more about what happened yesterday. Who was the teacher who showed you the 'lightning bolt' spell?"

"It wasn't a teacher."

"Who was it?"

"Great Grandma."

"*Great Grandma*?" I exploded. "Was she at CASS?"

"Yeah, she took me into the woods at lunchtime."

"And showed you the 'lightning bolt' spell?"

"Yeah. Can I go and play now? Please!"

"Okay, off you go."

"Jill!" Jack said. "Don't do anything—"

"Didn't you hear what she just said?"

"Yes, but I—"

"Did you know about this last night?"

"No, of course I didn't, or I would have told you. When I asked her what she had done at CASS, she just said nothing much, like she always does."

"I'm going to kill that woman." I pushed my half-eaten bowl of cereal away and stood up.

"Don't you think you should take a moment to compose yourself first?"

"No, I don't. I'm going to strangle her with my own bare hands."

"As opposed to someone else's hands?" He grinned, but not for long. Once he saw the look on my face, he quickly backpedalled. "I'll just—err—check on the goldfish."

I don't remember walking up to the hotel, but the next

thing I knew, I was standing in front of the reception desk.

"Hi, Jill, your grandmother said she isn't to be disturbed this morning. Sorry."

"Not as sorry as she's going to be."

"Jill, you can't—"

I headed straight for her office and threw open the door, to find her sitting at the desk, which was covered in piles of coins.

"Do you mind? I told Mary I wasn't to be disturbed."

"I don't care." I slammed my hand down onto her desk, causing the piles of coins to spill.

"Look what you've done now. I've just spent the last hour counting those."

"How dare you?"

"Someone has to count them."

"I don't mean that. I mean how dare you teach Florence the 'lightning bolt' spell?"

She sighed. "I thought you might have something to say about that."

"You've done some questionable stuff in the past, but this? What were you thinking? Never mind, it's obvious you weren't thinking. Why else would you teach a young child one of the most lethal spells that exists?"

"For her protection?"

"What are you talking about?"

"I'm talking about the day of burning. We've been so focussed on looking out for ourselves that we're both guilty of overlooking Florence."

"Are you serious? The witch-finders would never take a child."

"Are you sure about that?"

"I—err—"

"I wouldn't put anything past those lowlifes."

"They would have to come through me first."

"What if you aren't there? What then? Florence needs to be able to protect herself. And not just against the witch-finders."

"What do you mean?"

"Braxmore is still out there somewhere, or have you forgotten? Wouldn't you feel happier knowing your daughter is able to defend herself?"

"Err, I—err—yes, of course."

"There you are, then. We're agreed. Florence learning the 'lightning bolt' spell is a good thing."

"How did that go?" Jack asked.

"She's right."

"Sorry?"

"Grandma's right. Florence needs to be able to defend herself in case I'm not here to do it."

"What about me? I won't let anyone hurt her."

"I know you'd defend her until your dying breath, but you wouldn't stand a chance against some of the forces that you'd be up against. Teaching her the 'lightning bolt' spell was the right thing to do."

"Now you've got me worried about her."

I put my arms around him and gave him a hug. "There's no need, honestly. She's going to be fine."

"Promise?"

"I promise."

***

In all the excitement over the 'lightning bolt' spell, I

hadn't got around to having a drink before I left the house, so I decided to drop in at The Corner Coffee Shop before going into the office.

Marcy was behind the counter, but otherwise, the shop was deserted.

"Good morning, Jill. A caramel latte?"

"Yes, please."

"To go?"

"No, I'll drink it here before I go into the office."

"No problem."

Normally, I would have taken a seat near the counter, so I could chat with Marcy, but my head was still spinning from my earlier encounter with Grandma, so I deliberately took a seat by the window, so I could sit in silence for a while.

I had hoped the coffee might re-energise me for the day ahead, but curiously it seemed to be having the exact opposite effect; I could hardly keep my eyes open. Marcy walked by me to the door and turned the sign over. I didn't understand why she would be closing up so soon after opening, but I was too tired to say anything. I tried to stand up, but my legs felt like jelly.

"Marcy, I don't feel—" The words died on my lips.

The last thing I remember was seeing something on the back of her neck: a tattoo.

It took all my energy just to open one eye. My head was thumping, and my mouth felt as dry as a desert.

"She's coming around." A female voice floated around my head.

"I'm telling you. It's her," said another female voice that I didn't recognise.

I eventually managed to open both eyes, and when they'd become accustomed to the light, I saw that I was in a room with white walls, a white door, and no windows. I was lying on a white couch, and across the room, on an identical couch were three women, all staring at me.

"Are you okay?" said the middle one of the three.

"Where am I?" I pulled myself into a sitting position, but immediately regretted it, as the nausea kicked in.

"We don't know."

"Are you Jill Maxwell?"

"Yeah." I glanced around. "How did I get here?"

"They brought you here."

"*They*?" As I spoke, I had a flashback: I had been in the coffee shop. As Marcy had turned over the closed sign, I'd spotted something on the nape of her neck. A tattoo. A tattoo of a goblet. "Witch-finders."

"Yeah."

"They're going to burn us." The youngest of the three burst into tears.

"No, they're not, Judy." The woman to her left put her arm around her. "Jill is here now; she's the most powerful witch in Candlefield. She'll know what to do."

"If she's so powerful, how come she let them take her?"

It was a good question. How could I have been so stupid as to let my guard down like that?

"Tell her, Jill. Tell her that we're going to be okay."

"Yes, of course we will," I said with as much confidence as I could muster under the circumstances.

"I'm Denise," said the woman who was still trying to comfort the young witch. "This is Judy."

"And I'm Alice."

"Alice Allison?"

"Yes, how did you know?"

"I believe you're a friend of my Aunt Lucy. She told me that you'd been taken. She's been really worried about you."

"That's so sweet of her, but then Lucy was always the best of us."

"Are there only the three of you here?" I asked. "Only, my grandmother mentioned that a Belinda Berrymore had also been snatched."

"There's only ever been the three of us in this room, but we've heard other voices so we think there may be others being held close by."

"I never thought they'd be able to snatch you, Jill," Denise said. "What hope is there for the rest of us now?"

"It's my own stupid fault. I let my guard down. I should have realised there was something not right about that coffee shop."

"Coffee shop?"

"It's not important. We just need to get out of here and rescue the others."

"How are we supposed to do that?" Judy snapped. "Our magic doesn't work inside this room."

"What? Are you sure?"

"It might work for you," Alice said. "Try it."

I did. It didn't.

Oh bum!

But then I remembered the gizmo that Grandma had given me.

"It's okay, I can get us—" I looked around for my handbag but there was no sign of it. Why hadn't I carried the gizmo on my person?

And before you lot chime in, I already know the answer:

because I'm an idiot.

"What were you going to say, Jill?" Alice said. "Do you know how to get us out of here?"

"Not yet, but I'll come up with something. How often do they come in here?"

"The witch-finders? We never see them."

"What about when they brought me in? You must have seen them then?"

"Every time they bring someone new in, they pipe some kind of gas into the room and knock us out."

"What about when they bring food and water? Don't you see them then?"

"They just slide it through that slot." She pointed to an area next to the door. Until then, I hadn't even noticed the small, hinged cover that was the same colour as the walls.

"Okay, well they'll have to come into the room when they try and take us to the—err—"

I stopped short of saying the word burning, for fear that I might set Judy off again.

"Can I have a word, Jill?" Denise stood up and beckoned me to follow her to the far side of the room.

"I didn't want Judy or Alice to hear this," she said in a whisper. "But I don't think they'll need to take us out of this room when it comes time to—err—you know."

"What do you mean?"

"Listen." She tapped her knuckles on different parts of the wall, which all sounded the same, until she reached a certain point.

"That sounded like metal," I observed.

"There are several of those all around the room."

"I don't understand."

"I hope I'm wrong, but—" She hesitated.

"But what?"

"What if the burners are behind there?"

"You think they're going to burn us in here, don't you?"

"Shush!" Denise glanced over at the other two, who thankfully hadn't heard my outburst.

"I hope I'm wrong."

So did I.

I kept my own counsel for the next couple of hours. I'm sure the others thought I was trying to come up with a cunning plan to get us all out of there, but for once the queen of cunning plans was all out of them. Little did they know that I was actually thinking that this was not the way I'd expected to meet my end. And what about Braxmore? With me out of the picture, there would be nothing to stop him targeting Florence. The thought of never seeing her or Jack again was too much to bear, and it was all I could do not to cry.

"Have you come up with a plan yet, Jill?" Judy said.

There was no point in giving them false hope. I had to tell them that there was nothing I could do to get us out of there.

"I don't think—"

I didn't get to finish the sentence because an explosion blew the door off its hinges, and it came sailing across the floor, narrowly missing Belinda. The smoke that filled the room made my eyes smart.

"What are you lot waiting for?" Grandma said. "Do you want to get out of here or not?"

"Grandma?" I wiped my eyes. "How did you know where we were?"

"There's no time for that now. Come on, let's get

going."

We were all seated in a park, just around the corner from the building where we'd been held captive. In total, there were seven witches, all of whom wore the same relieved expression.

"Take some time to recover," Grandma addressed the others. "Then make your way home. Your loved ones have been worried about you."

Over the next twenty minutes, each of the witches thanked Grandma, and made their exit.

"How did you know where to find us?" I asked when we were alone. "I didn't have the tracking gizmo with me."

"It's just as well that I know you as well as I do, isn't it? I knew you couldn't be trusted to keep it with you at all times. That's why I implanted another one in your neck."

"You did *what*?"

"You heard me."

"When you slapped me?"

"Correct."

"You said it was a wasp."

"What can I tell you?" She grinned. "I lied."

"Thank you." I threw my arms around her and gave her a big hug.

"Put me down!" She tried to pull away. "If I'd known you were going to do that, I'd have left you in there."

"You saved my life."

"Let go of me, woman." She forced open my arms and stepped away.

Somewhat dazed by my ordeal, I made my way to my

office. As I passed by the car park, I noticed that The Corner Coffee Shop had disappeared. In its place was a derelict building.

Aunt Lucy called me.

"Jill, I've just heard from Alice. She told me that she and the others are safe, and that it's all thanks to you."

"I didn't have anything to do with it. It was Grandma who rescued everyone. Me included."

"Whoever did it, I'm so glad you're all okay."

"Me too. I'd better get going. I'm already late for work."

Chapter 27

"Are you alright, Jill?" Mrs V said.

"I'm fine."

"Are you sure? Your eyes are bloodshot."

"Just a bit of hay fever. I'm okay, honestly."

"Tea, or would you prefer coffee?"

"Definitely not a coffee. Tea would be nice."

"That new eye makeup of yours isn't working." Winky grinned.

"Very funny."

"What happened to you?"

"I'd rather not talk about it."

"Please yourself. Hey, guess how much sponsorship money I've had pledged already?"

"One-hundred pounds."

"Not even close. Try four-hundred and sixty smackeroos."

"How did you manage that?"

"What can I tell you? I'm Mr Popular."

"Nah, it can't be that. The parachute jump is next week, isn't it?"

"No, it's this Friday. And you promised to drive me there, remember?"

"I'm not sure I'll be able to. I'm really busy."

"You promised. You can't let me down now."

"Okay, but it had better not take all day."

Mrs V brought my tea through. "Mr Rich called just before you arrived. He asked if you would call him with an update on his case. I said I'd tell you but that I wasn't sure what time you'd be in."

"Okay, thanks. I'll call him later."

What I was going to tell him, I had no idea, so while I drank my tea, I reviewed the case and my progress, or lack of it, so far. I had spoken to Cutter's fellow-members of WCAS, Tex and Hank, as well as his assistant on the sweet stall, Rose Merry. I'd also spoken to his sister, Anita Hedge, and his neighbour, Brenda. None of them had had a bad word to say about Cutter, although there was a consensus that he hadn't been particularly happy in the months leading up to his disappearance. Money problems on his stall seemed to have been weighing heavily upon him. One thing all of them had agreed on was their disdain for Cutter's recent lady friend, Sarah. Having interviewed her myself, I could understand their feelings; she didn't come across as the most likeable individual. Of all the people I'd spoken to, she seemed the least concerned by Cutter's unexplained disappearance.

The truth was I was no further along than I'd been when I first met Sam Rich. I had no idea where Cutter was; I didn't even know if he was still alive. My train of thought was broken when Winky jumped onto my desk.

"I've been thinking," he said.

"Careful. You don't want to go giving yourself a migraine."

"I think you and I should start a syndicate."

"What kind of syndicate?"

"For the lottery. We'll both throw in a few quid each week and share any winnings."

"The lottery is a waste of money. I bought a ticket the other week and didn't win a sausage."

"You can't expect to win every week. You have to pick a set of numbers and play the same ones every time."

"I don't like that idea. What if you miss a week and find

out you would have won?"

"We won't miss any."

"If you're so keen, why don't you do it yourself?"

"And how am I supposed to walk into a shop and buy a lottery ticket?"

"Good point, but I still think it's a waste of time and money."

"You never know." He produced a copy of The Bugle. "Look at this."

He'd opened it on a feature about the anonymous local winner who had scooped a small fortune. The newspaper had invited readers to write in and say what they would have spent the money on if they'd won the jackpot.

"This idiot says they'd buy a year's supply of custard creams," Winky said.

"Where does it say that?"

"Gotcha."

"Very funny. I'd take Jack and Florence on a world cruise."

"What about me?"

"What about you?"

"You wouldn't leave me behind, would you?"

"In a heartbeat."

"You can be so cruel sometimes. So, what do you reckon about the syndicate?"

"Hang on. I'm still reading."

As well as asking readers what they would have bought with the winnings, it also discussed the merits of the winner's choice to remain anonymous. The readers seemed to be evenly split between those who would have done the same and those who would want the world to know.

"I'd shout it from the rooftop," Winky said.

"I think I'd keep it quiet." I turned the page where the article continued. "Are those the winning numbers?"

"Yeah. Just think, those six numbers were worth almost eight million."

"Is that how much it was?"

"Yeah. Can you imagine it?"

"Not really." I looked again at the winning numbers. "Was there only the one winner?"

"Yeah, just the one. So, are you up for it or not?"

"Go on, then, but I'm only playing one line per game."

"We'll never win with only two lines between us."

"It's that or nothing."

"Okay." He handed me a twenty-pound note. "Let me know when this runs out."

"Will do."

"And don't forget to buy the ticket."

"I won't. What numbers are we going with?"

"I say we go with these." He pointed at the winning numbers printed in the article.

"That's stupid. They'll never come up again."

"You really don't understand the concept of randomness, do you?"

"Are you sure you want to go with those?"

"Positive."

"Okay, let's do it." I scribbled down Winky's numbers and then added six random numbers of my own.

"Good luck to us."

Winky settled down on the sofa, allowing me to refocus my thoughts on the Cutter case. One thing was still nagging me, and that was Sarah's BMW, her designer clothes and the world cruise that I saw her booking. Until recently, she'd been working on the vacuum spares stall in the market. There was no way that would pay her enough to afford all of those luxuries. It appeared that she had come into some serious money, and I had a hunch I knew how, so I called Anita Hedge.

"Anita, it's Jill Maxwell."

"Any news on Cutter?"

"Nothing as yet. Sorry. I wondered if you knew whether Cutter has any life insurance."

"He definitely doesn't."

"You seem very sure."

"I am. Cutter had a thing about insurance companies. He has always said they are crooks who will do anything to avoid paying out. The only insurance he has is for his car."

"You don't think there's any chance he might have taken out a life insurance policy without telling you?"

"Zero chance. I know my brother. Why do you ask?"

"It doesn't matter. It was just a longshot. Thanks, anyway."

"You thought that woman, Sarah, had done away with him, to claim the insurance, didn't you?" Winky said.

"You shouldn't be listening to my phone calls, but yes, I thought it was a possibility."

"No, it wasn't. No insurance company would have paid out until there was solid proof that the man is dead."

Winky had a point: I wasn't thinking clearly, which was hardly surprising given my earlier traumatic encounter with the witch-finders.

I couldn't put it off any longer, so I gave Sam Rich a call.

"I'm sorry I haven't been in touch before, Sam."

"That's okay. I just wondered if you had any news."

"Not really." I gave him a quick recap of the investigation so far.

"It sounds like you're no closer to finding out what happened to Cutter."

"You're right, but I haven't given up yet."

"What's your next course of action?"

"I'm going to take another look around his house. Maybe I missed something the first time."

"Okay, and you'll keep me posted, won't you?"

"I promise."

Midway through the afternoon, I received a call from Francesca Artichoke.

"Jill, we're just in recess at the court, so I thought I'd take this opportunity to check how things are going."

"I'm not going to lie to you, Francesca, I'm no closer to finding your chickens yet."

"That's disappointing. No leads at all?"

"I wouldn't say that. I've discovered that your chickens aren't the only ones to have disappeared in this area."

"Really? Do you think there could be a connection?"

"It's possible."

"They've just called us into court, but I have a free day tomorrow. Do you think you could pop over to discuss what this means?"

"Sure. What time?"

"Afternoon would be best for me. One-thirty?"

"Okay, I'll see you then."

***

The first thing I did when I walked into the house was

throw my arms around Jack and give him a hug.

"Are you okay, Jill?"

"I'm fine. Where's Florence?"

"In her bedroom, playing with Jay."

I hurried upstairs, to find Florence and Jay, on the bed, playing snakes and ladders. I gave her a big hug and an even bigger kiss on top of her head.

"I love you so much."

Jack had followed me upstairs and was eyeing me suspiciously.

"I need to roll the dice, Mummy." Florence pulled away.

"Could I have a word, Jill?" Jack gestured for me to follow him out of the room.

Before I did, I gave Florence another big kiss, much to her annoyance. Jack ushered me into our bedroom and closed the door behind him.

"What's going on?" he said.

"What do you mean?"

"You know what I mean. Normally, when you get home from work, you ask what's for dinner. Or you ask me to make you a cup of tea. Today, you're all kissy and cuddly."

"There's nothing wrong with that, is there?"

"No, but it's just not you. We're not leaving this room until you tell me what's going on, so you may as well do it now."

"It's nothing, honestly. I just realised how lucky I am to have you and Florence. That's it, honestly." I started for the door, but he stepped forward to block me.

"Nice try. Now, how about you tell me the truth. What's bothering you?"

It was no good. Jack knew me far too well to try and pull the wool over his eyes. I slumped down onto the bed, took a deep breath and then told him about my abduction. When I'd finished, he sat down beside me, and put his arm around my shoulder.

"No wonder you're out of sorts."

"When I was sitting in that room, trying to figure out what to do, all I could think of was that I might never see you or Florence again."

"But you're here with us now, so everything is okay."

"Thanks to Grandma. I hate to think what might have happened if she hadn't had the foresight to plant that tracker in my neck. I'll never say a bad word about her again."

"Really?" Jack raised his eyebrows. "I'll believe that when I see it."

"One good thing came out of my ordeal at least."

"What's that?"

"It's made me more determined than ever to destroy Braxmore. I can't allow anyone or anything to hurt this family."

"Are you still planning on doing it this weekend?"

"Yes, while Florence is at Wonder World."

"Have you told your grandmother about your plans?"

"No."

"Don't you think you should?"

"No, this is my battle."

"There's no point in trying to be a martyr."

"That's not what I'm doing."

"Then tell your grandmother. She'll want to help."

"I'll think about it."

"Promise?"

"I promise."

Chapter 28

I'd slept like a log. I hadn't even heard Jack get up and have his shower. When I did eventually make it downstairs, he was alone in the kitchen.

"Where's Florence?"

"She's already had her breakfast. She's playing with Jay in her bedroom. How are you?"

"I'm fine."

"Are you sure? I was worried about you last night."

"Honestly, I'm okay. Those witch-finders actually did me a favour."

"How do you make that out?"

"I've become complacent recently. They made me realise how fragile life actually is. I won't let my guard down like that again."

"Have you thought any more about what I said about telling your grandmother that you intend to confront Braxmore this weekend?"

"Yeah, and you're right."

"Thank goodness you've seen sense. I wasn't sure you would."

"I'll nip up to the hotel before I go to work."

"Fancy a fry-up?"

"I'd love one." I gave him a kiss. "You're the best."

Feeling much better for having eaten Jack's world-famous fry-up, I gave him and Florence a kiss, and then made my way to the hotel. To my surprise, Grandma was seated behind the reception desk, and she didn't look happy.

"Good morning, Grandma."

"What's good about it?"

"How come you're on reception?"

"Because that useless lump, Brenda, called to say she was going to be late."

"Did she say why?"

"Her bus broke down, so she's waiting for another one."

"That's hardly her fault, is it?"

"It certainly isn't mine. Is there a purpose to this visit or did you just drop in to annoy me?"

"There's something I need to talk to you about."

"This is not one of those grandmother/granddaughter cosy talks, is it? I don't do cosy."

"You do surprise me. No, it isn't. This is really important."

"I'm so sorry, Ms Millbright," said a red-faced Brenda as she came running into reception.

"I expect my staff to be here on time," Grandma snapped.

"Sorry, the bus—"

"Excuses, excuses. I've heard them all before. Get behind this desk. I have important work that I should be doing."

"Sorry."

"Well?" Grandma said to me, as she started towards her office. "Let's get this over with."

"Take no notice of her," I whispered to Brenda. "She doesn't really mean it."

"Yes, I do." Grandma countered. "Are you coming or not?"

"You shouldn't have been so hard on Brenda," I said, once we were in her office.

"When I want your advice on how to run my hotel,

I'll—no wait, I'm never going to need your advice. So, what's this about?"

"Florence is going away with Kathy, Peter and the kids this weekend."

"Fascinating, I'm sure, but—"

"For once in your life, will you be quiet and listen?"

Almost as stunned by my outburst as I was, she took a seat at her desk and said nothing more.

"While Florence is away, I'm going to confront Braxmore once and for all."

Still keeping her own counsel, she waited for me to continue.

"I can't predict how it will go, so I—well, Jack, actually, thought it would be a good idea if I had you there as back up."

After another long silence, Grandma finally spoke, "May I speak now?"

"Sorry, I didn't mean to snap at you."

"Do you want me there with you?"

"I just said I did."

"What you said was that *Jim* thought it would be a good idea. My question is, do *you* want me there?"

"Yes."

"Are you sure?"

"Positive. If it hadn't been for you, I'd still be locked up, waiting to be burned."

"That's true."

"So, will you help?"

"Of course. What's your plan?"

"I—err—I don't actually have one."

"Give me strength. Are you telling me you intend to go up against Braxmore, possibly the evilest force known to man, and just wing it?"

"I'll have the compass stones."

"Big whoop. How are they going to help, exactly?"

"I don't actually know."

"Okay, let me make sure I've understood this correctly. You've just spent months collecting these compass stones, but you don't know how or if they're going to help. Is that right?"

"Martin told me that to breach Braxmore's defences, I'd need them."

"And?"

"That's it."

"But he didn't actually say how you were to use the stones?"

"No."

"Brilliant."

"I came here looking for your help, Grandma."

"And that's precisely what I'm trying to do. From what I've heard so far, your plan is to turn up on Braxmore's doorstep, carrying a handful of stones, in the hope that he sees them, and raises the white flag. Please tell me if I've got that wrong."

"Okay, so what should I do?"

"That's what we need to figure out. Sit down and I'll organise a drink for us."

"I'm supposed to be working this morning."

"Is that really more important than this?"

"No."

"Good." She picked up the phone. "Brenda, how about you try and redeem yourself by making Jill and me a nice cup of tea? And don't make it as milky as you did yesterday. Yes, in my office. Where did you think I wanted it?"

"I don't know how that young woman stands working for you."

"It'll be the making of her. Working alongside me builds character."

"Hmm."

"Why don't you start by telling me how you intend finding Braxmore?"

"According to Martin, he—"

"That brother of yours again? It seems all of this hinges upon information he has provided."

"It's all I have."

"Let's hope it turns out to be reliable. Carry on."

"Martin reckons Braxmore is hiding out in Sunville."

"That's that other world that Florence went to, isn't it? Do you know how to get there?"

"Yeah, Florence told me how to use the spell she devised."

"What happens once you're there? In Sunville."

"I'll find Braxmore."

"How?"

"I don't know."

"This gets better and better."

There was a knock at the door.

"Come in, Brenda."

"I didn't put too much milk in this time, Ms Millbright."

"I'll be the judge of that." She took a look at the tea. "That'll have to do, I suppose. Are you still here?"

"Sorry, Ms Millbright." She scuttled out of the room as quickly as she could.

Grandma took a sip of tea, then turned back to me. "Did I understand you correctly? Did you just say you didn't know how to find Braxmore?"

"I'll ask Ding Dong."

"Who?"

"He's a Bing Bong."

"If you're not going to take this seriously, I—"

"I *am* being serious. Ding Dong is from Sunville. I helped him get back there, so I figure he owes me a favour."

"And you know how to find this Ding Dong?"

"Of course," I lied.

"Okay, now we're getting somewhere. Carry on."

"Once I know where Braxmore is, I'll try to sneak up on him."

"What then?"

"I'll use the compass stones."

"How?"

"I'm not sure."

"Don't you think it might be an idea to find out?"

"How?"

"Your brother was the one who told you that you needed them, so how about you ask him?"

"Martin. Right, yeah, I'll do that. What if I can't get hold of him?"

"You have to."

When I'd agreed to ask for Grandma's help, I hadn't envisaged undergoing the third degree, but on reflection, it was just what I'd needed. Grandma was right. I hadn't thought any of this through, and I couldn't afford to try and wing it. The stakes were far too high for that. As I walked back to the house to get the car, I made a call to Martin, but as always, I got his voice mail.

"Martin, it's Jill. I'm planning to confront Braxmore this

weekend, but I need to talk to you first. Please call me back as soon as you get this message."

***

I'd spent more time with Grandma than I'd expected, so instead of going into the office, I drove straight to Cutter's house for a second, more thorough, search. Everyone I'd spoken to about Cutter had suggested that he had fallen on hard times recently, and yet, he clearly hadn't been tempted to sell any of his cowboy memorabilia. Although the pieces in the display cabinet were not to my taste, I suspected that they'd probably have raised a few quid. On my previous visit, I'd only made a cursory check through the various drawers and cupboards. This time, I emptied out each one in turn, going through everything in the hope that I might find something—anything, that might give me a clue as to his whereabouts.

In the bottom drawer of a rather dated sideboard, I found a pile of bills, which were a mix of household and business. Many of them were overdue and several were final demands. His money problems were much worse than I'd imagined, and once again, I wondered if it had all become too much for him. If so, had he done a runner? Or something much worse.

I spent most time in his spare bedroom, going through box after box of all-manner of stuff. Most of it was rubbish, but I did stumble across two photo albums. They contained photos taken when Cutter was a young boy. A few of them were of him alone, others were of him with his sister. Judging by their ages, the photos must have been taken before his mother died. Cutter's smile beamed from all of the photos; he had clearly been a happy child at that age. The most poignant of the photos was one of Cutter when he was about seven or eight, in which he was wearing a cowboy outfit and holding a toy gun. Clearly, his obsession with cowboys had started very early in his life.

Despite searching every nook and cranny of the house, I'd found nothing that might help me to locate Cutter. Having seen the pile of unpaid bills, I was beginning to think that he probably had decided to disappear. Before leaving the house, I took one final look in each of the downstairs rooms. It was then that something on the fridge freezer caught my eye. I'd seen it on my earlier visit, but I hadn't realised the significance of it at the time. Now, though, I saw it for what it was: the missing piece in the jigsaw puzzle.

That was the good news.

The bad news was that I was now almost certain that Cutter was dead.

Chapter 29

I had an appointment at one-thirty with Francesca Artichoke, at her house. Before that, I planned to grab a bite to eat and to drop into the office. I was bored of eating at the same old places, so decided to take a walk through town, to see if anything caught my eye.

I hadn't been walking for long when I spotted a new shop not far from Vinyl Alley. Called Sandwich Surprise, the shop's luminous orange and green décor was eye catching, to say the least. I approached the window, expecting to see a list of the sandwiches they had on offer, but there was none to be seen. As the shop was deserted of customers, I figured I might as well go inside.

The young man behind the counter was wearing a uniform, complete with baseball cap, in the same orange and green colours.

"Welcome to Sandwich Surprise. Would you like a regular, large or giant?"

I glanced at the wall behind him, expecting to find a menu of sandwiches, but there was nothing.

"What sandwiches do you have?"

"That would be telling." He grinned.

"Do you have egg and cress?"

"We might have. Then again, we might not."

What was wrong with this guy? Was he trying to lose a customer?

"How am I supposed to order anything if I don't know what you do?"

"This will explain." He handed me a leaflet, which I quickly skimmed.

"Are you telling me that I'm supposed to order a

sandwich without knowing what I'm going to get?"

"That's right. Hence the name: Sandwich *Surprise*."

"What if I don't like the sandwich you make for me?"

"In that unlikely event, we'll be more than happy to exchange your sandwich."

"For something I do like?"

"Hopefully."

The whole premise seemed ludicrous, but I decided to give it a go. Erring on the side of caution, though, I ordered a small sandwich.

"Drink?"

"Yes, please."

"What would you like?"

"Do I get to choose my drink?"

"Of course, otherwise you might end up with something you don't like."

"Right? I'll take a Diet Coke, please."

Moments later, he handed me my drink and a sandwich wrapped in orange and green greaseproof paper.

"Thanks. I think." I unwrapped the sandwich and was about to lift the bread to check the contents when he held up his hand.

"No! That will spoil the surprise. Take a bite."

Still not totally convinced, I took the smallest of bites.

"Mmm, that's good."

The young man beamed. "I told you, didn't I?"

The sandwich, which turned out to be turkey with stuffing and cranberry sauce, was delicious and I was tempted to go back for another, but then I remembered the motto by which I lived my life: Everything in moderation.

With my appetite at least partially sated, I drove to Little Biggly. The gates of Too Gusty began to open before I even had chance to press the intercom. Francesca, who was standing by the front door, had obviously seen my approach.

"Not in court today?" I said.

"I should have been, but my client jumped bail. Why don't we go inside, and you can bring me up to speed?"

"Sure."

After Francesca had served us both tea, I ran through my findings so far, such as they were.

"And you're sure my neighbours aren't behind this?"

"As sure as I can be. And the fact that this isn't an isolated incident makes that even less likely."

"I must admit I was rather surprised when you said that this has happened to other people. I wouldn't have believed there was a black market for chickens."

"Neither would I. In fact, I still don't."

"But you think the incidents are connected?"

"I'm sure they are. It's too much of a coincidence for this to have happened so many times in such a short period of time, and all in a thirty-mile radius."

"It's so weird." She took a sip of her tea.

"Everything about it is weird. Not least the fact that in each case, the only thing left behind was a number of tiny eggs."

"Are you able to tell me anything about the other people who had their chickens taken?"

"I don't see why not. I proceeded to tell her about Mrs Harvington-Smythe and the chickens she had kept on her allotment. Then I told her about Mase and his life-long affection for chickens.

"He sounds like a nice man," Francesca said.

"He is, and he's truly heartbroken. Don't get me wrong, I realise this incident has upset you too, but for him, the chickens were practically family. He actually had framed photographs of all of his chickens in his living room."

"How sweet." Francesca smiled. "Mind you, he isn't the only one to take photographs of his brood." She took out her phone, tapped at the screen and then handed it to me.

The gallery of photos were individual shots of her chickens, which she had obviously taken in her back garden.

"They're fine-looking birds," I said.

"I can't bear to look at them anymore. I find it too upsetting."

"Freddy!" I blurted out.

"Sorry?" Francesca was clearly surprised by my sudden outburst.

"This is Freddy." I nodded at the photo of the rooster.

"No, his name is Roger."

"Mase called his rooster Freddy."

"I see."

"I don't think you do. I'm saying this is Mase's rooster, Freddy."

"Now, I'm totally confused."

"Look at that thing on top of his head."

"The comb? What about it?"

"Do you see how it kind of droops to one side?"

"Yeah, I put that down to his age."

"Freddy's is identical. Do you remember who you bought your chickens from?"

"I still have the invoice."

"Could you get it for me, please?"

The invoice was from Feathers And More; the same people that Mase had purchased his chickens from.

"What is it, Jill?" Francesca asked.

"Just give me a minute." I called Mrs Harvington-Smythe.

Just as I suspected, she confirmed that she too had purchased her chickens from Feathers And More.

"What now?" Francesca had overheard my conversation.

"I think it's time I paid a visit to Feathers And More."

"Will you keep me posted?"

"Of course."

***

I'd just got back to my car when I got a call from Martin.

"Jill, I'm sorry I haven't got back to you before, but I've only just noticed your message. You said you're planning to go after Braxmore this weekend?"

"That's right, but I don't feel like I'm fully prepared."

"Is there something I can do to help? Would you like me to accompany you?"

"No, but I do need more information about the compass stones."

"What kind of information?"

"You were the one who told me that they'd weaken Braxmore's defences, but you didn't say how."

"I don't actually know."

"How did you even learn about the compass stones?"

"I spent ages finding out as much as I could about Braxmore. As part of that research, I read about Master

Klim."

"Who?"

"He's one of the elders here. He has spent a lifetime studying the dark forces of the sup world, including Braxmore. He was the one who identified the potential of the compass stones in defeating Braxmore."

"That's all fine and dandy, but what good are they to me if I don't know how to use them?"

"Point taken."

"Are you still in touch with this Master Klim guy?"

"Yes and no."

"What's that supposed to mean?"

"I know where he is, but the last I heard he was gravely ill and not expected to live much longer."

"He's dead?"

"I'm not sure."

"Can you find out? And quickly."

"Sure. I'll make some enquiries and I'll get back to you as soon as possible."

"Okay, but I'm going to Sunville on Saturday, come what may."

"Message received and understood."

I was annoyed with Martin, but I was even angrier with myself. Why hadn't I asked Martin for this information long ago? All I could do now was to keep my fingers crossed that Master Klim was still alive, and that he knew how to use the compass stones against Braxmore.

As soon as I'd finished on the call with Martin, I rang the number on the invoice for Feathers And More. It rang out for some considerable time, and I was expecting it to switch to voicemail, but then a man answered.

"Hello?"
"Is that Feathers And More?"
"Yes, how can I help?"
"I'm looking to buy some chickens."
"You've come to the right place. How many were you looking for?"
"I'm not sure. I was thinking of keeping them in my back garden."
"Is it a big garden?"
"Quite big, yes. I was thinking maybe twenty or so."
"That sounds about right."
"I'd like a rooster too."
"No problem."
"Would it be possible for me to come and see them before I make a decision?"
"Absolutely. I'm tied up for the rest of the day, but I'm free tomorrow afternoon."
"Excellent, I'll pop around then. What time?"
"Two o'clock?"
"That's fine."
He confirmed his address and we agreed we'd meet at his place the next day.
"Just one more thing," I said.
"Yes?"
"I didn't get your name."
"It's Solo. Marco Solo."
"Okay, Marco. I'm—err—Becky. I'll see you tomorrow."

***

I could tell something was amiss the moment I walked into the kitchen and saw Jack's expression.

"What's wrong?"

"It's nothing to worry about."

"Now, I'm really worried. Is Florence okay?"

"She's fine."

"What is it, then?"

"We have a bit of a tree problem."

"A tree—what are you talking about?"

"Take a look for yourself." He gestured to the garden.

I squeezed by him so that I could see through the open doors.

"What the—"

"I'm sure she didn't mean to do it."

The top half of the tree, which was the centrepiece of our garden, was now lying on the lawn. Fortunately, it had been far enough from the house that it hadn't fallen onto the building. To anyone else, it would have appeared that the tree had been brought down by a lightning strike from an electrical storm, but I knew better.

I turned on Jack. "What were you thinking?"

"Me? What did I do?"

"Why did you let her do it?"

"I had no idea she was going to do it until the tree came crashing down. I thought she was looking for worms."

"I'm going to have words with that little madam."

"Hold on." He put his hand on my shoulder. "She was pretty upset when it happened."

"But she was the one who did it."

"I know, but I honestly don't think she expected it to be so dramatic. All I'm saying, is take it easy on her."

"Okay."

I headed straight upstairs but then lingered outside her bedroom long enough to take a deep breath and compose myself. When I stepped inside, I found Florence sitting on her bed; she looked like she'd been crying.

Jay, who was sitting beside her, said, "Florence didn't mean to do it. Please don't be angry with her."

His words broke my heart. He might only be a jelly monster, but he was a real friend to my daughter.

"I'm not angry."

"I didn't mean it, Mummy," Florence said.

I took a seat next to her on the bed and put my arm around her. "Why don't you tell me what happened?"

"Great Grandma said I should practise the 'lightning bolt' spell as much as possible."

"I'm sure she meant you should do it when you're at CASS."

"I did, but I have lots of lessons there, so I don't have much time."

"So, you decided to practise in the garden?"

"Yeah, but I didn't mean to break the tree. I just thought it would burn a small hole in it, but then it came crashing down. Are you mad?"

"No, but you can't do it anymore. Someone might see you."

"Will the tree be okay?"

"I think so, but it might take a long time to grow again."

"Sorry."

"It's okay. Don't worry about it." I stood up. "I'll give you a shout when dinner is ready."

"How is she?" Jack asked.

"Okay. I think it just scared her."

"I'm not surprised. It scared me too."

"I can't believe she was able to slice the tree in half like that. The 'lightning bolt' spell isn't an easy one to perform, but for Florence to generate that amount of power blows my mind."

"Did you talk to your grandmother about Braxmore?"

"I did, and she said that you were right to make me do it."

"Your grandmother actually said *I* was right about something?"

"She did, but she still insisted on calling you Jim."

"I'll take that. What did she have to say?"

"She told me a few home truths."

"Such as?"

"Such as although I have the compass stones, I have no idea what to do with them. I've been in touch with Martin who will hopefully be able to find out more on that score." I sniffed the air. "Is that what I think it is?"

"If you're thinking steak and kidney pudding, then yes."

"Excellent."

Chapter 30

The next morning, Florence was on her best behaviour.

"Would you like some more cereal, Mummy?"

"No, thank you, darling."

"I'll put my bowl in the sink." She jumped down from the table.

Jack and I exchanged a look, but neither of us spoke.

"May I go up to my bedroom now?"

"You may."

As soon as we heard her bedroom door close, we both laughed.

"What was that all about?" Jack said.

"I think she's still feeling guilty about the tree."

"She never puts her bowl in the sink."

"Make the most of it. I doubt it will outlast the day."

"I have to say, you're looking much brighter this morning," he said.

"Against all the odds, I've made some progress on both of my cases. If things pan out the way I hope they do, I might be able to put them both to bed before the end of the day."

"That's great news. If you do, you'll be able to have a nice relaxing weekend."

"Except for the small matter of facing off with Braxmore, one of the evilest beings in the sup world."

"Oh yeah, sorry. I forgot about that for a minute."

"I wish I could."

After kissing Jack and Florence goodbye, I made my way out to the car, but before setting off, I gave Edna the surveillance fairy a call.

"Edna, it's Jill Maxwell. Could you spare me a minute sometime today?" The words were no sooner out of my mouth than she appeared on my shoulder. "I do wish you wouldn't do that."

"Stop complaining, woman. I assume you have a job for me?"

"I do, but I would need you to start immediately."

"That's not a problem. Provided, that is, that you are willing to pay the expedited engagement supplement."

"Which is?"

"Two packets of custard creams."

"Over and above your normal fee, I assume?"

"Of course."

"Okay, I agree, but I'll have to pay you later."

"Hmm, I'm not sure about that."

"Come on, Edna, you've dealt with me enough times by now to know that I'm good for them. And besides, I'm hardly likely to keep custard creams here in the car, am I?"

"I thought you never went anywhere without them. Okay, I'll allow it this once."

"Thanks." I took out a photograph and showed it to her. "This is the woman I want you to follow."

"Am I supposed to be watching for anything in particular?"

Once I had provided Edna with all the relevant information, she disappeared just as quickly as she'd appeared.

***

Armi was in the office with Mrs V.

"Hi, Armi, long time no see."

"I hope you don't mind me popping in to see Annabel."

"Of course not. I hear you might be going to Australia next year."

"Possibly, but I think Annabel might be getting cold feet."

"I never said that," Mrs V snapped. "I just pointed out that there are a lot of spiders there."

"I'll leave you two to it." I didn't want to get in the middle of the argument that seemed about to erupt.

As I walked into my office, I saw Winky push something under the sofa.

"What was that?"

"What was *what*?" he said, all innocent-like.

"The thing you pushed under the sofa."

"Nothing. I was just—err—hey, what are you doing?"

Ignoring his protests, I dropped down onto my knees and looked underneath the sofa where I found a small cardboard box.

"What are these?"

"They're not mine."

"Really? In that case, would you like to explain how a box of plastic spiders happened to get under here?"

"The old bag lady probably planted them there, to get me into trouble. She's vindictive like that."

"Or, just possibly, you planned to put these in Mrs V's office, to scare her silly."

"I don't know how you could even suggest such a thing."

I took the box over to the open window and emptied the contents onto the street below.

"Hey, I paid good money for those," Winky blurted out.

"I thought you didn't know anything about them."

"You've become a real killjoy; do you know that?"

Fifteen minutes later, when I left the office, Armi was nowhere to be seen.

"I hope you two haven't fallen out," I said.

"Of course not."

"So, you're not having second thoughts about Australia?"

"Of course I am, but that's beside the point."

"Right? I'm going to The Jewel Hotel. Then, this afternoon, I'm going to see a man about buying some chickens."

"I didn't realise you were thinking of keeping chickens at the Old Watermill."

"I'm not. I'll explain later."

"I hear they have a very strict dress code at The Jewel." She looked me up and down. "Just saying."

"It's okay. I'll get changed before I go there."

When I told Mrs V that I would be getting changed, I'd been telling the truth. What I hadn't told her, though, was that I would be changing into someone else altogether. Using recent photographs of Cutter, I used the 'doppelganger' spell to make myself look like him—minus the cowboy outfit. Once I was in position outside The Jewel, I waited to hear from Edna.

I didn't have long to wait because five minutes later she called.

"The target has just entered the restaurant."

"Okay, thanks."

I walked confidently into the hotel, through reception, and towards the restaurant. Sarah, dressed in another designer outfit, was seated close to the window. There were no more than a dozen people in there, so I had my choice of tables. I chose one close to the door, some distance away from Sarah, who was studying the menu. I too was holding a menu, just low enough so that I could see over the top of it. When she'd placed her order, I bided my time until she looked in my direction. Only then, did I lower the menu, so she could see my face.

Her face was a picture, as she stared at me, open-mouthed, in disbelief. While she was still staring at me (AKA Cutter), I cast the 'invisible' spell. That really freaked her out, and she looked frantically all around the restaurant. I gave her just enough time to convince herself that she'd been imagining things, and then I took a seat at a table on the other side of the restaurant. After reversing the 'invisible' spell, I waited until she spotted me again. It didn't take long. This time she closed her eyes and rubbed them, presumably in the hope that she was just having some kind of bad dream. But when she opened her eyes, I was still there, smiling at her.

Totally freaked out, she stood up, just as her breakfast arrived. Pushing the waiter to one side, she hurried out. Moments later, Edna called me.

"Something weird is going on," she said. "The target just rushed out of the restaurant like someone possessed."

"Really?" I hadn't bothered to tell Edna about my plans to turn myself into Cutter. "Stay with her and let me know where she goes."

"Okay, will do."

Once outside, I found a secluded spot and reversed the 'doppelganger' spell. Now all I had to do was to await Edna's call. While I waited, I treated myself to a strawberry smoothie from a shop, directly opposite the hotel, called Too Smooth For You. I'd only been there a few minutes when my phone rang. I assumed it would be Edna, but it turned out to be Martin.

"Jill, I have good news and bad news."

"I don't like the sound of that."

"Master Klim isn't dead."

"But—?"

"He's not long for this world. He's drifting in and out of consciousness."

"Did you manage to speak to him?"

"Just about, yes."

"And?"

"He managed to tell me the stones should be placed on the ground, according to their compass points. Then you have to stand inside of them."

"That's it?"

"That's what he said. I think."

"You aren't exactly filling me with confidence here."

"I'm sorry, but it took all of my time to get that much. Is there anything else I can do? Would you like me to come with you on Saturday?"

"No. I've asked Grandma to act as backup."

"Okay, be careful, Jill. I'll be thinking of you."

"Thanks, Martin."

I'd no sooner finished on the call than my phone rang again; this time it was Edna.

"How am I supposed to call you if you're gabbing to your friends all the time?"

"Sorry, it was an important call I had to take. What's happening?"

"My stomach is rumbling because I haven't eaten a

custard cream in ages."

"I meant what's happening with the subject."

"Oh her. She grabbed a taxi when she left the hotel."

"She didn't take her own car?"

"I think I know the difference between her car and a taxi."

"Sorry. Where did she go?"

"He dropped her off in the back end of nowhere."

"Is he waiting for her?"

"No, she paid him and he left."

After Edna had provided me with her location, I magicked myself straight over there. So quickly, in fact, that I made her jump.

"Did you have to do that?" she said, visibly shaken.

"Now you know how I feel when you do it to me." We were standing on a narrow country road with woods bordering either side of the road. "Where is she?"

"About twenty yards in that direction."

"Can you lead the way?"

"I've only just got all the twigs and leaves out of my hair."

"Please?"

"Okay, but you're going to owe me so many custard creams."

"That's fine. Just get going."

Edna flew ahead as best she could through the dense foliage. It took me all of my time just to keep up with her. After a few minutes, she stopped, put a finger to her lips, and nodded to a spot ahead of her. At first, I couldn't see anything, but then I saw a shape moving around.

I gave Edna the thumb's up and mouthed the words, "You can leave me to it now."

She didn't need telling twice and quickly disappeared.

As silently as I could, I made my way through the undergrowth. When I reached Sarah, she was on her hands and knees with her back to me.

"I assume that's where you buried Cutter," I said.

In her effort to turn around, she stumbled onto her backside, and stared at me in disbelief. "I don't know what you're talking about."

"The game is up, Sarah. The police are already on their way, so you'd better get your story straight."

"It was an accident."

"Really? You accidentally killed Cutter, drove his body out here to the middle of nowhere, dragged it through the wood, and buried him. Is that really the story you're going with?"

"You don't understand."

"I understand more than you might realise. I know that Cutter's numbers came up on the lottery. Unfortunately for you, you'd already broken up with him by then, hadn't you? I'm guessing you realised he'd won because he kept a sheet of paper with his regular numbers on, stuck to his fridge. The rest, I can only speculate. Did you ask him to take you back, so you could get your hands on some of the money?"

"I—err—"

"Did he tell you to sling your hook? I'm guessing he did. Cutter probably realised with that kind of money he wouldn't have any shortage of female admirers. I can't imagine you took that very well. Is that when you killed him?"

"It wasn't like that."

"How was it, then?"

"He and I came out here for a picnic once, when we were still an item."

"This place?" I glanced around. "I find that hard to believe."

"It's true. On the other side of the road, about fifty yards into the wood, there's a clearing with a pond."

"But the two of you didn't come out here for a picnic that last time, did you? In fact, you'd already finished with him by then, hadn't you?"

"I thought coming back here might get him to change his mind about us."

"But he saw straight through you, didn't he? Cutter realised you just wanted him back so you could get your hands on his money. That's why you killed him."

"I didn't mean to do it." She began to cry. "He wouldn't listen to me. He laughed at me and waved his winning ticket in my face."

"So, you killed him?"

"I've already told you it was an accident. I got angry, yes. I pushed him and he tripped and hit his head on a log. When he didn't get up, I thought he was messing about, but then when I checked his pulse—" She looked down at her feet and mumbled, "I didn't mean to do it."

"If it was an accident, why didn't you call the police?"

"I was scared."

"Not too scared to take his lottery ticket and claim the winnings, though?"

She didn't get the chance to answer because we were interrupted by the sound of sirens. Having resigned herself to her fate, Sarah didn't resist when I led her back to the road and handed her to one of the two uniformed officers.

"What's the story, Maxwell?" Big Mac said.

"I'll show you."

I took him back to the spot where I'd found Sarah.

"You'll find a man called Lorne Mower buried under there."

"*Lorne Mower*? This had better not be some kind of wind up."

"If you check your records, you'll find he was reported missing recently. His nickname was Cutter."

"And the woman?"

"Her name is Sarah. She was in a relationship with Cutter, but she ended it not long before he won the jackpot on the lottery. When she realised that he'd won, she tried to get back with him."

"I'm guessing he wasn't interested."

"Can you blame him? She says she didn't mean to kill him, but she had no problem taking the lottery ticket and claiming the winnings for herself."

"Nice lady."

"Can I leave it with you? There's somewhere I need to be."

"For now. I'll be in touch if I need you."

"Okay." I started back towards the road, but then I hesitated and said, "Sorry?"

"I didn't say anything."

"My mistake. I thought I heard you say *thank you.*"

"Don't push your luck, Maxwell."

As soon as I got the opportunity, I called Sam Rich.

"Sam, it's Jill."

"Any news?"

"Yes, but it isn't good I'm afraid. Cutter is dead; he was

murdered by his ex-girlfriend, Sarah. She has just been arrested."

"But why?"

I told him about Cutter's lottery win, and how Sarah had killed him when he'd refused to take her back.

"And she actually had the nerve to claim the money for herself?"

"Yeah."

"I hope they lock her up and throw away the key."

"I'm sorry it wasn't a better outcome."

"Me too, still I'm glad you uncovered the truth. Painful as this is, it would have been even worse never to know what happened to him. You'll let me have your bill, I assume?"

"I will."

Chapter 31

Feeling quite pleased with my morning's work, I grabbed a sandwich and then headed to Feathers And More. I was pretty sure I'd figured out the scam he was running. If I was right, it meant that Marco Solo would turn out to be a wizard, so I cast a spell that would block him from sensing I was also a sup. I had no reason to believe that Solo would recognise me, but on the off chance that he was a Jill Maxwell fanboy, I changed my appearance so that I looked like Kathy.

What? Of course I have fanboys. You can't be the most powerful witch in Candlefield without attracting a certain following.

When I arrived at the address that he'd given me, I wasn't totally sure it was the right place because it turned out to be a small farm, called Breezy Brook. I pulled into the driveway. Before I'd even had the chance to get out of the car, the door of the farmhouse opened, and a man wearing blue dungarees over a checked shirt stepped out. As soon as he appeared, I sensed that he was a wizard, just as I'd suspected.

"You must be Becky," he said as he strode towards me.

It was just as well he'd called me Becky because I'd totally forgotten what name I'd given him during our telephone conversation.

"Marco?"

"That's me, but everyone calls me Polo."

"After the explorer."

"Sorry?"

"I assume they call you Polo after the explorer?"

"No, it's because I'm addicted to these." He took a

packet of Polo mints out of his pocket. "Would you like one?"

"No, thanks."

"You said on the phone that you might be interested in buying some chickens."

"That's right. I'm fed up with bland supermarket eggs. I like the idea of collecting them from my own hens each morning."

"Good call."

"I didn't see a sign for Feathers And More when I drove in just now."

"Feathers And More is really just a sideline for us. This is a working farm." He spread his arms wide. "All the land you see is ours."

"That must keep you busy."

"It does. Unfortunately, it isn't very profitable. That's why we've been forced to look for other ways to boost our income. Feathers And More was Judy's idea—Judy is my wife. She was convinced that there were people out there who would like to have their own chickens. I wasn't sure at first, but it turned out that she was right. Shall we go around the back and take a look at them?"

"Yes, please."

Parked in the yard, behind the farmhouse were two tractors, one of which looked like it hadn't moved off that spot in several years.

"The chickens are in there." He pointed to the smaller of two barns.

Even before he pulled open the door, I could hear the sound of clucking. Once inside, he stepped to one side and asked, "What do you think?"

"There aren't as many as I expected. I thought you'd

have hundreds of them."

"I try to keep the numbers to manageable levels. I find the birds thrive better that way."

I'm not a big fan of chickens, but I did my best to look and sound enthusiastic.

"They certainly look healthy enough."

"You won't find healthier birds anywhere in Washbridge."

"What kind of yield can I expect?"

"It will vary from hen to hen and the time of year, but it's quite possible to average four to five eggs per hen per week."

"Excellent."

I glanced around. "Is that rooster over there okay?"

"He's fine. Why do you ask?"

"That thing on the top of his head is a bit wonky."

"The comb? That's nothing to worry about."

"What's his name?"

"I don't give any of the animals on the farm a name."

"He looks like a Roger to me. Or maybe a Freddy."

"Right? Well, if you decide to buy him, you'll be able to call him whatever you like."

"How quickly could you deliver them?"

"How many would you want?"

"I think I'd like to take them all. I have a lot of friends who I'm sure would be delighted to get fresh eggs from me."

"In that case, I can probably get them to you this weekend."

"And how soon afterwards will you take them back again?"

"Sorry, I don't follow."

"After you've sold the chickens to me, how long is it before you steal them and bring them back here?"

"Why would I do that?"

"So that you can sell them to another unsuspecting punter, I assume."

"Where is this coming from? Who are you?"

"My name isn't Becky. It's Jill Maxwell."

"I don't care what your name is. I think you'd better leave."

"I'm afraid I can't do that."

"Why not?"

"I was hired by a customer of yours. A lady by the name of Francesca Artichoke. Do you remember her?"

"Of course. She was delighted with the birds she bought from me."

"You're right, she was, but then you stole them."

"That's nonsense. How am I supposed to have stolen chickens from her backyard?"

"That had me puzzled too for a while, but once I realised you were a wizard, I figured that you must have shrunk the birds. That would have made it simple to take them away. You might have got away with it too if it hadn't been for the tiny eggs that the birds laid as you were removing them."

"Are you a sup?"

"I am indeed. Sorry for the subterfuge."

"You can't prove any of this."

"I think the photos of the rooster taken by two of your customers is pretty compelling evidence. Still, we can let the rogue retrievers decide that."

"Wait! There's no need to involve them. I only did this because I was finding it hard to make ends meet."

"That's as maybe, but you can't cheat other people just because you're having a hard time."

"You're right and I'm sorry. Please don't call in the rogue retrievers. My family and I are settled here in the human world."

"I might be persuaded not to involve them, but I'm going to need you to return the chickens to their rightful owner."

"Okay, but which of the customers shall I return them to?"

"That's a good point. There are at least four people with a claim on the chickens that I'm aware of. Were there others?"

"No, just those, I promise."

"Here's what we're going to do. I'll give you a call and let you know who to return the chickens to, and then you're going to refund the payments to the others. Okay?"

"If I do that, do you promise not to tell the rogue retrievers?"

"You have my word."

***

The first thing I did after I'd left Feathers And More was to call Francesca Artichoke.

"Jill? You're lucky to catch me. The judge has just adjourned the trial for the day. Did you pay a visit to Feathers And More?"

"I did, and I think you'll be interested in what I discovered."

"Have you found my chickens?"

"I have."

"Are they okay?"

"They're fine. Where are you now?"

"I was just about to grab a coffee and then drive home."

"How about I join you for a coffee and I can tell you everything."

"Okay. Do you know The Scales? It's on Court Street."

"I'll find it. I'll be with you in five."

In fact, with the aid of magic, I was with her a couple of minutes later.

"That was quick," Francesca said.

"I was just down the road."

"Have you been in here before, Jill?"

"No."

"I should warn you that it's a little quirky."

She wasn't kidding: The shop was set out like the interior of a courtroom, and all of the baristas were dressed as *barristers*, complete with wigs and robes. When I ordered a coffee, the man behind the counter insisted I repeat after him: *I declare and affirm that I will drink all the coffee, and nothing but the coffee.*

"This place is insane," I said, once Francesca and I had found a seat in the jury box.

"I did warn you. It's proven to be a big hit with many of my colleagues, which is kind of weird when you think about it. We spend most of our time in court, then come in here to relax. But enough of that. Tell me about the chickens."

"As I suspected, your chickens are currently residing at Feathers And More."

"I don't understand. Are you saying that Solo guy somehow stole them back?"

"That's exactly what I'm saying. And he didn't just do it

once. I know of at least three other people who bought the same chickens from him, only to have them 'disappear'."

"That's outrageous, but how on earth did he manage to steal them without anyone seeing him?"

"I honestly have no idea," I lied.

"The man needs locking up."

"Normally, I'd agree, but—"

"But *what*?" She snapped. "The man is a crook."

"You're right, but the only people who will be hurt by sending him to prison are his family."

I explained to Francesca that Marco Solo was actually a farmer who had started the business because he had been struggling to make ends meet.

"That's still no excuse for cheating people out of their money, Jill."

"You're right and he knows that. He's agreed to wind up the Feathers And More business and to refund all those who purchased chickens from him."

"That's something, I suppose. What about the chickens?"

"He's happy to return them, but of course, there is only one set of chickens and several disappointed customers. As you're my client, I intend telling him that they should be returned to you."

"Hang on. What about the guy you told me about? The one who had framed photos of all the chickens?"

"Mase? He'll be disappointed I'm sure, but at least he—"

"Let him have them."

"Sorry?"

"Tell Solo to return the chickens to Mase."

"Are you sure?"

"Absolutely. I still have my goats, sheep and pigs. From what you told me, those chickens were his life."

"That's true."

"Okay, it's decided, then. Solo can give me a refund, return the chickens to Mase, and we'll say no more about it."

"That's very generous of you."

"And you'll let me have your bill in due course, I assume?"

"I will. Thanks."

With that unselfish gesture, Francesca Artichoke had gone some way to restoring my faith in human nature. As soon as I left the coffee shop, I called Polo and told him that the chickens should be returned to Mase. All that remained now was for me to deliver the good news.

"Is that Mase?"

"Speaking. Who's this?"

"It's Jill Maxwell. I came to see you about—"

"I remember. Did you have any luck finding your client's chickens?"

"I did, as it happens."

"Good for them. I wish I could afford to pay you to do the same for me."

"You don't need to. You're going to get them back anyway."

"Sorry, I don't understand."

"Unfortunately, I'm not at liberty to go into all the details, but what I can tell you is that Freddy and the hens will be back with you, probably as early as tomorrow."

"I don't know what to say." The words caught in his throat as though he was about to burst into tears. "Thank you. This means so much to me."

***

"It sounds like you had a good day," Jack said after I'd finished telling him about my two cases.

"The best. It isn't every day that everything comes together like it did today. Mase was so happy when I told him he was going to get his chickens back. It was as if he'd won the lottery."

"Talking of which, who stands to get the money from Cutter's winning ticket?"

"I think it will go to his sister, Anita, but it will probably take a long time to sort out."

"Not a bad windfall for her."

"True, but I'm sure she'd rather have her brother back."

Chapter 32

"Daddy said you're going to jump out of an aeroplane," Florence said, in between mouthfuls of muesli.

"Daddy is wrong. I definitely won't be jumping out of any planes. Ever."

Florence considered this and then said, "I don't think I'd like to jump out of an aeroplane. It would be cold."

"That's true."

After Florence had finished her breakfast and gone outside to play on the half tree that was still lying in the garden, I confronted Jack.

"Why did you tell her I was going to jump out of a plane?"

"I didn't want to tell her that Winky was the one doing the parachute jump in case she decided to tell everyone at school."

"Fair enough."

"You're still going through with this insanity, I assume?"

"I don't really have any choice. I promised Winky I would take him, and he's collected a ton of sponsors."

"How many cats will be doing the jump?"

"Winky and a couple more, I believe."

"What happens if someone sees them?"

"It won't matter if they do. They'll just think it's raining cats and dogs."

"That's terrible."

"You're just jealous of my comic genius."

***

"Why do I have to go in that horrible basket?" Winky moaned.

"Because I say so."

"It smells."

"The only thing it smells of is you. Either you get in or I don't take you to the parachute jump."

"So degrading." Somewhat reluctantly, he crept into the cat basket.

"Off out, Jill?" Mrs V eyed the cat basket. "He's not ill, I hope."

"No, he's fine. I promised I'd take him to see Florence for a few hours."

"Are you sure? You never know what might be living in that fur of his."

"It'll be fine. I might not be back until after you've left. If so, have a good weekend."

"You too, dear."

"Did you hear that?" Winky said, as I walked to the car park.

"Hear what?"

"She said: *I hope he's not ill.*"

"What's wrong with that?"

"It was the way she said it. She obviously hopes I am ill. She's probably got her fingers crossed that that's the last she's seen of me."

"That's rich coming from you."

"And how dare she insinuate that I have fleas? Goodness knows what's lurking in that wig of hers."

"Okay, that's enough. I don't want to have to listen to this all the way to the airstrip."

"Can I at least get out of this basket in the car?"

"If you promise to sit in the back seat and not distract

me."

"Okay, deal."

We'd been driving for about an hour when I snapped, "What did I say about not distracting me?"

"Sheesh, I was only trying to play I-Spy."

"Well don't."

"Can I sing?"

"Definitely not."

He spent the rest of the journey sulking, but at least he remained quiet.

"I assume this is the place," I said.

"What gave it away? Was it the planes?"

"No need to be a smart Alec."

I parked the car next to a hangar, standing outside of which were half a dozen cats.

"That's Bernie!" Winky waved excitedly. "And that's Tommy. Come on. Let me out."

"Have some patience, will you?" I got out of the car and opened the back door for his highness.

So eager was he to join his friends, he leapt out, but then pulled up.

"Ouch!" He began to hobble.

"What have you done?"

"It's nothing." He tried to walk, but it was obvious that he couldn't put any weight on his front paw.

"Winky, what have you done?"

"I turned my paw when I landed."

"That's it, then. You can't jump like that."

"I have to. I can't let down the Abandoned Kittens Shelter."

"They'll understand."

"I'm doing it." He tried again to walk but couldn't manage more than a couple of steps.

"You're not doing it and that's final. It would be suicide."

"You'll have to do it for me, then."

"Me? Are you insane?"

"We can't let down the abandoned kittens."

"*We*? Since when did I have any part in it?"

"Look." He took out his phone and showed me a photograph of several of the most pathetic looking kittens I'd ever seen. "Are you really going to let them down?"

"That's emotional blackmail."

"Is it working?"

"People have sponsored you, not me."

"That's okay. You can change yourself into me. No one will be any the wiser."

"Let me get this straight. You want me to change myself into you, then throw myself out of a plane, with only a bit of fabric tied to my back."

"You're the best. Haven't I always said so?"

Winky struggled back into the car and hid on the back seat. Meanwhile, muggins here turned myself into him and headed towards the hangar. If confirmation was ever needed that I was insane, this was surely it.

"Hi, Winky!" the cat Winky had earlier identified as Bernie, shouted to me.

"Hi there."

"Ready for this?"

Not really. "As ready as I'll ever be."

"You'll be okay, buddy," said the other cat, called Tommy. "I hear there's only a fifty percent chance that the 'chute doesn't open." He laughed.

"Great."

"Did that two-legged of yours bring you down here this morning?" Bernie asked.

"Yeah."

"Is she really as bad as you said? She sounds like a nightmare."

"Jill? No, she's okay. In fact, she's one of the best."

"That's not what you said last time we saw you," Tommy said.

Before I could respond, the pilot, a wizard called Alfie, called us over to the plane.

"Everyone ready?"

Tommy and Bernie nodded enthusiastically.

The next few minutes are something of a blur. The next thing I remember is looking out of the window of the aircraft and thinking how tiny my car looked on the ground below. Surely, we weren't supposed to be this high up.

"Okay, guys, this is it," Alfie said.

Tommy pulled open the door, turned back to us, and said, "See you down below."

With that, he threw himself out of the aircraft.

"You next, Winky." Bernie nudged me towards the door.

"No, after you."

"Don't be daft. Off you go." He gave me a gentle shove and the next thing I knew I was plunging towards the earth.

In the couple of minutes I'd had with Winky before heading to the plane, he'd just had time to show me how to pull the rip cord. Doing it while I still had my feet on the ground was one thing; trying to do it while spinning through the air was quite another. What if it didn't open? Would I have time to use magic to stop my fall?

I pulled the cord.

Phew! The parachute had opened, and I was now drifting slowly towards the earth. My relief at avoiding certain death was short-lived as I realised that I had no idea how to steer the stupid thing. Below me, Tommy was waving frantically. Winky had said something about using the toggles to steer, but I had no clue what I was supposed to do with them, so I drifted further and further away from the airfield.

In a scene reminiscent of Peter's parachute jump, I found myself headed towards a field full of haystacks. If I could manage to land on one of those, it should at least break my fall.

Missed!

I overshot the haystack by several feet and landed with a thump on the ground. Remarkably, I didn't appear to have broken any bones, but I was covered by the canopy. While I was still trying to fight my way out, I heard approaching voices.

"Winky, are you okay?" Tommy said.

Bernie pulled the canopy off me. "He's okay."

"Thank goodness. Why didn't you steer?"

"I think the parachute must have been faulty."

"Are you okay?"

"A bit bruised, but yeah, I'm okay."

After saying my goodbyes to Bernie and Tommy, I made my way back to the car.

"What do you call that?" Winky said. "Why didn't you steer it like I told you?"

"I don't know how you've got the brass neck to criticise after I just risked life and limb to help you." I reversed the spell and transformed back into myself. "I'm covered in bruises."

"Sorry, I really do appreciate what you did. And the abandoned kittens definitely do."

"Let's go home. I'm going to need a long soak in a hot bath."

First, though, I had to take Winky back to the office. As soon as I let him out of the basket, he jumped onto the sofa.

"What happened to your injured paw?"

"I—err—it's still really painful." He pulled a pained expression.

"Were you faking that injury all along, just to get me to do the parachute jump?"

"How can you suggest such a thing? I'm gutted that I couldn't do the jump."

"I don't believe you. You chickened out, didn't you?"

"No, I didn't. I'm injured. If there had been any way that I could have done the jump, I would have. I wouldn't lie to you."

"Hmm. And another thing, how come you told your two friends I was a nightmare?"

"My paw is throbbing again. I think I need to get some sleep."

"You haven't heard the last of this."

***

"I'm glad you find it so funny," I snapped at Jack who

was doubled over with laughter.

"Come on, Jill. Even you have to admit it's hilarious."

"I could have been killed."

"Did they take any photos?"

"Is that all you can think about?"

"I'd just love to see you, as Winky, floating down to earth on a parachute."

"Crashing down to earth, more like."

Florence came charging into the kitchen; she'd been keeping watch through the front window.

"Auntie Kathy is here!"

Jack gave her a kiss. "Don't be upset while you're away from home. You'll soon be back with Mummy and Daddy."

"I'll get it." Florence rushed to open the door before Kathy even had a chance to knock (not that she ever did).

"Someone's excited," Kathy said.

"Mummy turned into a cat and jumped out of a plane," Florence blurted out. "Can I go and get in the car?"

"Sure. Take your bag and go and sit next to Lizzie. I'll be there in a minute." Kathy turned to me. "Turned into a cat? Jumped out of a plane?"

"Kids." I laughed. "What imagination they have."

"She seems excited about this weekend."

"She certainly is," Jack said. "She's been counting down the days."

"Don't worry about her because she's going to have the time of her life."

"Thanks for doing this, Kathy."

"No problem. And you two, don't go wearing yourselves out this weekend." She gave us what I assumed to be a knowing wink, and then went on her way.

Chapter 33

It was Saturday morning. Neither Jack nor I had been able to face breakfast, and we'd barely spoken a dozen words to one another.

"What time did your grandmother say she'd come over?"

"First thing. I'm surprised she isn't here already."

"In that case, I'd better make myself scarce." He came around the table and gave me a kiss. "Be careful."

"I will. Don't worry about me."

"Easier said than done. I think I'll go for a walk until it's all over."

As he left the house, I couldn't help but wonder if that might be the last time that I'd ever see him. Although I'd tried to put on a brave face and appear blasé about the whole thing, I was really nervous. More than nervous—I was scared of what lay ahead. Since I'd discovered I was a witch, I'd come up against many adversaries, and I'd always managed to prevail, but Braxmore was next level. What if he was more than a match for me, even with the compass stones? What would happen to Florence if I failed to defeat him? That's what scared me more than anything else.

"I thought you'd have a cup of tea waiting for me." Grandma appeared in the kitchen doorway.

"I couldn't face anything to eat or drink this morning."

"I've just had a delicious sausage cob. Where's Jim?"

"Jack has gone for a walk."

"Does he know what you're going to be doing today?"

"No. You and Martin are the only people who know."

"Talking of whom, where is that useless brother of

yours? Left you to do it all by yourself, has he?"

"He wanted to help, but I wouldn't let him. And besides, I'm not alone. I have you to back me up."

"We might as well get this thing over with. Have you got those stones?"

"They're in my pocket."

"And do you know what you're supposed to do with them?"

"I think so."

"You *think* so? That doesn't exactly fill me with confidence."

"Master Klim told Martin how to use them."

"Klim? Is he still alive? I thought he died centuries ago. Come on, then. Let's do this."

I led the way up to Florence's bedroom.

"Why are we in here?" Grandma said.

"So I can call up the gateway to Sunville."

"Couldn't you have done it downstairs?"

"No—maybe—I'm not sure. Anyway, we're here now." I took out the notepaper on which I'd written down the complex spell, which Florence had used to conjure up the circle of mist.

Looking over my shoulder, Grandma asked, "What's that?"

"It's the spell to call up the gateway."

"It looks complicated."

"It is. Florence devised it all by herself."

"She's a chip off the old block, that one. Go on, then, crack on."

Probably because Grandma was making me nervous, I managed to screw up my first attempt at the spell.

"Are you sure you wrote it down correctly?" she

snapped.

"Yes, I'm sure. Just be quiet and let me concentrate."

My second attempt succeeded in calling up the circle of mist.

"I'll go first, Grandma, then you follow."

"Okay."

I stepped through the circle and found myself in what I assumed was Sunville. I wasn't sure what I'd been expecting, but it looked just like one of the country lanes to be found around Middle Tweaking. There was not one, but three suns in the blue sky, which probably accounted for why it was so hot. I turned around, expecting to see Grandma behind me, but there was no sign of her.

"I can't get through!" Grandma's voice echoed from somewhere behind me.

"What do you mean?"

"I mean when I try to get through the mist circle, something is forcing me back."

"What is it?"

"My guess would be Braxmore. Come back here until we work it out."

"No, I have to go on."

"You can't do it by yourself."

"I have to. I might never get another chance. Keep trying to get through."

"Where will you be?"

"I'm not sure. I'm going to follow this road and see where it takes me."

"Be careful."

"I will."

I'd been walking for almost fifteen minutes and hadn't seen another soul, but then a familiar little creature, which resembled a cross between a gerbil and a kangaroo, came bounding across the road in front of me.

"Hey, Ding Dong, wait!"

The creature stopped dead in his tracks and looked at me with a puzzled expression.

"Who are you?" he said.

"Don't you remember? I'm Jill. I helped you get back here after you slipped into our world."

"I think you may have the wrong Bing Bong. What did you call me?"

"Ding Dong. DD."

"That explains it. I'm Ting Tong or TT for short."

"Do you know DD?"

"Everyone knows DD. He's something of a celebrity since he got sucked into your world. Is it true that he was presented to your king?"

"I—err—"

"He says he was the guest of honour."

"Right. You wouldn't happen to know where I can find DD, would you?"

"I can take you to him if you like."

"I wouldn't want to take you out of your way."

"It's not a problem. I was just headed back there anyway."

"Great. Lead the way, then."

It turns out that Bing Bongs are pretty fast on their feet, so I was forced to run to keep up with him. He led the way through a dark wood and, a couple of times, I almost lost sight of him. Eventually, though, we arrived at a clearing in which was a small village made up of straw houses. The village was bustling with Bing Bongs rushing this way and that, but they all stopped when I appeared.

"This is Jill," Ting Tong announced. "Does anyone know where DD is?"

"I'm here."

The crowd of Bing Bongs divided to allow DD to come to the front.

"Jill, what brings you here?"

Before I could reply, Ting Tong chipped in, "I was just telling Jill about your stories of meeting the king of her world."

"Err, yeah—I—err."

DD looked like a rabbit caught in the headlights.

"The king still talks of him," I said, coming to his rescue.

Relieved, DD said, "Why don't you come with me, Jill, then you can tell me why you're here?" He led the way to one of the straw houses. Once inside, he said, "Thanks for not ratting on me."

"Why did you tell them you'd met the king of my world?"

"No one took much notice of me before. I figured if they thought I'd done something special that they might see me differently."

"It seems to have worked."

"You won't tell them it's a lie, will you?"

"Your secret is safe with me."

"Thanks. So, what are you doing here?"

I told him about Braxmore, the compass stones, and my mission to defeat the tyrant once and for all.

"He sounds like a terrible person. Why would anyone want to hurt an innocent child like Florence?"

"He derives his power by absorbing the power of others, and Florence is already one of the most powerful witches the world has ever known."

"But she's so young." DD shook his head. "What makes you think Braxmore is here in Sunville?"

"My brother, Martin, has been keeping tabs on him while I gathered the compass stones. It was Martin who told me he was here. I was kind of hoping that you might have some idea of where I could find him."

"I wish I could, but I have no clue."

"That's a blow."

"Mind you." He hesitated.

"What?"

"No one has seen the king for several weeks."

"Is that unusual?"

"Very. He usually makes an appearance at least once a week. Rumour has it that he might be ill. Unless—"

"Unless someone is preventing him from doing so."

"You don't think this Braxmore guy might have done something to the king, do you?"

"I hope not, but I wouldn't put anything past him. Where does your king live, DD?"

"In Sunville Castle. It's about an hour's walk from here."

"Would you take me there?"

"Of course. I'll gather together all the Bing Bongs of fighting age, and we'll go with you."

"No."

"Why not? If our king is in danger, we have to help him."

"That's very noble, but Braxmore would destroy all of you before you had the chance to get close to him. This is something I have to do alone."

"I don't like it."

"I'll be fine, I promise. Now, will you show me where

the castle is?"

"Of course."

Just like Ting Tong, DD moved at pace.

"DD, slow down. I can't keep up."

"Sorry, Jill, we Bing Bongs are used to rushing everywhere. We're almost there now."

A few minutes later, we came to a rickety-looking bridge across a raging river.

"That's the castle up there." DD pointed to a magnificent building perched upon the hill on the other side of the river. "I should warn you, it's a steep climb."

"I can see that. Are you sure this bridge is safe?"

"It's safe enough for Bing Bongs, but I'm not sure whether it will take your weight."

Cheek!

"Actually, you can leave me here," I said.

"No, I'll take you all the way."

"It's not necessary, honestly."

"Okay, but be careful."

"I'll be fine."

"Will you drop by the village on your way back to let us know if the king is okay?"

"Of course."

I waited until DD had left, and then took a shortcut to the castle, courtesy of magic. Up close, the castle was even more impressive than it had appeared from down in the valley. I expected to have to use magic to gain entry, but to my surprise, the two huge doors were wide open. It was almost as though someone was expecting me.

That wasn't good.

Tentatively, I stepped into a colossal hall. There was no

sign of life and no sounds other than my own footsteps as they echoed around the stone walls. There were three staircases, one directly in front of me, and one to either side. Why would the king's residence be unguarded, and the doors wide open?

I was still wondering what to do next when a figure appeared at the top of the staircase to my right. The man was very tall, at least seven feet, and dressed from head to toe in black.

"How very good to meet you at last, Jill. I've been looking forward to this moment for such a long time." The smile on his face was scarier than anything I'd ever seen.

I reached into my pocket, took out the compass stones, and placed them on the stone floor around me, as per Master Klim's instructions.

For such a huge man, he seemed to glide down the staircase, and was soon standing opposite me.

"This ends here, Braxmore," I said. "Your reign of evil is over."

"How very cute." He laughed uproariously. "You almost sound like you believe that. Tell me, how is that beautiful daughter of yours?"

"Don't you dare—"

"Her name is Florence, isn't it? Much as I've enjoyed meeting you, I'm looking forward to getting acquainted with her even more."

"Shut up! You don't get to say her name."

"This is so disappointing. I thought we might at least have an interesting conversation before I killed you, but you're boring me already."

He raised his hand so quickly that I didn't have time to react before he'd fired a lightning bolt at me. What an idiot I was. I'd allowed my anger to get in the way of my judgement, and now it was too late. I braced myself for the inevitable, but the fatal impact never came. Instead, the lightning bolt exploded a few feet in front of me. Incredibly, but much to my relief, the compass stones had done their job and put up an invisible shield around me.

"What?" Braxmore stared at me in disbelief.

"No one threatens my daughter," I screamed at him, and then mustered all my power to unleash the most powerful lightning bolt I had ever fired.

It hit him smack bang in the centre of his chest, sending him stumbling backwards. He screamed in agony, dropped to his knees and then fell forwards. Before I could go and check if he was still alive, his body began to glow and then he combusted before my eyes. It was over; I had rid the world of Braxmore, but more importantly I had removed the threat that had hung over my family for so long.

"Very impressive." The voice, which was accompanied by the sound of applause, came from behind me.

I spun around to see a fat, diminutive figure walking down the last few steps of the central staircase.

"Who are you?" I said. "Are you the king?"

"The king?" He laughed. "No, I'm not the king. His majesty is a little under the weather, I'm afraid. He's been prescribed bedrest."

"Who are you, then?"

"I rather fancy that I'm the person you came to see."

"I don't understand."

"Come on, Jill, I gave you far more credit than that. Why don't you have a little think and see if you can work it out."

"You're Braxmore?"

"There you are. That wasn't so difficult, was it?"

"Then who's—" I glanced back at the glowing embers, which were all that remained of the man I had assumed to be Braxmore.

"Don't worry your head about him. He was just something I conjured up for my own amusement. I have to say that I didn't think you'd fall for it so easily."

"Don't come any closer."

"Or what? You'll fire a lightning bolt at me?" He scoffed. "Correct me if I'm wrong, but I rather suspect that you have used up most of your energy already."

He was right. I had put so much into the first lightning bolt that if I was to use it again, it would be much less powerful.

"Don't beat yourself up, Jill, it wouldn't have made any difference. You are no match for me."

"You think an awful lot of yourself, don't you?"

"I'm only stating facts. I have accumulated power from a thousand witches. None as powerful as you, granted, but cumulatively they have bestowed on me a power you can't begin to imagine. And just think how formidable I'll be when I've absorbed your power and that of your daughter's."

"You lay one finger on Florence and I'll—"

"You'll do what?" He laughed. "You won't do anything because you won't be here." He unleashed a lightning bolt, the likes of which I'd never seen before. I wasn't worried, though, because the compass stones would shield me.

I felt like I'd been hit by a freight train. The force sent me flying backwards across the floor. The pain was so intense that I could hardly catch my breath.

"You look surprised, Jill." He was striding slowly towards me. "Were you really expecting those silly stones to save you?" He laughed again. "Those were just my little joke. I didn't actually think you'd fall for it."

I tried to get back to my feet, but all the strength had drained from my body. One more lightning bolt like that would spell the end for me. All I could think about was Florence and how I'd failed her. She would stand no chance against this evil man.

"Fun as this has been, it's time for me to take my leave." Braxmore was standing over me now. "There's a certain little girl who I need to pay a visit."

"Please, don't hurt her."

"Are you begging?"

"Yes, I'm begging you to spare her."

"I'd love to do that. Honestly, I would. But you see, it's my destiny, and you can't argue with destiny."

"Please."

"Goodbye, Jill." He raised his hand and pointed it straight at my head.

The explosion was so loud that I thought my eardrums would burst. And the heat was so intense that I felt it singe my hair. The room was full of smoke, and I could barely see my hands in front of me. When the smoke eventually began to clear, I saw Braxmore lying on the floor. Where his chest had once been was now just a large, smouldering hole. I tried to understand what had just happened, but my head was still spinning from the impact of whatever had killed Braxmore. The only thing that made any sense was that Grandma must have managed to get through the circle of mist and come to my rescue.

"Grandma? Grandma, where are you?" There was no reply, but I saw a small figure, walking towards me through the smoke. "Grandma, I'm over here."

"Mummy!" Florence rushed up to me and threw her arms around me.

"Florence? Where did you come from?" I was beginning to think that this was a dream. It couldn't be Florence; she was with Kathy.

"That nasty man hurt you and he was going to do it again."

"What did you see?"

"I saw him hurt you, so I hurt him. Am I in trouble?"

I pulled her close to me and gave her a kiss. "No, you're not in trouble. Are you okay?"

"Yeah, but I don't like all this smoke."

"Me neither. Let's get out of here."

From somewhere, I summoned up the strength to get up on my feet, and the two of us started towards the doors.

"Don't you want your stones, Mummy?"

"No, darling, we'll leave those here." Once I was outside in the fresh air, my head started to clear. "How did you get here, Florence?"

"I was with Lizzie at the toffee apple stall when I saw the man."

"Which man?"

"The bad man in there." She pointed back inside the castle.

"He was at the funfair?"

"He wasn't really there. I just saw him in my head. I saw you too and I knew he was going to hurt you."

"Did you magic yourself here?"

"Yeah."

My phone rang, causing me to almost jump out of my skin. It was Kathy.

"Jill, it's me." I could tell by her voice that she was upset, and I didn't need two guesses as to why.

"What's wrong, Kathy?"

"It's Florence. I—err—we don't know where she is. She was with Lizzie getting a toffee apple and then she just disappeared. Jill, I'm so sorry. I don't know what to do."

"Hold on a second, Kathy." I put my hand over the phone and whispered to Florence. "It's your Auntie Kathy. She's worried about you. Do you think you can magic yourself back there?"

"I don't want to leave you. What if that man gets up?"

"He won't. I'm fine now, honestly. You need to get back to Auntie Kathy because she's really upset."

"Okay."

"And don't tell her anything about what happened just now."

"I won't."

I gave her a kiss. "Off you go, then."

"Jill, are you still there?" Kathy screamed down the phone.

"I'm here."

"Jill, did you hear what I just—hang on a minute. Florence, where did you go to? We were really worried about you. Jill, it's okay. She's here now."

"Is she okay?"

"She's fine. I'm sorry to have scared you like that."

"That's okay."

On my way out of Sunville, I dropped in on DD and the other Bing Bongs, as I'd promised I would. I explained that Braxmore had taken control of the castle, but that he was now out of the picture. I also told them that I hadn't had a chance to check on the king, but I believed he was still alive. They thanked me and immediately despatched a party of men to check on his wellbeing.

"Thank goodness you're okay," Grandma said when I stepped back into the bedroom. "What happened?"

"Braxmore is dead."

"I take it those stones did the trick?"

"No, they were completely useless."

"But you managed to kill him, anyway?"

"I didn't. Florence did."

I'd not often seen Grandma lost for words, but on this occasion, she was well and truly struck dumb.

Chapter 34

By the time Monday morning came around, I'd just about recovered from my encounter with Braxmore, although my ribs were still painful, particularly if I coughed or laughed.

Florence had already finished her breakfast and had gone to play in her bedroom. Jack and I were still at the breakfast table.

"What do you reckon?" Jack said.

"About what?"

"Florence. Do you think she'll be okay to go to school?"

"Why wouldn't she be? She's not poorly."

"I know. I was just thinking about what she went through this weekend."

"It sounded like she had a great time at Wonder World. She's done nothing but talk about it since she got home."

"That's just it. Don't you find it kind of weird that she's never mentioned *him* once?"

"Braxmore?"

"Shush, she might hear you. I mean, she killed a man. You do realise that, don't you?"

"Of course I do. I was there. Remember?"

"So, shouldn't she be traumatised?"

"She's fine. You can see that for yourself."

"Yes, but—"

"As far as Florence is concerned, she stopped a bad man from hurting her Mummy. That's it."

"Don't you think we should have a conversation with her?"

"How would that help? She's much more interested in telling us about the Twirl Ride than she is about discussing Braxmore. I say we leave it alone. If she ever brings up the subject, or if there are any signs that it's adversely affected her, that's the time we should talk to her about it. For now, we should just be grateful that she no longer has that threat hanging over her."

"Okay, you're right. Are you going to take a couple of days off?"

"Why would I?"

"To give your ribs a chance to mend."

"I'll be fine as long as no one makes me laugh."

***

I was practically doubled over with laughter. And with the pain from my ribs.

"It's not funny, Jill," Mrs V snapped.

"I really wish it wasn't, trust me."

"Can you get them out, please?" She bent forward over her desk.

"How on earth did you manage to get staples in your bottom?"

"The stapler was stuck, so I stood up and hit it on the desk. It flew open and all the staples dropped out onto my chair."

"But why sit on them?"

"Armi called me, and he was waffling on for ages about a new cuckoo clock he's bought. By the time he'd ended the call, I'd forgotten all about the staples and I sat on the chair."

All of this must have happened just before I'd walked through the door because I'd found Mrs V jumping around, as though she was doing some kind of crazy rain dance.

"Stand still and don't move." I pulled out each of the staples that had gone straight through her dress. "There, that's it. All out."

"Thank you." She sat down but jumped straight back up again. "I think I might stand up for the rest of the day."

"Probably as well."

"What have you done to your ribs?"

"It's nothing. I just hurt myself while I was gardening."

"Since when did you do any gardening?"

"I thought I'd give it a tidy while Florence was away for the weekend."

"Oh yes, how did she get on?"

"She had a blast."

Winky had a concerned look on his face.

"What's up with you?" I said.

"I think you should sit down."

"What now? What have you done?"

"Honestly, it would be better if you sat down first."

"Tell me. Right now."

"Okay. Well, you remember how I told you about the takeover at Fun Rat?"

"Is this about my investment?"

"Yeah."

"I'm guessing it's not good news. I suppose the takeover didn't happen."

"No, it did."

"So, what's the problem?"

"Everyone thought Fun Rat was going to take over Drop Jaw."

"And?"

"Someone else actually took over Drop Jaw."
"So Fun Rat's share price fell?"
"Correct."
"How much?"
"Quite a bit."
"Ten percent?"
"More."
"Twenty?"
"More."
"How much, Winky?"
"Forty-six percent."
"What? Are you telling me that we've lost forty-six percent of our investment?"
"I only lost twenty percent."
"How come?"
"I got out as soon as I found out."
"And you didn't think to tell me?"
"I tried to call you, but you didn't answer your phone."
"What am I supposed to do now?"
"Sell those shares before they drop any further."
"Great. Just great."

I wasted no time in disposing of my shares, but I still ended up taking a loss closer to fifty percent. How was I going to break the news to Jack? What had I been thinking? What kind of idiot takes investment advice from a cat?

Mrs V came through to my office.

"Miss Lockjaw is here. She wondered if you might spare her a minute."

I'd undertaken a case for Roberta Lockjaw some time ago. I'd managed to track down jewellery that she'd inherited, but that had subsequently disappeared. In a moment of madness, I'd agreed to take the case on the understanding that I would receive five percent of the value of the recovered jewellery when it was sold. Unfortunately, Miss Lockjaw then decided not to sell the jewellery and went AWOL. The woman had a cheek showing her face around here again.

"Send her in, would you?"

"Shall I offer her a drink?"

"Definitely not."

Vindictive? Me? You bet your life I am.

Miss Lockjaw looked a million dollars; a far cry from when I'd first met her in Smallwash when she'd been wearing fingerless gloves and earmuffs.

"Jill, how lovely to see you again."

"Hello, Miss Lockjaw."

"You really must call me Roberta. May I take a seat?"

"Sure."

"I must apologise for not being in touch before, but I decided to take a world cruise. It's something I've always wanted to do, but never had the money."

"Does that mean you decided to sell some of the jewellery after all?"

"I did. I know I was hesitant at first, but then I thought about all the things I could do with it, so I actually sold it all."

"Everything?"

"Yes, that's why I'm here today. If I recall correctly, I promised to give you five percent of the sale value."

"Would you like a drink, Miss—err—Roberta?"

"A cup of tea would go down a treat."

I buzzed Mrs V on the intercom. "Mrs V, would you

make Roberta and me a cup of tea, please. Use the best cups. Oh, and bring through the biscuits too."

"But you said—"

"Thank you, Mrs V."

Roberta continued, "I believe I told you that the jewellery was worth approximately two million."

"That's what you said."

"That turned out not to be the case."

I might have known. "How much did it fetch?"

"It actually went for three point two million."

"Three point two? Million?"

"That's right, which means that your share is one-hundred and sixty thousand pounds." She reached into her handbag, took out a cheque, and handed it to me.

For the longest moment, all I could do was sit there and stare at it.

"Are you alright, Jill?" Mrs V said when she brought through the drinks.

"What? Err, yeah. Never better."

Long after Roberta Lockjaw had left, I was still staring at the cheque.

"That's a lot of money," Winky said.

"No kidding."

"It just so happens that I've had an ironclad tip about a new startup company. If you get in quick, you're bound to double your money within a year."

"You're joking, I assume."

"No, I'm deadly serious, but you'll need to act quickly."

"Watch my lips. I am never taking investment advice from you again. Ever."

"You won't get a better opportunity."

"Forget it. I know exactly what I'm going to do with this money."

Season Five

The next book (Witch Is The Nest Now Empty) begins season five of the Witch P.I Mysteries. In that book, we will rejoin Jill and her family six years on from the conclusion of this book.

In the intervening years, there have been many changes, but some things never change:

i) Jill is still crazy busy solving mysteries.
ii) Winky is still crazy (but even he has seen some changes).
iii) The laughs will keep coming thick and fast.

ALSO BY ADELE ABBOTT

The Not-A-Date (a sweet romantic comedy)

I'd just been fired, so the last thing I needed was some guy hitting on me, and I told him so in no uncertain terms. Then he goes and offers me the job of my dreams.

Pushing All My Buttons (a sweet romantic comedy)

I got stuck in a lift with this guy who then tried to hit on me, so I told him he was a jerk. A few days later, I started a new job and discovered he was my boss.

So Not The One (A sweet romantic comedy)

I was devastated when my old boss had to take early retirement. But that was nothing compared to how I felt when I discovered who his replacement was.

The Witch P.I. Mysteries (A Candlefield/Washbridge Series)

Witch Is When... (Season #1)

Witch Is When It All Began
Witch Is When Life Got Complicated
Witch Is When Everything Went Crazy
Witch Is When Things Fell Apart
Witch Is When The Bubble Burst
Witch Is When The Penny Dropped
Witch Is When The Floodgates Opened
Witch Is When The Hammer Fell

Witch Is When My Heart Broke
Witch Is When I Said Goodbye
Witch Is When Stuff Got Serious
Witch Is When All Was Revealed

Witch Is Why... (Season #2)
Witch Is Why Time Stood Still
Witch is Why The Laughter Stopped
Witch is Why Another Door Opened
Witch is Why Two Became One
Witch is Why The Moon Disappeared
Witch is Why The Wolf Howled
Witch is Why The Music Stopped
Witch is Why A Pin Dropped
Witch is Why The Owl Returned
Witch is Why The Search Began
Witch is Why Promises Were Broken
Witch is Why It Was Over

Witch Is How... (Season #3)
Witch is How Things Had Changed
Witch is How Berries Tasted Good
Witch is How The Mirror Lied
Witch is How The Tables Turned
Witch is How The Drought Ended
Witch is How The Dice Fell
Witch is How The Biscuits Disappeared
Witch is How Dreams Became Reality
Witch is How Bells Were Saved
Witch is How To Fool Cats
Witch is How To Lose Big
Witch is How Life Changed Forever

Witch Is Where... (Season #4)
Witch is Where Magic Lives Now
Witch Is Where Clowns Go To Die
Witch Is Where Squirrels Go Nuts
Witch Is Where Rainbows End
Witch Is Where Unicorns Cry
Witch Is Where The Lights Went Out
Witch Is Where Fairies Wing It
Witch Is Where Roses Bloom Early
Witch Is Where Decisions Are Made
Witch Is Where Gnomes Rules
Witch Is Where Cats Always Win
Witch Is Where Chickens Go To Roost

Susan Hall Investigates (A Candlefield/Washbridge Series)
Whoops! Our New Flatmate Is A Human.
Whoops! All The Money Went Missing.
Whoops! Someone Is On Our Case.
Whoops! We're In Big Trouble Now.

Murder On Account (A Kat Royle Novel)
Her boss has been murdered. Now she must find his killer. Smart, sassy and kickass tough, private investigator, Kat Royle, is nobody's fool, but does she have what it takes to keep the agency afloat, and find the murderer?

Web site: AdeleAbbott.com
Facebook: facebook.com/ AdeleAbbottAuthor

Printed in Great Britain
by Amazon